FACE THE MUSIC

A Novel

By

Alexandra Y. Caluen

FACE THE MUSIC

FACE THE MUSIC

Contents

Part 1: Break You: The Playlist   1
    Chapter 1   2
    Chapter 2   10
    Chapter 3   19
    Chapter 4   27
    Chapter 5   36
    Chapter 6   47
    Chapter 7   58
    Chapter 8   66
    Chapter 9   77
    Chapter 10   90
    Chapter 11   99
Part II: Flight: The Playlist   113
    Chapter 12   114
    Chapter 13   124
    Chapter 14   135
    Chapter 15   145
    Chapter 16   155
    Chapter 17   169
    Chapter 18   181
    Chapter 19   193
    Chapter 20   203
    Chapter 21   217
    Chapter 22   230
Part III: Face the Music: The Playlist   243
    Chapter 23   244
    Chapter 24   255
    Chapter 25   268
    Chapter 26   283
    Chapter 27   294
    Chapter 28   304
    Chapter 29   316

PART I: BREAK YOU

The Playlist:

Short Skirt Long Jacket - Cake

You Oughta Know - Alanis Morissette

Stiletto Cool - Brian Setzer

My Prerogative - Britney Spears

Trapped in the Web of Love - Royal Crown Revue

These Precious Things - Tori Amos

+

Rock Star - N.E.R.D. (Jason Nevins remix)

+

Save Me – Queen

CHAPTER 1

August 2014

Paula didn't often get emails from Kelli on her work account; when she did, they tended to be invitations to come in to talk with HR about a complaint. Not that Paula got a *lot* of complaints, but she'd had a few. They were always about her 'attitude,' and they were generally justified. She assumed that's what this was about, though she couldn't remember having given anyone shit in any actionable way since the last little chat, so her first reaction was to think, what the fuck, I didn't even do anything.

But the email actually read:

> **Hi Paula - we have a new LAA and I'd like you to take him out for the orientation lunch. Set it up with him, please, and then let me know where you're going and when. The firm will reimburse you. His name is Michael Borodin, he goes by Mike, and fyi he's a dancer too. That should give you something to talk about! Thanks - Kelli**

Maybe she'd passed a test if they were letting her orient people now. Paula snickered to herself and got on with the next task on her desk. Toward the end of the day, she copied Mike's email address from Kelli's note and composed a message:

> Hi Mike – We haven't met yet but HR asked me to take you to lunch. I see IT hasn't got your profile finished. Ping me back about where they have you

stationed, I'll come to collect you. I usually take lunch 2-3 but if earlier works for you, that's fine with me. Any day in the next five is good. Welcome to the team – Paula Ross

She got a reply back before leaving for the day.

Hi Paula – thanks for the note. I've got more training the next couple of days and they don't leave much time to get out. How's Monday? 2-3 is fine for me. Btw I'm at 1636-A. Look forward to meeting you – Mike

She put the meeting in Outlook and sent him an invite, then an email reply.

Hi Mike – Monday 2:00 it is then. I'll scoop you up a few minutes before. Any dietary restrictions? – Paula

His answer came back almost immediately, right after the invite was accepted.

LOL Nope, you can feed me anything – Mike

And then, following orders like the good little soldier she wasn't, she sent a note to Kelli.

Hi Kelli – taking Mike out on Monday, 2-3, we'll go to Toscanova. – Paula

By Monday, IT had Mike's profile finished. All the staff, including 'legal administrative assistants' (a.k.a. secretaries), got a head shot. Paula looked at the picture they were using and thought, Hello. Even in the tiny thumbnail attached to the intranet profile, he was gorgeous. Probably gay. If not, he was going to need a chastity belt around here. There were a lot of ravenously single women in the support-staff ranks. This usually amused Paula, but maybe that was because none of the men in the firm looked like her personal catnip. At least, not till now.

She fully intended to Google him later, to find out more about his dance history (if any of it was online), but her bosses had stuff to do and she ran out of time.

Meanwhile, Mike had been Googling Paula, because Kelli had let slip that Paula was a dancer, and Mike was desperate to find other dancers to talk to. He hadn't expected to find the video from a performance captioned 'Underground Cabaret - Tubular Bells - Oct 2012.' And he *really* hadn't expected this dancer to be a striptease artist. The routine betrayed a lot of jazz dance experience, but the performance seemed at odds with the personality required for full-time employment in a law firm, even though it didn't end with full nudity. He wondered if the firm knew about Paula's double life. Wondered how long she'd been there. Suspected that a lunch hour was almost certainly not going to be enough time for him to learn as much about her as he wanted to.

She showed up at his desk at 1:50 on Monday. Mike wondered later if he had *felt* her approach; there was no other reason to have looked up, watching as she came down the hall. He got to his feet almost without meaning to. She was above average height, slim, wearing a long close-fitting blazer over a short skirt, bare legs, and motorcycle boots. Her hair was light brown, medium-long, twisted up with an octopus clip. The ends were dyed bright red and orange. Her face was square-ish, with strong eyebrows and large hazel eyes and a chin that

4

had the potential to be belligerent. She was the first white woman he'd seen in L.A. who wasn't wearing any makeup. Her skin was perfect. "You look different," he said after a moment. "From your profile picture."

"It's a shitty picture," Paula said, glad he had spoken so she could simply respond, instead of having to invent something. Her brain had glitched for a second at how impossibly much better he looked in real life. He had to be tall, too? "They had this whole glamour team that held me down and did makeup. Ready to go?"

"Yeah." He found his access key card and his sunglasses, following as she walked away without another word. What the hell, he thought, almost offended despite his fascination. Apparently she didn't believe in small talk.

They barely spoke on the way over to the mall; he was starting to wonder why this particular person had been asked to take him out. HR probably thought 'dancer' would give them both something to break the ice, something to talk about. Maybe they didn't know Paula very well. He resigned himself to a non-informative, non-friendly, but at least free lunch.

So he was surprised when, after they gave their orders to the server, Paula looked at him and said, "It's nice to meet another dancer. Did you know Kelli dances too?"

"She mentioned it in the first interview. She seems like the kind of person who tries to find a tribe for people."

"Yeah, pretty much."

"So. I Googled you. Because she told me you were a dancer. I saw this clip," he began, then stopped.

5

"The 'Tubular Bells'? That's always at the top of the results."

"Yeah. That one."

"What did you think?"

"Honestly?"

"No, Mike, fucking lie to me. Of course, honestly."

Yikes. "Um, okay. The first time I watched it, I thought it was really sexy, which, well, you were stripping." He'd lowered his voice, because this wasn't the kind of stuff you said to someone in public. She nodded, expressionless. "Then I watched it again because it gave me the creeps despite being sexy." She nodded again. "And then I watched it *again*, because the more I got used to it the more I thought I saw what you were doing. I found other performances from that show, it was Halloween, right? And I thought, she's stripping because she's about to dismember somebody and doesn't want her clothes to get messed up." She blinked. "And I thought it was, well, genius."

Her eyebrows went up, then her chin; he thought there was the slightest flicker of a smile. She seemed about to reply, but then their food arrived and all she said was, "Eat. Then I'll interrogate you."

"Okay." They both addressed their food for a while. Mike noticed Paula checking her Swiss Army wristwatch. "We still have almost a half-hour, right?" he said.

"Yeah. So. Age, education, orientation, and why the fuck are you working in a law firm?"

"You first." He smiled for the first time.

Good Christ, she thought. The height and the body were bad enough, but add the soft low voice, the blond

6

hair, the incongruously dark-lashed gray eyes, the ... *well, let's face it, that's The Face.* And she needed to answer the question. "Thirty-four, too much, bi, couldn't make it as a pro, but I can type really fast."

"Do you ever ... temporize?"

"You mean am I ever tactful? No."

He bit his lip, trying not to laugh. "Okay then. Thirty-two, not enough, straight, broke half my body in a car accident and lost my place in a company."

"Well, that sucks."

"Yes it does."

"Before I ask for details, I'll be tactful and ask if you mind giving details."

"I don't mind."

"But first, one more question. Are you single?"

He nodded. "You?"

She nodded. "You should know that you're likely to get *majorly* harassed in this place. There are hordes of single women in the firm. And a few single men."

"I'm used to being harassed." He wondered if that was why she was the way she was.

"Yeah, I'll bet."

"So, the details. I was a passenger in a van going back to home base from a performance. The van got t-boned on my side, someone ran a red light. The person behind me lost her spleen, had a couple ribs broken, and had her right leg broken in three places. And I ... broke my ankle, femur, pelvis, humerus, several ribs, and skull. Almost bled to death from a lacerated liver." His voice was matter-of-fact, but he wasn't looking at her.

"Jesus *fuck.*" She'd thought 'half his body' might have been an exaggeration.

7

"Well, the other driver and his passenger were killed, so it could have been worse." He looked up now, with a small smile.

"How long were you out of action?"

"Two years. I still see a trainer and a therapist, but I'm back in class now."

"Jazz?"

"It's my preference. How'd you guess?"

"You could read that strip routine. Anything else?"

"I did some ballroom in Minneapolis."

"No kidding."

"It's social. I need to find a studio, I don't really know anybody."

"Why come to L.A.?"

"Because I didn't know anybody."

"Starting over, huh."

He nodded. No need to mention the pressure to join the family business, or the breakup of his long-term relationship. "How are we doing for time?"

"We'd better wrap this up." She signaled the server.

"So, this is only the second firm I've worked in. Is this the kind of place where co-workers can talk on the job, or would after-hours be the way to go?"

Her chin went up again and her eyelids lowered. There was something seductive about the expression. She answered indirectly. "I work nine-thirty to six."

"Me too." The server brought the check; Paula handed over a credit card. *Might as well ask*, he thought. "Do you ever date co-workers?"

She looked at him sharply, as if she hadn't expected that. "I've fucked a few," she said. "Never dated."

8

A completely NSFW mental image caught him by surprise. Arousal, out of nowhere; Mike went hard under the table. He looked away and took a few deep breaths, hoping his reaction wasn't obvious.

He blushes beautifully, Paula thought. *Because of course he does.* Something made her add, "But then, I don't really date."

He looked back at her. "Why not?"

"Because I don't like dating."

"Neither do I."

The server came back. Paula signed the check, adding a good tip. She tucked her card in her pocket, stood up, tipped her head toward the door. Then she walked away. After a moment, Mike pushed back from the table and followed her out. Halfway back to the office he was about to ask her to stop for a second, when she did, turning around so suddenly he almost crashed into her. Her chin went up again; her gaze dropped from his eyes to his mouth. He had to take a step back, because he wanted to kiss her right there, and that wasn't like him at all. A smile crept into her eyes when she looked up to meet his. "There's a thing some of us do," she said.

"What kind of thing?"

"Fridays, after six, when there's no clients in house and no other events. Go to office 1850."

"Whose is that?"

"Facilities manager."

"And why?"

"Because occasionally leftover booze is liberated from meetings or events, and our buddy Dylan likes to share."

CHAPTER 2

They didn't work on the same floor, so Mike didn't see Paula again the rest of that week. His email thanking her for lunch got no reply but a smiley face. Given that he couldn't remember her really smiling at all, he thought this might have been ironic. Then, at five minutes to six on Friday, she sent a message: 1850 in fifteen

He wasn't sure if it was a good idea; suspected that it might not be. By now almost acclimated to the firm, he couldn't quite believe that after-hours on-site boozing was a thing anyone was really getting away with. But by five minutes past six, the sixteenth floor was a ghost town. He shut down his workstation, went to the bathroom, then headed upstairs.

The eighteenth floor seemed mostly deserted, but he heard voices, then a door closing. He turned toward the sounds. The door of office number 1850 was closed; he knocked. A moment later, Paula opened it a couple of inches. When she saw it was him, she opened the door wide enough for him to come in, then closed it again.

Six people were already crammed into the room. They all introduced themselves. Mike shook hands with everyone, knowing he'd met a couple of them before. "I apologize in advance if I forget anybody's name," he said. "Or more like *when* I forget. Head injury."

"What happened?" said the big guy from Records.

"Car accident."

Dylan winced, as if he knew about car accidents. "If you'd been here a couple years ago, you would have seen me after mine. I was messed up."

"Yes you were. Dish it out, Dylan," said the other woman, who'd introduced herself as Susan. "Gotta get over to the mall."

"Me too," said Paula. "What've we got today?"

"Patrón Silver," said Dylan. He brought out an open bottle, half-full. Everyone produced a shot glass. Mike felt awkward.

"I brought one for you," said Paula. "You can make it up to me later." She gave him that look with her chin tipped up and her eyelids lowered. Everyone else in the room made stifled laughing noises. She handed the extra shot glass to Dylan; it said 'Alcatraz.'

"Is that where I'm likely to end up if I hang out with you guys?" Mike said.

"Aw hell no," said Billy, the Records guy. "They closed it down a long time ago." He gave Mike an interested look.

"He's straight, Billy," said Paula.

"God *damn* it."

Mike smiled. Susan said, "You know, sometimes I wish *I* were straight."

"Susan, you're the only person in this room with a functional relationship," said Paula. "Relax and enjoy the scenery."

"Oh, I will."

Dylan finished filling the shot glasses. Everybody took theirs; Paula took the Alcatraz glass and handed it to Mike, then clinked her glass against it. "Salud," she said, then tossed back the tequila. "Fuck!" She coughed, half-laughing. Mike was so busy enjoying her face that he forgot to drink until she pointed at him. He cautiously sipped the tequila, grimacing at the taste of it.

11

"This boy doesn't know how we do it," said one of the other guys.

"He's from Minnesota, give him a break," said Paula. She raised her eyebrows at Mike, who thought, *welcome back, peer pressure*, took a deep breath, and tossed back the liquor. He swallowed, painfully. Clamped his eyes shut against the burn.

"God, that's awful!" he said finally, voice thready, eyes watering. Everyone was snorting with muted hilarity, except Paula. She was actually smiling as she reached up to wipe under his eyes with her knuckles.

"You never have to drink it again," she said. "But it sure takes the edge off a week in this joint."

"How was it, anyway?" said Susan. "I remember my first couple of weeks. Ugh."

"It wasn't that bad," he said. "I mean, it wasn't *fun*, but that's why they call it work, right?"

"I'm going over to Rock Sugar to meet my wife," she said. "You want to join us?"

"Trying to set up a three-way, Susie?" said one of the guys.

"Gross, no." She glared at him. "I am simply being nice to the new guy."

"You weren't that nice to *me*."

"Because you don't look like *that*," said the other guy whose name Mike couldn't remember. Susan snickered, shrugged, didn't deny it.

Dylan said, "I heard there's always a traffic jam around your desk, Mike. Suddenly all the ladies find a reason to be going that way."

"Don't worry," said Susan. "Nobody will blame you. The female appetite in this place is legendary."

"Why don't the lawyers shut it down?" he asked.

"Somebody pointed out to them that as long as the work gets done, letting people have a little fun is a good way to reduce employee turnover."

"Well, thanks, Susan. I'd be happy to join you for dinner."

"Great. Anybody else?"

"I gotta get home," said Dylan. "My relationship may be dysfunctional, but it'll be nonexistent if I go out with someone else on a Friday."

The other men also made excuses. Paula, the last to answer, said, "I could go. I was heading over there anyway." Mike thought, *Yes, thank you God.*

"Anybody want another before we break this up?" said Dylan, wagging the bottle.

Paula made a face. "Ugh, no. If it was Casamigos, I'd be fighting you for it."

"If it was Casamigos, I wouldn't have invited you moochers up here." Dylan faked a rim shot off his monitor. They all shuffled out and headed for the elevator.

"So Paula," said Susan on their way over to the mall. "What were you headed over here for?" Mike was grateful, because he'd been curious, but didn't want to ask.

"My after-work walk. You know I don't sleep unless I'm worn out."

"Still? Have you seen a doctor about that?"

"I've seen *all* the goddamned doctors. The diagnosis seems to be 'thinking while female.'" She glanced over at Mike. "A friend who's a cancer survivor recommended cannabis, but I hate smoking."

"Me too," he said. "And brownies are too fattening." She and Susan both laughed, which felt like a victory. They arrived at the restaurant, where they met up with Susan's wife Janice. Dinner was the most fun Mike had had since moving to L.A.

"So you remember that video?" Paula said to Susan, when the remains of their food had been taken away and two out of four of them were having coffee.

"What, the creepy sexy one? Who could forget? Are you doing another one of those?"

"I'm working with a couple dancers at this studio near me, we're going to submit a jazz piece for the Halloween show. If we get in, you want to come?" She was talking to Susan, but she looked at Mike.

"Sure," said Janice. "That's at the place in Hollywood, right?"

"Yeah."

Susan turned to Mike. "Do you know our Paula's little secret?"

"I saw that video. We haven't really talked about it though. I mean, we only met a minute ago."

"I've done a few shows with the Underground Cabaret," said Paula. "The first time was that strip routine. But right after that I started learning trapeze, so I've done a couple of trapeze things. Last Halloween it was a jazz thing. I think hooking up with that company may have kept me from blowing up Century City." Susan snickered. "I mean, I even got this job through that connection."

"I'd like to see one of the shows," Mike said. "I saw a promo card at the studio where I do class, but it didn't really register."

"Look for Underground Cabaret on YouTube. Lots of the routines are on there. Sometimes the music owners make them take something down, but all of mine are still up." *Good*, Mike thought, *I didn't miss any.*

"So you're a dancer, too?" Susan asked him.

"I was. Before the accident. Since rehab, I've only danced for exercise."

"That must be hard," said Janice. "That was your career?"

"For twelve years." He tried to say it lightly.

"There's a different show next month at the club," said Paula. "All ballroom. And a dance concert I'm dying to see, I heard about it from a friend and thought, you know, shit! I wanna be in that! It sounds really cool."

"I'll go see anything," said Mike. "It's time I started to enjoy dance again. I mean, even if I can't do that for a living, at least there's a lot of ways to participate. I'm not ready to live without it entirely. I really do need to find a ballroom studio, I guess." He became aware that he'd said more than he meant to. Appreciated the sympathetic attention from Susan and Janice. Had no idea they were both thinking about how notoriously-prickly Paula wasn't being prickly.

"I quit going to ballroom dances," said Paula, which surprised him all over again. "The guy I used to meet up with met up with somebody else and I didn't like going stag."

"I'll go with you." Mike saw Susan and Janice glance at each other with eyebrows raised. He looked each of them in the eye, didn't look at Paula. "She told me she doesn't *date* co-workers. She never said she wouldn't *dance* with them." That earned him a pair of amused looks.

"Well played, Mike," said Paula. "But if I do ballroom with you, you have to do jazz with me."

15

"Oh, that's a problem." His face said that it clearly was not.

Susan and Janice laughed again. "You may be getting more than you bargained for, Paula," said Janice.

"I'm tough," she said, looking tough. "I can handle it."

Mike left the restaurant with Paula, walking with her as she started hiking all over the mall. She didn't tell him to get lost and the movement felt good. After a while, he said, "So why did you do that first routine, the Tubular Bells?"

"You mean why was it strip?"

"I guess."

"Huh. Good question. I'd been scratching around for solo things I could do, somehow tripped over the Cabaret audition post, and thought, I want to try that. Since it was a Halloween theme, and I'd been watching a lot of 'Dexter,' the jazz choreo I originally put together took a turn. I mean, I'd seen some great performance films of striptease artists. Tried to steal what I could from those, but mostly it was just, well." She didn't go on.

He thought he understood. "Unbearable frustration? Free-floating hostility? Homicidal rage?"

She glanced over at his face for a second. His expression was remote and his eyes looked dark. "I guess you probably know about some of that."

"It's one thing to miss out on a role. It's another thing to be told you'll never get another chance." They were quiet for a while, walking fast.

"You don't seem like an angry guy. I mean, I know how *I* come across," she said. "I hear about it a couple times a year from HR. You're not like that."

"I'm from Minnesota. We repress." She huffed out a laugh. Mike glanced over. "Also, I'm a guy, and I'm tall, and I have this physicality. It's not what it used to be, but it's not nothing."

That's for sure, she thought. Couldn't stop herself from saying, "You move like a mountain lion."

Mike felt himself blush, glad it was dark. "Anyway, a man with rage can be scary. I don't want to be scary."

"People sometimes think it's cute. A woman with rage."

"They shouldn't."

After another few minutes, silent except for their own footsteps and the music piped around the mall, she said, "There is one hard and fast rule."

"Only one?"

She glanced at him. "Yeah, only one. You can say, or not say, anything. If you don't want to say something, don't. But when you do say something, always tell me the truth."

"Even if it's tactless?"

"Especially if it's tactless. I'm so sick of prevaricating, mendacious, mealy-mouthed morons with agendas, I can't even tell you."

He said, "I have an agenda."

"Which is?" She thought she knew.

"I don't want to say it yet."

"Fair enough." They'd arrived back at the bridge that would take them over Avenue of the Stars. She stopped walking and looked up at him. The outdoor lighting made the most of the narrow, slanting planes of his face. His eyes were in shadow, but he was looking directly at her. "Give me your phone." He fished it out of his pocket. "Is it passcoded?"

"No."

She added her contact information. Then she got her own phone out and handed both to him. He slid his into his pocket, then entered his number and email address in her phone, handed it back. "I'll send you my dance schedule," she said. "You can decide what, if anything, you want to do."

"What if I want to do everything?"

"If I think it's too much, I'll tell you."

"Yeah. I guess you will."

She gazed at him for a long minute. Through his stillness she could sense power humming, but she also could almost feel his bones ache. "You're tired. Go home. I'm going to do another lap." He didn't know if he'd ever felt so thoroughly *seen*. He wasn't willing to leave it at that, so he was glad when she spoke again. "So why shouldn't people think female rage is cute?"

"Because the only reason women haven't laid waste to the earth is, you still believe you can fix it. Men have got *nothing* on female rage." She didn't say anything, but her gaze was suddenly hungry. He stared back at her, wanting so much more than to go home alone. "You're the first person outside my family who's ever said they want me to tell them the truth." She moved her head slightly, closing her eyes for a second. It was as if he could hear her thinking, *fuck them all*. He nodded, then headed over the bridge, not looking back.

CHAPTER 3

When Paula got home, sometime after ten, she went online to send an email to Kelli's home address.

> DO YOU KNOW WHAT YOU'VE DONE? I thought I couldn't sleep BEFORE. This may be a bad idea but Mike and I are going to be hanging out at some dance shit. You'll probably see us around. If the office building burns down it's because I caught him in the file room at a moment of low resistance.
>
> Btw tell Vince not to actually break a leg working on that show. It's a figure of speech.

Then she got down on the floor to stretch, put on Turner Classics, and eventually went to bed. The next morning, there was a reply.

> **ROFLMAO**
>
> Is he not amazingly good-looking?! The second I saw him in interview I was like damn, we'll never be able to peel all the women off this guy. Is he nice? He seemed nice. No boning in the file room plz and just generally do not burn down the building.
>
> Vince and the gang are working with spears. He's got bruises in the weirdest places but he's loving it. He helped choreograph one of the numbers and it is SMOKING HOT. I can't wait to see the show. Are you coming? To the show I mean :-)

Paula sipped coffee while she composed a reply.

> Ha ha very funny, yes I wouldn't miss the show. Yes Mike is nice. Probably too nice for me, at least before he got smashed up. Now he's got a layer of hatefulness that really works for me, because I am twisted. It's down pretty deep though, you'll probably never have to call him in to HR. He really misses dancing.

Kelli must have been home and online, because a reply came quickly, but via text. Paula's phone was right next to her as usual, so she picked it up.

> **He mentioned an accident, said he has memory glitches sometimes. How bad was it?**

> Confidentially, if it wasn't for a good trauma center he would be dead

> **Yikes. At least his face didn't get wrecked. And he appears to be fully functional**

> Well, you know, 'fully functional' for an average joe is a little different from 'fully functional' for a dancer

> **Yeah. Maybe hanging out with you will show him some new doors. I never expected to be dancing in shows and competitions after thirty**

> Me neither. Btw I have to re-do my condo. Had dinner with Rory & Dana a while back, like last year, and they did this hella cool harem thing in their dining room that I'm finally resolved to copy somewhere

> **Hmm could that be because you think somebody might be seeing it soon??**

I admit nothing. :-)

Mike had gone home tired and confused and thrilled. After a shower, a painkiller, and some stretching, he realized he was having the same set of feelings that he used to have after a first rehearsal. He thought that Paula was a wild card, but had the feeling, if he followed her lead, that some kind of door had opened.

When he woke up the next morning and logged on, there was an email from Paula with a list of the dance events she proposed to attend, or participate in, for the next couple of months. She'd included a couple of ballroom social dances. Out of habit, he checked his calendar, but he already knew he didn't have any conflicts. He wrote back:

> *Any or all. If you put something on here I assume you don't mind if I tag along. Unless I hear otherwise, I'll meet you.*

As of Monday, he hadn't heard back. *Okay*, he thought. *I guess that's how we're doing this.*

The first item on Paula's list was a no-details entry for 'Jazz,' after work that Wednesday. The address was a studio up in Hollywood. Mike found it all right, located an open parking place that didn't look like an invitation to break into his car, walked back to the building and up the stairs. An Argentine tango class occupied the main room, so he looked around and saw a smaller room behind an office. The door was ajar. He went to it and looked through.

Paula was already there, with two other women, all in black leotards, tights, and Dance Paws. They

21

were working with no music, only a metronome, on a synchronized phrase. He watched silently for several repetitions, until they stopped and one of them went to lock down the metronome. Paula met his eyes; he could tell she had known he was there all along. "Come on in. This is for the thing we're planning to submit for Halloween."

"Am I watching?" He'd worn a close-fitting tee and dance jeans, just in case.

"Unless you want to improvise something. We have most of the choreo but there are a few pieces missing. Ann, Bonnie, this is my friend Mike."

"Hi Mike," both women said. The one he thought was Bonnie added, "Paula told us you'd be coming. It's fine if you only want to watch. She said it's been a while since you did anything but class."

"Could I hear the music and see what you have?"

The one he thought was Ann went to a boombox and fed in a disc. Mike closed the door. "Can you start it for us? It's just the one track," she said.

"Sure." He went over to the little stereo and sat on the floor beside it. "Let me know when."

The three women took their starting positions, three points of a triangle facing the wall of mirror behind Mike. Ann looked at him; he pressed Play. The track was David Bowie's 'Putting out Fire with Gasoline,' the theme from 'Cat People,' which made him smile immediately. They had almost the whole song choreographed. The vocabulary was familiar and the phrasing logical. He watched with concentration through to the end, wanting to get up and dance with them.

"Do it," said Paula, as if he'd asked. He hadn't even been aware she was looking at him and didn't care if this was an invitation or a challenge. He took off his shoes, then started the track again, skidding into place in the middle of the triangle and catching up with their first phrase. They went through the whole thing again, Mike always a step or two behind. It was both frustrating and exhilarating.

"Again," said Bonnie. She started the track. Mike had almost the whole thing this time through. When they finished, all four of them were sweating and breathless. "You pick shit up fast."

"Thanks ... Bonnie, right?"

"Right. Why haven't you been dancing?" She brought him a bottle of water.

"Thanks," he said again. "Paula didn't tell you? I got smashed up in a car accident. Tail end of rehab now."

"Your team must have been great. I wouldn't have known you were hurt."

"I was lucky. Mostly broken bones, not soft tissue injuries."

"Only a dancer," said Ann, shaking her head. Bonnie nodded. "You know, if you did it by yourself I'll bet we could lock down what's missing. Or if you did it with Paula."

"Okay," Paula said. "Once more unto the breach." She took her position and waited for Mike to join her. He moved into position behind her, already tired and a little sore, but nearly drunk with being back in action. Completely unable to say No. Bonnie started the track. He let the shape of the dance play in his head while he moved, watching Paula, feeling the music in a way he hadn't for many months. The closing lyric brought tears to his eyes. *Been so long, so long, so long ... .* When they finished he had to

23

turn to the wall for a minute to compose himself. "Sorry," he said, turning around. "Thanks."

"Want to hang out while we finish this fucker? We still have half an hour," said Paula.

"I'll hang." He sat down again and watched while they worked out the last few pieces. All three of the women wore expressions of satisfaction at the end.

"I think we'll be able to put this on tape next week, don't you?" said Ann.

"No doubt," said Bonnie. "Same time, right?"

"Yep," said Paula. "Mike, the men's room is at the far end of the main teaching area. Mine is down the hall past that shitty waiting room. I'm going to go change and then head out." He felt like this was an unusual amount of detail for her to be giving. Wasn't sure if she meant he should wait for her. Decided to believe he should, went to the restroom, then waited for a few minutes. He was soon lost in thought. Ann and Bonnie both came out, waving as they passed him. He acknowledged them with an absent, reflexive smile.

A few more minutes later, Paula came out in jeans, a tee shirt, and sneakers, with her dance bag over her shoulder. She looked him over for a second, noting the fatigue in the lines of his face and body, before he registered her appearance. Maybe she shouldn't have pushed him. "I walked over here," she said. "Can you give me a lift back?"

"Of course." She didn't say anything else as they exited the building and walked to his car. "Thanks for that," he said when they got there. He opened the passenger door for her.

"The girls said it was very helpful to see you do it. It's easy to get stuck when you don't have a fresh input from time to time."

24

"I remember." He got in, fastened his seatbelt, and started the car. Paula gave him directions to her place, a small condo complex a dozen blocks from the studio. "I found an apartment near a studio, too," he said. "Down on Pico."

"Near Genesee?"

"Yeah, how'd you know?"

"I think I know all the studios on the west side now. That's where you take class?"

"Yeah."

Aaaaah I can't help it. "Maybe you should start working on something."

"Maybe I should." He pulled up at the curb and turned to look at her. She had that world-class poker face on and he was grateful. If she had smiled, or said anything else, he might have started bawling. Instead, she looked into his eyes for a moment, nodded, then got out of the car. He watched her go up to the gate and scan a card for entry. She didn't look back.

Mike didn't see Paula again until the next week, when he again went to the Hollywood studio. This time he did the routine twice with the women before stepping out to watch one more run-through, then record it for them. He was aware that he was approaching morning class differently, but didn't realize that from one week to the next, his movement had changed. All three women noticed.

Paula and the others had a brief discussion while changing out of their dancewear. Ann and Bonnie knew Paula well enough to know that for her to invite a 'friend' to a rehearsal was unexpected to the point of unthinkable. To then invite him to dance with them was in the realm of fantasy. They'd been willing to let it play out, admittedly because of the way he looked. After seeing how fast he picked it up they'd known there was something interesting going on: it was professional-level acquisition, the last thing they'd expected. But once they'd seen him move on the second night, Ann asked, "What is the actual story?"

Paula said, "He was in a company. Then there was the accident and they let him go. And he thought he was done, but I just." She shrugged, out of words.

"I just, too," said Bonnie. "How old is he?"

"Thirty-two."

"Jesus, they didn't ask him back?"

"Nope." It wasn't enough, and she knew it, so she fought past her habitual reticence and said, "We work in the same office. I, well, you know my story. His is worse. He wasn't mad enough to suit me."

"So you're pushing him," said Ann, while Bonnie shook her head, half-laughing.

"He should be dancing," said Paula, then clammed up. The others nodded, changed their clothes, and went away.

Mike gave her a lift home again, and would never have guessed that after getting to her condo, Paula changed into her swimsuit and went to the pool to do lap after lap until she was so exhausted she could hardly move. *Fuck you, brain*, she thought as she dragged back up the stairs. *Fuck you very much.*

CHAPTER 4

The dance concert Paula was so excited about, 'Green Darkness,' was playing at the end of September. One of the performance dates had been on the list she sent Mike. He'd checked out the club information online, with a link to the show's production page, and agreed it sounded well worth the price of admission. But the weekend before it started there was another dance show at the same club, that she hadn't put on the list. He sent her a text the Friday before, not at all sure this was the way to proceed, but figuring it was worth a try: *Chrome, Sunday, Mating Dance: Bandstand. I could pick you up if you want to go.*

After about a half hour, a reply pinged: **Yes**

He didn't want to think about why this felt like a major victory. So instead, he bought two tickets online, then sent an email to a dancer he'd been talking to at the studio where he took class. She was a few years older; turned out she'd worked with the star of the upcoming concert. He'd gotten her email address from the studio owner.

> *Hi Ms. Jarvet - wanted to ask if you ever do coaching. Ready to start working something up. Thanks in advance - Michael (Mike) Borodin*

He didn't hear back until that night, but when the reply came in it was exactly what he was hoping for.

> **Hi Mike - I Googled you and would LOVE to work with you. Solo? Duet? Audition? Let me know what your availability is. Btw here's my phone number ... text is easier. - Alison**

Okay, he thought. *Now, what do I want to do?* He couldn't decide. He looked over Paula's list again, noting the pattern and the blank spaces it left in his schedule, then composed a reply via text.

Hi Alison, thanks! Not sure what yet. Going to a couple shows in the next few weeks and then I should have some ideas. Nearly always available Mon Tues & Thurs after 7:30 p.m., 10-5 Sat-Sun. Let me know if any of that works for you.

Hi Mike, I'm married with child so weeknights are not great. Saturdays anytime and Sundays 1-5 are open.

Could we do Sundays 3-5 to start? Beginning 2nd week of October?

Don't you want to ask about rates?

Nope :-) Still spending insurance settlement. Best possible therapy, right?

LOL Gotcha. See you at the studio

Paula had been getting through the workdays by concentrating hard. As a consequence, her desk was unusually clean and she was well ahead of her work requests. This left her a little too much time for viewing YouTube videos. She had watched everything she could find of Mike's. He'd been a powerhouse on stage, with solid contemporary and jazz technique, plus sex appeal that was off the charts. It wasn't only her opinion, either; the comments on the videos were unanimous.

But the way he had moved at the studio, especially the second time, was not that much different from before; it looked like 'out of practice' more than 'broken.' He must have trained, from the minute he could, as if he expected to go back to his dance career. Obviously things still hurt, but she couldn't make herself believe that he was no longer physically capable. Somebody must have sold him the 'you're done' story; it made her angry. But, given the chorus of discouragement that she'd received as she started to age out of casting calls, she guessed she knew why.

He sent a text when he arrived at her condo on Sunday, a simple *I'm here*, and she went out to meet him. She was wearing jeans and a long-sleeved tee with a scarf wrapped around her neck, even though it was hot. Mike wondered if the club was usually cold. Then he noticed how tired she looked. Remembered how he always felt cold when he was fatigued. "Are you okay?"

"It's been a bad couple of weeks for the insomnia."

"Sorry." He had programmed the club's address in his GPS; it was not very far from the condo. They got there in fifteen minutes and he turned the car over to the parking valet. "This is my treat tonight," he said as they went up to the Will Call stand. She didn't say anything, only raised her eyebrows. "To say thanks for the jazz nights. I got in touch with a woman who dances at the studio near me. We're going to start working something up pretty soon."

"Good for you." *I will not, will not, will not ask who or what*, she thought, and immediately caved. "Would I know her?"

"Her name is Alison Jarvet. She's the one who worked with Mary Bassey on this show we're seeing next week."

"Oh! Cool." She was hard to read, but he thought she relaxed a little. They didn't talk much beyond ordering drinks, with some snacks from the bar kitchen. Then the show started.

Mike enjoyed it; it reminded him of 'Burn the Floor,' on a smaller scale. The program card identified all the cast as local ballroom dancers, some pros dancing with students or non-pro partners, but mostly pro couples. The setting was a 1940s military base and the routines included everything from big-band jitterbug to slow foxtrot. The closing number was a heartbreaking adagio set to 'I'll Be Seeing You.' At the end, he slid off his barstool and joined Paula – and half the crowd – in a standing ovation.

"God, that last couple," he said, when things quieted down. He was still standing.

"I know," said Paula. "That's one of the Cabaret principals, Michelle, with her ballroom partner Dmitri. He owns the Shall We Dance studio over in WeHo. They're the World Professional Smooth champions. He's, like, fifty-five? And she's thirty-seven."

He turned to face her, tapping his fingers restlessly against his empty glass. He didn't need to ask why she'd mentioned that last pair of facts. "Why did I think I was done?"

His eyes had that dark look that she'd started to associate with inner demons, the ones he kept so well controlled. It secretly thrilled her. "Is that a rhetorical question?"

"Not really."

"If I had to guess, I would guess that a bunch of people told you you were done. And you were hurt and scared, so you believed them."

He nodded. For the first time ever, Paula saw some of that rage in his face. After a moment he said, "I'm an idiot."

"No," she said emphatically. "That's our culture. You can be a shining star from age six to age eighteen, but after that you'd better buckle down and suck it up and join the rat race. Forget about your dreams. I mean, even on So You Think - they'll audition people up to age thirty, but most of them who make it to the show are under twenty-two. They're billed as being at the start of their careers, but ... as much as I love the show, in a way it's saying you have to *already be a star* in order to get that start. What does that say to the older dancer?"

"It says sit down and shut up and watch these pretty young things."

Boy, he really is mad, she thought, almost gleefully. She didn't even realize that she'd shifted closer to him, that they were nearly touching, until he set his hand lightly on hers. It was only for a second, then he slid his hand up to wrap around her wrist, gently squeezing, as if to take her pulse, then let her go. "What was that for?" *Jesus, he could break my arm without even trying*. It didn't scare her. The energy conducted by that touch had been anything but hostile.

He was about to say something else when he remembered he'd promised to always tell her the truth. "I just wanted to touch you." *Take that how you want*. He looked around; house music had started. He didn't really want another drink. "Do you want to hang out?"

"No, let's go."

For whatever reason, Paula slept better the next week. When Mike picked her up again the next Sunday she was in high-energy mode. "Wow," he said when she slid into the car. She was wearing a short, snug camouflage-print dress, with high heels and loose hair. "You look phenomenal."

"I haven't worn these shoes for months and I'm regretting it already. Good thing I don't have to walk much. Who designed these fuckers, anyway?" She yanked one off and studied it as he pulled away from the curb. "Oh, no wonder."

"Who?" he said, smiling.

"Jessica Simpson." He laughed. She shook her head and put the shoe back on. "I need to chuck out all this shit and wear dance shoes everywhere."

"If they get too bad, I'll carry you."

"You would, wouldn't you?" He looked over at her for a second, then back at the road. *Fuck. That's some agenda you've got there.* Given her history, it was a little alarming. *I do not want to burn this*, she thought suddenly. *Oh help.*

Halfway through the first number of the show, Paula and Mike were both leaning forward, riveted. By the end of the second, they were both dying to be up on stage. It was a re-imagining of 'Beowulf;' they could tell the storyline wasn't going down the traditional path.

They didn't exchange any of the small observations or comments that they might have, because neither of them wanted to take their attention off the stage. At the end of Act I, when Grendel had been executed, all they wanted to do was throw themselves down in front of the show creators and beg for work. A minute into intermission, they finally sat back and looked at each other, then at the program. Beowulf was played by a massively tall man with long red hair billed, appropriately, as Red Warner. Both Grendel and his mother – here called Kali – were played by a six-foot-tall black woman named Mary Bassey. Her chemistry with Red was electric.

"God damn," said Paula. "I need some primal-scream therapy right now." Mike made a gesture of agreement before flagging down a server for drinks.

A minute later, Kelli found them. "Guys! Can you even believe this?!"

"Not really," said Paula. "The choreography is killing me. That Beowulf solo was like, *ungh*." Kelli made an 'I know!!' face. "Had you seen any of this before?"

"I saw a lot of the rehearsal footage, they were posting it on a Dropbox all along and Vince would study at home. I love, love, love all that shit with the spears. But you are going to die when you see what's coming. Mike, you look a little shell-shocked."

"I am. I'm not used to seeing work like this. It's really exciting."

"Can you two hang out for a little while after the show? Vince and I were planning to go next door for pizza. He'll be all wired, probably talking a mile a minute about this whole thing."

Mike looked at Paula; she shrugged. He smiled a little. "I think that's a yes, Kelli, thanks. I want to hear all about it."

They chatted for the rest of intermission, then Kelli left to get back to her own seat as the lights went down. As soon as he heard the music start, 'Paint it Black,' Mike thought, *these are my people.* Halfway through, as Kali flew around the stage wreaking havoc on the warriors, he realized that Paula's hand was clamped around his wrist. He didn't take his eyes off the stage until, as a segue started, she let go of him. He glanced over at her. She said, "Sorry," very low, not looking at him.

"No worries," he said quietly, turning back to the stage. Then the next number began. Within seconds he felt like he was drowning. It was a solo for Mary and she was the embodiment of fury. Her movement was so powerful that he sat back as if he'd been pushed, thinking helplessly, *I have to dance that.* He didn't even know if he could.

Paula tried to watch Mary, but Mike's physical reaction had gotten her attention. At the end, he closed his eyes for a second, opening them when he felt her light touch on his arm. He looked over and she raised her eyebrows, nodding toward his hand, in a fist on the table. He shook his head, opened his hand, took a deep breath.

The rest of the show was every bit as good. The tango that Vince had helped choreograph was, Paula thought, exactly as Kelli had said: smoking hot. And the finale, in which Kali killed Beowulf, was ferociously sexy, even more terrifying than her solo. They both joined the standing ovation at the end, then sat silently for several minutes while bar traffic started up again.

Just when Paula was thinking she should say something, Mike said, "I'm coming back next week. Should I pick you up again?"

Thank you. "Yes."

"What was it about 'Paint it Black'?"

"That flying stuff. I met some of those guys two years ago, they did a number in the same show I did

'Tubular Bells.' I have to learn that. I thought trapeze would be a substitute, but no, fuck, no." She considered him for a moment. "Are you going to try working on that solo?"

He looked up at her. "How'd you guess?"

"You looked like you wanted to *eat* it." He laughed, the line of his body relaxing. Kelli joined them a moment later; a few minutes after that her husband Vince came out from backstage with the rest of the troupe. Several of them decided to come along for pizza. Mike and Paula ate, listened to the rehash of the show, and thought deeply envious thoughts.

The next day, Mike bought another pair of tickets online, then sent a text to Alison: *Green Darkness, Rock Star. Can I use Mary's choreo? I have to try.*

She replied within the hour: **She says go for it. Prepare for pain**

I'm an expert on pain

Yeah guess so :-)

Paula had another 'Jazz' appointment that week, but this time Mike decided not to go. He liked the 'Cat People' choreography, but the state of tension he'd been in during Sunday's show had gotten to him. He wasn't willing to simply not show up, so he sent a text to Paula telling her he'd be seeing his massage therapist after work on Wednesday. She called him immediately on his office phone. "Everything all right?"

"Yeah, things got really tight and it's … I have to deal with it," he said softly, knowing that his office neighbor could hear.

"If you're not fit for the ballroom thing on Saturday, that's okay." *Gaaahh, shit, that sounds like I expected to go with him.*

Mike hadn't missed the implication. He smiled to himself. "I'll be fine."

"Good. Later." She hung up, reassured and obscurely, unwillingly, disappointed. *We are not dating*, she reminded herself. *He is not my partner. Fucking stop it.*

That Saturday was the ballroom social at Shall We Dance. Mike offered to drive again, and again Paula had said yes. Her place was well out of his way, but he didn't mention that and neither did she. They exchanged only a few casual words on the way.

The host at the party, Mateo, was a teacher at the studio, but Mike recognized him from the 'Green Darkness' troupe. He didn't hear what Mateo very quietly said to his partner for the evening, instructor Julia, when Mike and Paula first walked in: "Hold onto your ovaries." Julia smothered a laugh, looking toward the door. Her eyes went wide.

"I see what you mean," she said, equally quiet. She walked over to greet Paula, who'd rehearsed in the studio before but had never come to a social. Then she turned to the newcomer. "Welcome, I'm Julia. Our lesson tonight is foxtrot. Have you done any before?"

"Hi Julia, I'm Mike. I've been doing ballroom off and on for years. Looking forward to it." He smiled, feeling the reaction from around the room. It felt good. For months after the accident, people noticed him for the wrong reasons: the crutches, the brace, the awkward gait. Now, for the first time in a long time, he enjoyed it.

It had been sufficiently long since he'd gone to a ballroom social that he still felt awkward at the beginning of the introductory lesson; those moments of eye contact with strangers were as unsettling as ever. By the end of the half-hour, he felt like he was getting his groove back. He got back around the circle to Paula, who also appeared to be enjoying it.

"I missed this," she admitted. "It's so goofy, but it's fun."

"How long do you want to stay?"

"Whenever."

"Okay." They did the first dance, a foxtrot, together. Then they split up to dance with other partners. They had a rumba together about an hour later, then split up again for a few dances. Mike would have kept dancing to the end if he hadn't felt a headache coming on. He went to get some water, tipping his head back against the wall and closing his eyes for a minute.

"Are you okay?" It was Mateo.

Mike opened his eyes and smiled half-heartedly. "There's a lot of thinking involved," he said. "I was in a car accident a couple of years ago and had a skull fracture. Sometimes things still set it off."

"We've got the usual painkillers if you need something. Motrin? Excedrin?"

"Excedrin would be good. Thanks." Mateo got him a couple of caplets. By that time, Paula had noticed what was going on and joined them. She looked at him silently and he knew she was seeing everything. "We don't have to go if you want to stay."

She silently shook her head. Mike thanked Mateo again. They went to change back into street shoes before heading out. "Are you okay to drive?" she asked as they walked to the car.

"Yeah. Really. I think we caught it in time."

"Is it like a migraine kind of thing?"

"Only if migraines are triggered by excessive thinking. I guess it's more like your insomnia."

"Oh that's fucking great." She sounded so annoyed that he almost laughed. Then, "You didn't get a headache after the jazz stuff?"

"No. Maybe that was more feeling than thinking." The realization was a surprise (and a relief).

"Well, good."

The following evening, Mike collected Paula again for the second performance of 'Green Darkness.' She was wearing flats this time instead of heels. He didn't comment. In fact, they barely spoke on the way to the club. It wasn't until they were seated and had drinks on the way that he asked, "So what did you mean by too much education?"

She cast her eyes up at the ceiling for a second, then gave him a sidelong glance. *Quit that*, he thought, *you have to know how sexy it is*. "I have an MFA in dance from Smith," she said. "It's one of the things I'm maddest about."

"Why does that make you mad?"

"Because it represents a lot of wasted time and of course money. I'm mad at them for selling me this dream situation, which it really was, and making it seem like that *was* the dance life, which it really wasn't. I'm mad at myself for thinking that course was the safer thing, more likely to lead to a lifetime of work than hitting the auditions right out of the gate. So many of my decisions were based on what seemed practical, or logical, or safe. And they all led to me working in a goddamned law office."

"Where did you work after school?"

"No fucking where," she said disgustedly. "I spent two years trying to get a dance job, any kind of dance job. Then I moved out here, because the East Coast was clearly not working for me, and the best offer I got was to do a character at Disneyland. Which, Jesus, kill me now."

He managed not to laugh at her expression. "I never went to college. I went to work right out of high school. I'd been winning competitions and I got an offer to join the company."

"So you were with them for a dozen years?"

"More or less."

"Now I'm mad at *them*."

"Why?"

"Because they dumped you instead of trying to get you back."

"My girlfriend did too."

She looked incredulous. "You're *kidding* me."

He did laugh then. "No. She just couldn't handle it. I don't really blame her. Well, not anymore." Now he was glad. Paula was looking right at him. For once he could read her. *You're glad too, aren't you?*

Mike brought along a notebook and a pen, and this time had enough presence of mind to take some notes during 'Rock Star.' One or two elements would be new to him; others he hadn't attempted since the accident. Even though much of the vocabulary was familiar, this music, in that character, made it fresh. Exciting. He couldn't wait to get started.

At the end of the show, they were hanging around, not quite ready to leave because at that moment neither of them could think of a way to skate around what they really wanted to do, when Mateo came out from backstage and came to their table. "Hi guys," he said, "weren't you here last week?"

"Yeah," said Paula. "We both want to be in it, the best we can do is see it again."

Mike said, "I'd come back next week if it wasn't sold out."

Mateo looked pleased. "We're going next door for pizza if you want. Me and Sam, plus Vicky. Sam is my boyfriend," he told Mike. "And Vicky is, well, she's Vicky. Too bad Sharon isn't here tonight. The four of us went to the Gay Games this summer."

"No kidding! In dance?"

"Sam and I did Latin, Vicky and Sharon did Standard. They made it to the semifinal."

"How about you?"

"Well, not to brag, but bronze medal, baby!" Mike held up his hand and Mateo high-fived. "I'm still buzzed over it." Then Sam and Vicky came out together, making their way through the mob. Both were tall, strong, agile dancers in their thirties; Sam was mixed-race and Vicky looked like a Mafia princess. Mike smiled at the thought of how they'd moved onstage, as warriors. *Yeah, these are my people.* "Hey sugar lips," said Mateo as they arrived, lifting his face for a kiss. "Sam, Vicky … this is Mike."

"I heard about you," said Vicky, looking him over with clinical interest. "From Kelli."

"I can imagine," said Paula dryly.

"There was some bullshit backstage," said Sam. "People making bets."

"And giving me shit like I was going to throw myself at you," said Mateo indignantly. "I mean, okay, you're gorgeous like Sam, and you're tall like Sam, but you're not Sam, so with all due respect, no thanks."

Mike shrugged, smiling. "I'm straight anyway."

"That's perfect," said Vicky. "Now he can flirt with you with complete freedom. Let's go eat."

41

For the rest of October, Paula doubled up on rehearsal time with her team. Their submission had been accepted for the Halloween show of the Underground Cabaret. Mike heard, through Kelli, that several of his new friends would be in the show as well. If it was anything like the ballroom program they'd seen, he was in for a treat.

Meanwhile, Paula had gotten a text from Rory, another friend in the Cabaret: **Why have we not met this Mike person we are hearing so much about, what are we, CHOPPED LIVER? We were stage managing, not ABSENT**

Hi Rory. You know I'm not the apologizing type but I'm gonna apologize. Haven't set anything up because we're not officially dating

From the sound of things, you should be

Trying to keep it casual. You've heard about me and dating. It's always a shitshow

So what, you're "just friends"??

Um yeah. Anyway I'll introduce you at the show, he's going to be there, then maybe we could all have dinner and it wouldn't look like I'm trying to get all girlfriendy

Srsly why tf do you not want to be girlfriendy? I mean from what I hear he is prime, also totally into you

Who told you that?

EVERYBODY

LOL

So??

42

So me + relationship = bloodbath. Especially with men. I like him too much for that

You are one crazypants woman

So I've heard

Srsly EVERY FUCKING BODY

LMAO

Mike checked in with Paula to see if he should pick her up for the next ballroom social, the night before her show. She didn't respond to his text for a couple of hours. By an hour before the lesson was scheduled he was getting ready to go alone. Then, finally, an answer came: I'll get you this time, over your way already

Okay. Ready whenever. Here's the address

She pinged him again when she got there: On a red curb, can you hustle?

On my way

He grabbed his shoe bag, patted his pocket to confirm the presence of his phone, and hustled. It was the first time he'd seen her car but somehow he wasn't surprised; it was a filthy Subaru with rusted bottom panels, even worse than his own snow-maligned Jeep Cherokee. "Did you drive this out here across country?"

"And haven't been through a car wash since," she said. "Afraid the bottom would fall out." She put it in gear and started to drive. She looked sideways at him. "I pay the service center to clean it when I take it in."

"Yeah, I didn't think it really looked like it hadn't been washed *at all* in, what, ten years."

When they got to West Hollywood, Paula found a free space two blocks from the studio and parked. They started walking and she felt like she wanted to say something, but then she also wanted to hold his hand, or rather grab him and throw him onto a bus bench and have her way with him. *Do none of those things*, she thought, half-laughing at herself.

"What's funny?"

"You don't want to know."

"So what were you doing in my neighborhood?"

"I was down in Culver City, actually. Late lunch and meeting with one of the Kung Fu Flyers. Since I'm done with this jazz piece as of Tuesday, figured I'd try to set up some lessons." She gave him that quick sidelong glance again. "Have you started working with Alison?"

"Yeah. It's torture, but I'm loving it."

"Any headaches?"

"Not so far. We'll see how it goes tonight." She actually did catch his hand then, squeezing it quickly before letting go. He didn't say anything for a minute. Then, as they arrived at the studio, he asked, "What was that for?"

She didn't look at him. "Just felt like touching you." He didn't point out that they were going to be dancing together in a few minutes. He was too busy trying to hold back a flood of *want*. Keeping it casual, so as not to swamp her with his agenda, was getting more difficult all the time.

He was almost certain she knew. Almost certain that if he made a move it wouldn't be a disaster. But 'almost certain' wasn't enough, so he kept it light, kept it casual, and hoped that in those moments when he gave himself away (because there had to be some), she wasn't paying attention.

The Halloween show at Chrome was everything Mike had been hoping for. Everything and more, loaded with dance numbers in various styles, plus aerial and gymnastic burlesque numbers. The theme was 'Haunted Hollywood;' all of the music was from movies. A contortionist used 'Tubular Bells,' for a number in which she seemed to turn herself inside out. He supposed with two years in between, the audience probably wouldn't make the connection to Paula's strip routine.

He met nearly all the performers at the after-party. Fortunately he had his notebook and was able to write down the names so he wouldn't forget. Those he hadn't met before included Cabaret principals Stacey (aerial silk) and Rory (strip), Rory's girlfriend Dana (aerial pole), Vicky's wife Sharon, and the champion ballroom couple, Michelle and Dmitri.

"Are we going to get you into one of these things sometime?" asked Kelli when he caught up with her. She and Vince had danced an impressive tango-rumba segue to 'Red Right Hand.' Now Vince was hanging out with some other friends, including Paula, across the room.

"Maybe. Don't have any ideas of my own yet. Is it always like this, the variety?"

"Pretty much, yeah. They used to be straight-up burlesque, but since Michelle and the others took over, they've been incorporating more dance. The owner here, Tyrone? He's their number one fan. We did a special show for his wedding this spring." She looked at him hopefully. "Do you want to get the audition notices? 'Cause I'm pretty sure they'd be happy to put you on the list."

"Yeah, sure." He gazed at her with affection. "Did you ever think, when I was interviewing, that I'd end up over here, thinking about getting onstage?"

"Everybody I like seems to."

"So how long has your husband been dancing? He was great in 'Green Darkness,' and he was great in this too."

"Thanks! I'll tell him you said so. He was doing social salsa for a long time, well, basically all his life. His mother's from Mexico and taught him. Then when he met Vicky he started doing swing. After we got together we started learning Argentine tango."

Mike wanted to ask about Vince and Vicky, because that sounded interesting, but he had a more pertinent question. "Does he dance full time?"

"No, he's a mortgage broker."

Mike huffed out a laugh. "I'm getting such an education in what's *possible*."

He said as much to Paula on their way back to her place. "I know," she said. "I had the same feeling after I met all these people. And then I was kicking myself because for so long I'd thought I couldn't do anything on my own."

"What do you want to do next?"

"I don't know yet." It was all she could do not to say *something with you*.

She didn't say anything else on the way home, and because all Mike wanted to say was *do something with me*, he didn't say anything either.

CHAPTER 6

The next Friday, at five minutes till six, Mike got that email again:

1850 in fifteen

He seriously debated the wisdom of going up. If it was only one shot again, he thought he could handle it. On the other hand … *well, who am I kidding*, he thought. He hadn't seen Paula all week. He got the Alcatraz shot glass out of his desk drawer and went upstairs.

There were only five people this time, counting him; Billy and Susan weren't there. Paula had one of the guest chairs, sitting crookedly with her side against the backrest. She was wearing jeans and sneakers with a halter top. Mike's eyebrows went up. She read his face, as usual. "I wore a sweater at my desk."

"Did you hurt your back?"

"She already showed us," said Dylan. "Show him, Paula."

She sighed, as if exasperated. Stood up, turning her face to the wall. There was a big dark bruise all the way across her back. "It's no big deal." She turned around again.

"What happened?" said Mike. "Oh. Did you have a lesson with the Flyers?"

"Yeah. I crashed a few times. Once there was some stuff in my way. A Flyer, to be precise."

"But did you love it?"

"Fuck yeah," she said, grinning. Dylan and the other guys stifled laughter. Then Dylan pulled out the day's bottle.

"Check it out," he said. "We got the trippy stuff today."

"What even is that?" said Mike.

"It's Empress 1908 gin."

"It looks like medicine."

"It *is*," said Paula.

Dylan poured an ounce, with clinical precision, into each of the shot glasses. Then he produced a bottle of lime juice. "Picked it up special," he said. "Watch this." He added some juice to each shot; the blue gin turned pink. "Magic!" The glasses were claimed, clinked together, and rapidly emptied.

"Wow," said Mike. "That one actually tasted good."

"One more?" said Dylan.

"Uh ... I guess I could go take a walk at the mall before going home." He handed over his glass again, as did Paula and one of the other guys. Dylan refilled them. This time Mike tapped his glass only against Paula's. For a moment it was like nobody else was in the room. "Salud," he said softly. Drank this one slowly, looking in her eyes. Her chin went up and her lashes came down. She drank her gin and then licked her lips, still looking at him, and he thought, *damn this to hell.* Paula's eyes widened.

"Maybe you should take this one," said Dylan, breaking the spell. He capped the bottle. "I think you might need it. Better put that shit in here." He produced a brown paper bag and put the bottle and juice in it, then handed the bag to Mike.

"Thanks, Dylan. I'd better ... I have to go. See you around," he said to everybody. After he closed the office door, he heard three male voices chorusing

"Whoa" and "What was that?" He kept walking, reaching the elevator bank before Paula caught up with him. He turned, hearing and recognizing her footsteps. Stood there and stared at her.

"Want some company for your walk?" She cursed herself for saying something so inane, but his expression was nothing she'd ever seen. It wasn't angry, or hurt, or sad, but all of those things together, topped off with a longing so magnetic it scared the hell out of her.

"Paula. You know I'll take any time with you that I can get," he said, tired of not saying everything he wanted to say. "Why are we still doing this?"

She didn't ask what he meant. "I have to pick up some shit at my desk. Come along, or meet on the plaza?"

He signed. "I'm going to take this down to my car. I'll meet you out there."

"Okay." All the way to her desk, to the bathroom, and then down to the lobby, Paula was asking herself *Can I do this? Will it be worth it? How long will we have?*

She was waiting near the doors when he came back up from the garage. They looked at each other for a moment without speaking. He had what she now recognized as his public, calm face on, but his gaze was wary. *He's not sure why he's bothering with this,* she realized, with something close to panic. "Can we walk?"

Mike thought she was genuinely asking, as if maybe she thought he'd prefer to have this argument – or whatever it was – right here. He produced a confused gesture.

49

Paula said, "It's easier for me to talk if I'm moving."

"Then we can walk." They walked toward Avenue of the Stars, then down the block to the bridge, and she hadn't said anything yet.

Finally, after they crossed, still moving, she spoke. "You know how you survived that crash. You should have been dead. I'm glad you weren't," she added. "That's not what I mean. I mean, you're the boy who lived, aren't you? You're this kind of magical beast and you've had your life changed by circumstances beyond your control. And I ... I can't seem to change my life no matter what I do."

"I don't think you want a change like a car crash," he said.

"No, of course not. Who would? But it created this vacuum for a whole new life to rush into, and you didn't sit home and, like, nobly *suffer*, and start driving trucks or whatever. It would have been easier for you. Probably everyone thought you would."

So she did Google me, too, he thought. For some reason, that was encouraging. "It was a close call."

"Or maybe you'd have come back halfway, working in a studio in Minneapolis, teaching other dancers to grab for that piece of sky that ought to be yours."

"Maybe that's where I'll end up anyway."

She moved her head dismissively, like, *not a chance*. "Yeah, whatever. You moved on and said that's not for me, I want something else. You didn't know if you could have what you wanted, but you went after it anyway."

"Why do you think you're not doing that?"

50

"Maybe I am," she said after a few minutes. "Now. For the past two years, I've started to make things happen. I'm not used to it yet. Because for the fourteen, *fourteen* years preceding, nothing happened. Except a series of stupid, pointless, repetitive mistakes."

"What kind of mistakes?" he asked after a few more minutes. The mall music was too loud. It was annoying. All he really wanted to do was sit her down and look at her face and figure this out. But if she had to move, he'd move.

"Okay. You're the boy who lived. I'm the girl who *left*. Every time."

"Left what?"

"Left everything. Left before things could disappoint me. Which means they always disappointed me, because I never knew what could have happened."

There was a long pause before he was ready to speak again. "Paula. If things aren't right, you're *supposed* to leave. You're not supposed to stay in a situation that isn't working because maybe magically one day it will *start* working."

"But what if I'm the whole reason it wasn't working?"

"Are you actually insane?" he said, after a short silence in which she really wanted to look at his face but was afraid to. Now she laughed, kind of. "Have you always been like this?"

"Like what?" For once, she didn't want to assume she knew what someone was going to say.

"Insomniac. Compulsive exerciser. Angry."

"I've been angry for a long time. Since high school, when my boyfriend said 'it's not you, it's me' and then I saw him literally two days later kissing someone the polar opposite of me. Or since college when the *exact same fucking thing* happened again with a girlfriend."

He left that alone for a minute. Then, "You know Madonna's from up my way, right? Northern midwest. She's one of the people I thought of when you were talking about female rage. Nobody thought it was cute, even though she's tiny and beautiful, because right from the jump she looked like she would rip your throat out with her teeth if you fucked with her. Anyway, she married Sean Penn, right? And that didn't work out. And he turned around and married someone else and started a family. Same thing happened with Warren Beatty. Madonna, panic, marriage and family."

"What are you getting at?" Paula said after a minute, catching up from the point where he said 'fuck,' because he usually didn't.

"There's a lot of guys – a lot of people – out there who can't handle female power. And that is not the woman's fault. It's not the woman's *problem*. That's what I meant about if it's not right, you're supposed to leave. If those exes of yours turned around and made a beeline for someone who was everything you're not, that's because they couldn't handle you. Not because something was wrong with you. They were doing you a favor."

She stopped walking, so he did too. "Mike. Somebody else you know has rage. There has to be somebody. Who? What happened?"

"My sister was raped, and my mother lived for twenty miserable years with an abusive alcoholic. There's a lot of rage to go around."

"Jesus." She turned to look at him, finally. "That makes my little issue seem pretty trivial."

"That wasn't my intention."

"No, I know." She studied him. "So. Are you ready to tell me about your agenda?"

"My agenda." He nodded slowly. "Sure. If you really need to hear it."

"We've been talking in sign language for the past three months. I could really use some words right now."

"Okay." He looked around; they were in the middle of a traffic flow and hadn't even realized it. "Let's go over here where it's quieter." They walked a little way, to an area free of pedestrian traffic, where the music wasn't quite so loud. She stopped about four feet from him, *outside my reach*, he thought, *if I weren't a dancer*. He realized that even with all the dance shows and the ballroom and the coaching, it was the first time he'd thought something like that since the accident. He took another minute to think through what he wanted to say.

"Because of you," he said finally, "I feel like a dancer again. I want to dance with you. I want to watch movies with you. Sit in the dark and talk with you. Drink magic gin with you once in a while. I want to go to dinner with you, and walk on the beach with you, and someday, which I really hope is someday soon, I want to kiss you." He stopped. Her face wasn't at all hard to read in that moment. "I want to take you to bed," he said softly, "and get to know how it feels to have you naked against me."

The next silence seemed to last forever. Then he reached across the space between them, caught her hand, drew her a little closer. "Paula?"

"I want to sleep with you," she said, her voice breaking, and went to pieces.

She cried the entire time they were walking back to their building, down the elevator to the garage, and as he helped her into his car. She cried while he drove to his place and parked. It wasn't dramatic sobbing, more like she couldn't breathe without tears, but by this time he'd gone beyond concern and was well into alarm. He had to lift her out of the car and carry her into his apartment, sincerely hoping none of the neighbors saw them and called the police. He got some water into her, sat her on the bed, took off her shoes. It was as if she'd been trying to cry for years and never managed it, and now everything was coming out. She curled up in a ball of misery. He didn't know how to handle this, or if he should even try. All he knew was he couldn't leave her alone, and she wouldn't want anyone else to witness whatever this was. So he got ready for bed as quickly as he could, went back to her in his tee shirt and briefs, and lay down beside her, tucking her against his front and simply holding her. It seemed like ages before she finally stopped crying. They didn't speak. Eventually, incredibly, they both went to sleep.

Mike woke up when the morning light made it through the bedroom window. He didn't know what time it was. All he knew was that Paula was in his bed, still asleep. He got up quietly and went to refill the water glass, then pulled the bedroom door almost closed. Knowing it was an invasion of privacy, he then rummaged through her bag for her phone and woke it up, checking for any appointments that day. He didn't see any, so he turned it off and put it away again. Then he found his own phone and woke it up to send a text to Kelli.

Hi Kelli, this is not an emergency - I think - but I thought someone should know. Paula had kind of a breakdown last night. She's with me, she's safe, I'll stay with her. If you could ping me back when you're up I'd appreciate it. Keeping it quiet over here, she's sleeping. Thanks - Mike

He wasn't really hungry. With nothing else to do that wouldn't make noise, he spent the morning stretching, thinking, browsing on the Internet, occasionally checking on Paula. He got himself something to eat around eleven. By his estimate she had been asleep for twelve hours. He didn't know that much about her habits, but he guessed this was some kind of record. His phone buzzed not long after.

Hi Mike, just got your note. Everything okay?

She's still asleep. I'm trying to think what to do

Can I help?

Would you say she's probably going to want to pretend this never happened?

Good chance of that. Did you talk?

Before the dam broke

Did you tell her how you feel?

He didn't wonder how Kelli knew how he felt; he hadn't really been trying to hide it. *Yes*

And is that when shit happened?

Yes. But I don't think she was sorry to hear what I had to say

55

Of course not, she's not actually insane

Guess I'll do what I was going to do anyway

Which is?

Take care of her. And give her what she wants

You're a good man. Keep me posted

Will do

Mike was watching a movie with his headphones on when he caught movement off to the side. He glanced over, paused the movie, took the headphones off. Paula was standing in the bedroom doorway, staring at him. It had been so long since the crying jag that her face looked normal. He suspected it didn't *feel* normal, but there was nothing he could do about that. "Hi," he said. "How are you feeling?"

"What time is it?" Her voice sounded raw.

"Three o'clock. Saturday," he added helpfully. She flapped a hand at him. "Bathroom's that way." He pointed; she shuffled in that direction. The bruise on her back had lightened a little. He had time to send a quick update to Kelli before Paula came back out a few minutes later. "Hungry?" She shook her head. "Want me to take you home?" Another negative. "What can I do for you?"

"What are you watching?"

"'Ninotchka.'" He patted the couch beside him. When she sat down, they looked at each other. He brushed some unruly hair off her face. "I'll be right back." He went to the bathroom himself, then came back out, sat down with her, and un-paused the movie. Left the sound on this time, but not loud. After a few minutes, Paula leaned against his shoulder. It was such a clear request for a cuddle that he put his arm around her. A while later, she slid onto his lap and fell asleep again.

She woke up when he was well into 'Silk Stockings.' It took her a minute or so to regroup. "Double feature?"

"One of my favorites."

"What's another?"

"'The Artist' and 'Singin' in the Rain.'"

She smiled and sat up. Cyd Charisse was doing the lingerie ballet. "This is my favorite part."

"What, not 'The Red Blues'?"

"That's my favorite too."

He finally took her to the office to pick up her car at about eight, after a quiet (for L.A.) dinner in an Italian restaurant not far from his place. Before getting out of the car, she said, "I owe you a few more weeks' worth of dance stuff."

"You don't owe me anything."

"Okay, then let's say I want to set up another few weeks' worth of dance stuff."

"That works." He considered her. "I'm working on the big jumps with Alison and Mary tomorrow. Mary's going to demo and critique. Alison's going to spot me. Sam and Mateo are coming too. Three o'clock. You want?"

Her face lit up. "Fuck yeah!"

"You want me to follow you home?"

"No, I'm okay." She looked away for a second, then back at him. "Thanks."

CHAPTER 7

Once home, Mike decided not to think about what had triggered the episode and instead be glad he'd finally said what he wanted to say. Everything else was out of his control. He sat down with his laptop to review the video he'd taken during his latest sessions with Alison, since they'd started working the entire piece. Soon, he was totally absorbed, letting the shapes and the rhythms of the choreography wash through him, feeling his nerves fire even though he wasn't moving. On the second viewing, everything he'd been feeling for the past six weeks seemed to crystallize. *I am a dancer again*, he thought when he finally turned off the computer. *They were wrong.*

Meanwhile, Paula had gone home, taken a shower, gone through her usual plan-for-the-week routine, then sat herself down on the couch. Didn't turn on the TV, didn't listen to music, didn't read. Simply sat in the dark and thought about what Mike had said, and what she'd said, and what it meant.

She'd thought – okay, she'd *hoped* – he would kiss her Friday night. She knew he wanted to, had wanted to for a long time, from the first. And she had been *this close* to kissing him herself, so many times. At the ballroom socials, when he was holding her … especially during the Latin dances when he was looking right at her. Those eyes. That body. That physicality, which he'd said was not nothing, as if he had some idea, but he couldn't possibly. He couldn't possibly know that the way he moved in a dance was like a thunderstorm, electric, fresh, sometimes startling but always thrilling.

Then again it was even worse during the ballroom dances, when the communication was so purely physical, when her body had to read his not only without a word, but without a look. They'd danced a foxtrot at the last social that had been so telepathic she'd had trouble letting go of him when the music stopped. She hadn't wanted to come down to earth.

I understand him, she thought finally, *and he understands me. Even though I have so completely failed to explain myself.*

She'd said that she was the girl who left. This time, she was more afraid of leaving than of staying.

They didn't see each other at all for the next week, except for the coaching session the Sunday after what each of them thought of as That Night. Paula spent some time in the Hollywood studio with a video of that session and a video Alison sent her of the original blocking, learning the 'Rock Star' choreography herself. She didn't contact Mike, because she didn't know what the fuck to say.

Mike sent a text when they found out about a special party at Shall We Dance. Michelle and Dmitri were heading for the Ohio Star Ball to compete for the World Professional Smooth championship again. They were going to perform their competition show dance at the party.

SWD party? I can pick you up if you want to go was all he wrote. He knew she would have the details from the studio's email. The same language he'd always used, not 'if you want to go with me' or 'can I take you' or 'would you like to go with me.' Always careful not to frame it as a date. He was sick of it, but as far as he knew, That Night hadn't actually changed anything.

Yes was all she wrote in reply.

When he got to her condo he didn't even have to ping her; she was waiting by the gate. Paula pulled the door open and got into the Jeep, meeting his eyes briefly before looking away. It had been one thing to work with him and the other dancers at the studio. At this moment all she could think was *he knows what I look like when I break*, and the fact that he would still come for her almost broke her again.

"It's good to see you," he said quietly after a moment, pulling away from the curb.

She couldn't manage to speak until he was parking down the block from the dance studio. "Thanks for coming for me."

"I will always come for you," he said, with a little smile that she caught in her peripheral vision.

Paula thought *oh fuck me, The Princess Bride?* They'd given each other movie lines before, usually tweaked to fit a situation, but she hadn't expected one now. A flush of gratitude and relief had her laughing under her breath; she wracked her brain for a line to give him back. "It appears to me as if we're doomed, then." She couldn't remember if it was in the movie, and she had no idea if he'd read the book, but he suddenly laughed. She set her hand on his for a moment; his turned underneath it and he held it tightly for another moment more. Then he let her go and she got out of the car.

Mateo and Sam performed an hour into the party, with a rumba they'd been working on for January's Broadway-themed edition of 'Mating Dance.' They were dancing to 'Do I Love You Because You're Beautiful,' from 'Cinderella.' Paula and Mike sat on the floor at the far end of the studio and watched Sam as the prince, with Mateo in the Cinderella role. Mike was humming along with the music, and very softly sang the first two lines of the lyric on the reprise. "That song's about us." He wasn't looking at her.

"I'm not beautiful," she said after a pause. *Did he just say he loves me?*

"Wrong," he said absently, watching the dance. He didn't say anything else. He got to his feet when the performance ended, gave her a hand up, applauded with the rest of the crowd. The main show would come later in the evening. For now, there was more social dancing.

Paula let Mike monopolize her a bit, dancing with others occasionally. They did a rumba and he finished with a trick from Sam and Mateo's routine, spinning her into the curve of his arm and then taking her off her balance to a sliding split. She let him take her weight, trusting him completely, laughing. He didn't say anything, only smiled and set her back on her feet. Their faces were close; she thought, *now?* But he let Dmitri take her away for a foxtrot.

Before the main show, Dmitri announced to the gathered dancers that if he and Michelle won the championship again, he would be retiring from competition. His expression was more austere than usual, even when the whole room made a sound of sympathetic disappointment. At the end of the performance – the adagio set to 'I'll be Seeing You' – Michelle curled into Dmitri's shoulder, crying. He hugged her with his cheek against her hair, and then her husband came over to them, putting his arms around both her and Dmitri. Mike watched, thinking, *how hard must that be? To give up such an unbelievable partnership?* But knowing how old

61

Dmitri was, seeing his silver-haired husband Patrick across the room, he understood. And envied.

The last dance of the night was a waltz. Mike listened for a few seconds; it was Bob Dylan's 'When the Deal Goes Down,' one of his favorites. He looked for Paula, spotting her not far away. Someone else was approaching, so he got to her fast. "Sorry, my dance," he told the other guy, and swept her onto the floor.

"This whole I'm-in-charge thing is kind of working for me," she said. "Political incorrectness notwithstanding."

"Hush," he said. "Listen." She hadn't recognized the song. Mike was leading simply, so she turned off her dance brain. Concentrated on the lyrics. Thought, *oh my God.*

Finally the music stopped and the lights came up. They went to change back to their street shoes, then Mike held her jacket for her. She shrugged into it, looked up at him over her shoulder, started to say something. Her mind went blank at the look on his face.

He met her eyes for a second before his gaze went to her mouth. After that dance, after *everything*, it was too much. All at once his brakes failed and he kissed her. No preliminaries, no experiments; it was hungry, open-mouthed, passionate. The plundering, devouring, insatiable kiss Paula had read about in romance novels but never experienced. She was breathless and shaking when he finally raised his head. His eyes were dark. Under the hand that had landed on his chest, she could feel his heart pounding.

Their gazes locked for a long moment. Then Mike realized he had his hand on her throat, his thumb on one side of her jaw and his fingers on the other. He took a breath, let his hand slide down to her shoulder, and opened his mouth to speak.

Paula cleared her throat. "If you fucking *apologize*, I will kill you where you stand."

He let go of her and looked away, laughing silently. After a moment they both looked around. The few people still in the studio were carefully not looking at them. "What were you about to say?"

"I can't remember," she said. He tipped his head toward the door and she followed him out.

They didn't say anything to each other as they walked to the car, or as Mike drove east, or when he turned south toward her condo. He pulled up outside her gate, as usual. She didn't get out of the car. Instead, she turned to him and said, "Do you want to come in?"

He huffed out a breath, surprised. *Truth.* "Yes."

"Pull in the driveway, I'll give you my key card to open the gate." He followed directions. "You can park behind me in my space, it's a tandem." He drove slowly forward and she directed him to the space. She opened the passenger door and got out before he could get around to her. He locked the car and followed as she headed for a stairwell, scanning her card again to open the door. When it closed behind them she suddenly turned and moved into him, stretching up to kiss him, one hand plunging into his hair. He moved one foot back for balance, then leaned against the door, pulling her tight against him and diving into another drugged, oblivious, drowning kiss. Her slim, strong body was tense and she made hungry little noises that were driving him wild. His hands were on her hips, urging her, closing on the fabric of her dress and pulling it up little by little until he could touch her bare flesh. "Jesus!" she said, almost into his mouth. "We have to get out of here."

"Yeah," he said breathlessly. "Probably a good idea." He was fully aroused and felt lightheaded. All he wanted to do was things that could get them arrested. She stepped back as he reluctantly let go of her, both of them taking deep breaths while she tugged her skirt down. She was smiling a little as she turned around and started up the stairs. At the third landing she scanned her card again and pulled open another door, holding it for him. They walked down the hall. He wasn't keeping track of how many doors they passed. He couldn't think of anything except how much of *everything* he wanted.

Finally they were through a door. She threw her key card and her bag onto a table, not even looking when the card skidded across the surface and dropped off onto the floor. The nice midwestern boy he used to be would have held back for a moment and asked for permission. Mike set that on fire without regret, moving forward to wrap an arm around her, dragging her with him through the living area and down the short hall to the room he knew had to have a bed in it. She didn't say anything. When he stopped, she turned, her legs against the side of the bed. He set his hands on her shoulders and she sat down, reaching up to unfasten his pants, pushing them down without ceremony. He got his shoes and everything else off in the time it took her to remove her own shoes and the dress.

Then he got his fingers under the thin fabric of her underpants and pulled them off. Knelt down between her legs. "I've wanted to do this since the day I first saw you," he said, looking up at her face.

"I know. I've wanted you to do it." She was propped on her elbows on the bed, legs over the side, watching him. When he leaned close and touched her, kissed her, licked her, as decisively as he'd kissed her mouth at the studio, she let her head fall back. "Jesus fucking God, Mike, oh my God, that feels so *good*," and she kept talking, making him even crazier.

One hand pressed her thigh back till her foot rested on his shoulder. Two fingers of the other hand worked into her. She stopped talking with a moan that never seemed to stop, just caught and recycled until with a sort of panting scream she came, bucking hard against his mouth and collapsing onto the bed. He gently extracted his fingers and stayed with her until she relaxed, pressing his face against her thigh. She put her hand in his hair. "Tell me you have a condom," he said huskily. "I wasn't expecting this tonight."

"Who could have?" she said, half laughing. "In the nightstand." He shifted over to open the drawer, found the box, shook its contents onto the top of the little table. She had gotten her legs up on the bed; now she pulled down the covers and stayed there, on hands and knees, looking like a lioness about to tear into a downed gazelle as he stood up. "You gorgeous animal," she said. "Give me."

"Give you what?" He set one knee on the bed and leaned closer. She raised herself up and pressed her bare skin against his, shoulder to knee, mouth on his throat, taking him in her hand. "*Fuck*, Paula."

"That. Everything."

CHAPTER 8

Some time later, exhausted, hungry, thirsty, and still naked, they wandered out to the kitchen. They both drank water as if they'd been in the desert. Paula stayed close, as if she needed to feel his skin against her even though they were, for the moment, utterly spent. Her hands were too unsteady to cut up an apple, so he did it for her, dropping the slices into a bowl she took down from the cupboard. She doused the fruit with balsamic vinegar, then opened the refrigerator and found some cheese. He cut that up too, then tore some chunks off a loaf of challah. They ate standing up, touching at feet and knees and elbows. When they were done, he opened his arms to her and she leaned against him with a sigh. He stroked her hair back off her face and kissed her lightly.

"Your scars aren't bad," she said. "I don't know what I was expecting."

"They're all surgical."

"It's good you have those. Otherwise you'd be too goddamned perfect." He made an amused, dismissive sound. "How are you feeling these days?"

"You can't tell?"

"Okay, so you seem pretty damn strong. And flexible. And did I mention strong."

Mike smiled. "I feel great. I mean, stuff still hurts sometimes, but I'm so used to it now. It doesn't interfere."

"Your elevation is kind of incredible. No one would know you broke anything. And your extension is almost as good as mine." She sounded faintly offended, which made him laugh again.

"I really was lucky. I'm still lucky. I'm lucky I came to L.A., lucky I interviewed at this firm, lucky you were there. Lucky to be here."

"You think it's luck?"

"Actually that last thing I don't think is luck," he said after a moment.

"About being here?"

"Yeah. I think we've both worked for that."

She nodded, then stood back a little. "Now that we're a little more rational, what do you think of the place?"

"In a minute." He gave her a searching look. "Did you want this from the beginning?"

"I wanted to fuck you, like, immediately," she said. He laughed. "It wasn't until tequila night that I thought, uh-oh."

"I thought you changed your mind about something. When we were standing at the bridge, before I left."

"Yeah. When you said that about female rage, and then what you said about the truth, I thought holy shit, he gets it, if this guy isn't afraid of me then I can't do that thing I do. And I couldn't be that person who asks for the truth and then won't accept it." She looked away for a second, then back at him. It should have been awkward, standing there naked and talking like this. It wasn't. He'd already seen her. "I couldn't because I wanted more. I *wanted* the truth."

"But you were hung up."

"I was afraid of what the truth might be."

"So. Now that you have a better idea about that, how do you feel?"

"I want to dance with you. I want to do everything we've been doing, and everything we've just done, and everything else there is, and damn the consequences."

"Okay." The word ended on an up note, as if they'd reached some kind of agreement. He looked away then, slowly examining the main living space. It was a single room containing a lounge area, an eating area, and the kitchen. The walls were painted dark gray; the ceiling had sparkly acoustic 'popcorn.' The kitchen cabinets were white. On the wall over the couch were two framed Underground Cabaret posters flanking a Warhol-esque collage of four head-and-shoulder portrait images. Mike let go of Paula and walked over to get a closer look. Pictured, in four shades of high-contrast monochrome purple, were Nicolas Cage, Rhys Ifans, David Strathairn, and Leonard Nimoy. Mike couldn't help noticing that with a little makeup and a few years (or some hard living), he himself could be a reasonable facsimile of each of the actors. "So I guess you have a *type*."

Paula shrugged, walked over, and flopped down on the couch, pulling an afghan off the back. "Andy made that for me. He does the Cabaret posters and stuff." He sat down beside her and put his arm around her. She draped the afghan over their legs and rested her head on his shoulder. "So Borodin is a Russian name, right? There's some Russians back in my tree somewhere too."

"My father's family came from Russia back in the day, my mother's came from Norway." He looked to the left. He assumed there was a window under the wall of ornate drapery. There were side tables, instead of a coffee table, which left enough floor space for a tall person to stretch. Across from the couch was a big flat-screen TV flanked by racks of DVDs.

"I have a little bit of a movie problem," said Paula. "When I can't sleep, if there's nothing on TCM or whatever, I'll chuck in one from the library."

"Me too. How's that been the past couple of weeks?"

"I've been sleeping better than usual."

"That's good." They didn't talk for a few minutes. The room was quiet and dark; they'd only turned on the light from the kitchen's vent hood. "These drapes really muffle the street noise, don't they?"

"Yeah. And they look so much nicer than the vertical blinds. We're not allowed to remove the blinds, but nobody ever said we couldn't hang more shit over them to hide them. It's not like there's a view."

"The management company lets you paint, too. That's nice."

"They don't let renters paint. I own this one. Well, the bank and I own this one."

"How'd you swing that?"

"My first six years here in L.A., I was working as a litigation assistant. Logged a shitload of overtime and double time. Banked it all to buy a place, because renting sucks. When this one came up I liked the location. Plus it's the top floor and it's a corner, so I'm only sharing one wall. And it has a pool. That makes up for a lot of the shit that comes with living in L.A."

"It's great." He glanced at her. "I would think that kind of work would make a person even more ragey."

"Yeah, I suppose it did. Anyway, I left that job and got one as an entertainment assistant. After two years placing calls for those celebrity-adjacent dickheads, I moved over to where we are now. The corporate guys are not exciting, but they are also not dickheads."

"The real estate folks seem to be okay." He took another moment to enjoy being where he was, but realized he didn't know if she wanted him to stay. So, in the spirit of truth, he asked. "Do you want me to stay tonight?"

"Yes," she said. He kissed the side of her face. She turned so he could kiss her mouth. He took advantage of it, feeling like he would never tire of it. She put her hand on the side of his face, stroking down his neck to his clavicle, running two fingers along the sides of the bone. "Thanks for sticking with me."

"You know, you aren't actually horrible." She dropped her head to his shoulder, laughing silently. "If I had *only* been trying to get in your pants I might not have stuck. But we were doing things I wanted to do. If it wasn't *everything* I wanted to do, well. I'm not entitled to something simply because I want it."

She sighed and straightened up. "Could you please display some kind of flaw? Because honestly."

"Okay. I've been informed that I can be as stubborn as a mule. And I'm a lousy student. I barely graduated from high school. Probably would have flunked out of college. I'm a pretty fluent speaker, but writing anything longer than a text is painful. I got my first law job as a favor, and if law firms didn't use so many forms, I'd be screwed." He half-shrugged, smiling. "I basically never cared about anything but dancing, so that's the only stuff I paid attention to. Can I tell you something I learned about the dance life?"

"What's that?"

"It either knocks the bullshit out of you, or it magnifies your vices. I didn't like what I saw on the one side."

"You mean you were once an entitled little prick?"

"Yeah, kind of. I was good," he said. "And I looked good. Women liked me. Choreographers liked me. It would have been so easy for me to just mow through people."

"So what happened? Because, not to inflate your ego or anything, but you're still all of that."

"But I wasn't perfect for everything. There were parts I didn't get because my style was too edgy, or because I was too tall, or because they were looking for a more diverse cast and I'm about as white as you can get. Anyway, I had to learn how to see *why* casting decisions got made, and that made me see that a lot of my ... call it prominence, in the company, was strictly down to strength. It wasn't necessarily talent. I had skill, but skill is a different thing."

"You mean strength like literal strength? You had the lifting ability."

"Right. I was the muscle. All of the guys in the company had the technique, but with all the girls who were over five foot four, I was the one taking them up because I'm six one."

"That's one of the things that got me, being five seven," she said. "I thought, my God, he's actually tall enough for me."

"So what should we dance together?"

"I don't know yet. What are you doing with 'Rock Star'?"

"Alison says we should put it on video and throw it up on YouTube. Actually, she said we should do that and then I should reactivate my Facebook page and talk some smack."

Oh yeah, do that. "Like, I'm back, bitches?"

"Exactly."

"I am so there for that. When could we do that?"

"I guess we could do it next Sunday. I've got the room again."

"How were you affording all those hours?" Not that it was any of her business, but she'd been curious all along.

"Alison wasn't charging me. She said she was new to coaching and if it turned out the way she hoped, I'd be a good advertisement. So I've only been paying for the room at the studio. And, well. There was still money from the insurance settlement." He felt her react.

Paula hadn't thought about that. "The other driver's insurance?"

"Yeah. Anyway. We've taken a lot of rehearsal video. Elena, from Dmitri's studio?"

"Yeah?"

"Her husband Tony works on that Ovation series 'Live Work Dance' and he's been in, too."

"Jeez, talk about celebrity-adjacent."

"I'll let him know when you and I start working on something. He's always looking for new people to feature."

"Cool." She yawned. "Guess it's kind of late."

"Go get ready for bed." He kissed her again. Watched as she stood up, dumping the afghan on him. Watched her leave the room, still not quite believing they'd ended up here, like this, the way he'd hoped from the beginning.

She was already asleep when he got to bed.

Mike woke up at some point; the room was completely dark and very quiet, but a moment later he heard a car door close. He knew exactly where he was. Paula was breathing softly beside him, and he was painfully aroused. *Don't wake her up*, he thought. He sat up and moved as quietly as possible to the edge of the bed, intending to go take care of things himself, then stopped when her hand landed on his hip.

"Mike." Her voice was very quiet.

"Yeah."

"Where are you going?"

"Sorry … I was trying not to wake you up." She moved closer to him, then even closer. Her face was against his back and both arms were around him. One hand went to his chest and the other to his groin. He inhaled sharply as her hand closed around him. She kept hold of him as she moved, her mouth now on the back of his neck, one hand on his throat, the other still on him. "Paula." He tipped his head back against hers and she kissed his face.

"I'm getting back on the Pill immediately," she muttered. He laughed breathlessly. "Get one of those damn things, would you? I have to have you."

He hadn't thought he could be more turned on, but apparently it was possible.

The next time he woke up, the clock on the nightstand read ten o'clock, which meant – he thought

73

– that he'd slept over eight hours. Aside from that little intermission. The memory made him smile. He slid out of bed and found his shirt, then looked around the room. There were two windows in the bedroom, both covered with heavy, beautiful drapery matching the deep-purple walls. He hadn't noticed the night before that there was another portrait collage over the bed, this one in shades of blue; the images were Marisa Tomei, Michelle Yeoh, Jennifer Beals, and Angela Bassett. *Your type for girls, I guess*, he thought, untroubled.

The only furniture aside from the king-sized platform bed was an Art Deco vanity with curved wooden cabinets and a big round mirror, with a round stool upholstered in purple velvet. Over it hung a cluster of small chandeliers, all painted shades of blue, strung with blue and purple beads and crystals. He'd never really thought about what Paula's home would be like, but the colors and the textures surprised him. He wondered what else he'd be learning about her.

He looked over at the bed; Paula seemed to be deeply asleep. He left the room quietly, pulling the door nearly closed, going down the hall to the living area. When he checked his phone there was a message from Kelli, sent a few minutes before.

Michelle pinged me. Dmitri wants you and Paula for Mating Dance: Broadway Melody. He says Dancing in the Dark, the movie choreography. FYI it's pretty hard to say no to Dmitri :-)

Hi Kelli. You mean the Astaire/Charisse choreo? I'd love to try it. Would he coach?

Hey! I'm sure he would. Probably Michelle too.

I'll ask Paula. 80% chance, my guess.

Make it 100. I believe in you

LOL

Mike put down the phone on the side table and went to the racks to see if Paula had a copy of 'The Bandwagon.' Unsurprisingly, she did. By the time she came out to the living room, he'd watched it almost all the way to that number.

"What's up?" she said, coming over and flopping down beside him. He paused the movie, picked up his phone and lit up the text exchange, then handed it to her to read. "Hey! Cool!"

"You want?"

"I haven't done that style since college, but if someone like Dmitri says they want me to do something, I'm gonna try to fucking do it."

He smiled. "That's what I thought, too. So how'd you sleep?"

"Like a rock. Let's watch this thing." He put his arm around her and hit 'play.' They watched the dance twice, then let the movie play to the end. Paula turned to him and kissed his face, his mouth, his neck, his chest. He put his hand on her face and brought her mouth back to his. Her hands wandered. "You're a lively guy," she said, smiling.

"It's been kind of a long time."

"How long?"

"Since before the accident."

She pulled back, looking appalled. "That's like … two and a half *years*."

"Well, I was in and out of the hospital for a while, and it took months for the anesthesia to work out of my system, and, you know, things hurt. Then Sheri called it quits, so I had to get my head around that. Once I was in rehab, I guess I could have, but ... I didn't want to."

She played with him some more. "That doesn't seem to be a problem now."

"I don't think I have any problems now," he said, kissing her again. "And this was worth waiting for." She slid off the couch, tugged him to his feet, and started walking backward to the bedroom.

CHAPTER 9

The following Friday, they met up in Dylan's office again. Susan and Billy were there, not the other two guys. Susan looked Mike up and down, then studied Paula. "Uh-huh," was all she said. Paula bit her lip. Mike managed not to laugh out loud. Billy and Dylan were wheezing.

"It was that magic gin, I swear," Mike said. "Kind of a delayed reaction."

"Did you drink it all?" Dylan wiped his eyes.

"Saving it for emergencies." Mike glanced over at Paula.

Susan said, "Uh-huh," again, then added, "Magic gin, or somebody's magic wang?" and Paula clamped a hand over her mouth and turned to the wall, shoulders shaking. Mike looked at the ceiling and breathed deep. Billy cough-laughed.

Dylan shushed him. "Careful, some of the dudes are still here. Maybe just as well we have something different today." He lifted a tall bottle out of his bottom desk drawer. "Macallan 18. It is only because you are very special people that you are here for this."

"Oh, Dom and Sandor are going to be *bent* if they find out," said Susan, and they all lost it.

"God, I thought we were caught for sure," said Paula as they got on the main elevator to go down to the lobby. "I heard footsteps in the hall and was like, shit!"

"I was amazed how quiet we got. Dylan's face though," and Mike started laughing again. "Where did he even put that bottle?"

"Who cares, as long as he didn't knock it over. You could smell it all the way over by the door once he got the cap off. If it had spilled, he would have had to stay all night shampooing the carpet."

"Everyone would have come down the hall like," he put his nose in the air, sniffing. Paula snickered. "He would've been so busted. Doesn't anyone ever ask where the booze goes?"

"Honestly, I suspect they all know. It's like don't ask, don't tell, and for fuck's sake don't be obvious. That's why the group is small. Most of these people can't keep a secret."

"You hardly even knew me before you invited me," he pointed out.

"Yeah, it was a little risky. The truth is, I couldn't think of another way I could reasonably see you. Our paths don't cross in the office. Eh." She squirmed, embarrassed.

"Thanks for that," he said softly, his hand on her back. "Want company tonight?"

"Actually, I was wondering."

"What?"

"I've got a session with the Flyers pretty early tomorrow."

"I'm like five minutes from that gym. You could stay at my place."

"That's what I was wondering." She gave him that look, chin up, lashes down, very faintly smiling. He couldn't help it; he kissed her, taking his time over it.

Eventually, and really only because the elevator doors opened, he lifted his head. "I know I'm not supposed to do that on the premises."

"Says who? Kelli only told *me* 'no boning in the file room.'"

He raised his eyebrows, considering that. "Fine, then. I'll follow you to your place, you get your stuff, and we'll go in my car. Right?"

"Right."

Paula ended up staying at Mike's all weekend. It seemed practical, since she had gym time in Culver City on Saturday and he already had the studio near him booked for Sunday. On Saturday night they walked around his neighborhood and found a decent little restaurant for dinner. After getting back, he said, "I found a movie with one of your pin-ups. Have you seen this?" He held up the case for 'Good Night, and Good Luck.'

"Yeah, I saw it in the theatre. The only reason I didn't buy it is I had temporarily exceeded my storage and needed to get rid of a few. Then I got otherwise occupied. I'd love to see it again."

"Cool." After washing up, they settled down on the couch. Midway through the movie, Mike found he wasn't really paying attention to the acting because he was concentrating on the soundtrack. "This music is amazing."

"Does it make you want to dance?"

"Yeah, it does." Once the movie was over, he got online to order the soundtrack. And then he scooped Paula up off the couch and took her to his bed.

The next day started late. Mike couldn't seem to stop kissing Paula. She wasn't exactly fighting him off. After the morning's second round of sex, he fell back, out of breath and laughing. "I don't know what's gotten into me."

"Maybe your lizard brain is thinking of 'Rock Star.'"

"Yeah, maybe." He rolled off the bed. "And speaking of which, I'd better get away from you so I have a little juice left for putting that on tape."

"Oh, very nice," she said dryly. He leaned over her quickly, caging her with his arms. "Hey now."

"Maybe I'll fuck you in the studio after I dance," he said softly, leaning in to kiss her one more time. The thought of it made her hot all over again, but she gave him a little shove. He was smiling as he left the room. When the shower went on a few minutes later, she was strongly tempted to go get in with him. *Stop it*, she thought, laughing at herself. *He needs his strength.*

They stayed a safe distance from each other while she showered, they dressed, and they ate. He pushed the couch against a wall so they could both stretch. Paula wanted to run the routine one time herself, just for fun. There was one of the big tricks - the 540 - that she couldn't execute, so she'd substituted another move. Mike fully intended to put her on tape. It was one of those things for the 'yeah, I did that' archive, he thought. They assembled their gear bags and walked over to the studio a little before three.

"Okay," said Mike. "Warm-up first. Then you?"

"Okay." He put on some music and they did a standard warm-up together. Then he put the performance track on and they both marked it through. Paula said, "I'm ready." Mike stepped away and sat on a folding chair by his boom-box, getting his camera ready. "Are you taping?"

"Of course I'm taping," he said. "You're gonna want to see this when you're sixty-five."

"Whatever, okay." She paced for a minute, getting her head straight. Went to her mark and nodded. He started the camera, started the track, and watched as she completely nailed it. When she was done, on her knees, chest heaving, he switched off the camera and went to lift her up. He didn't say anything, only held her, because her breathing had hitched and he could tell she was trying not to cry. After a minute she pulled herself together. "How was it?"

"I think you might be surprised when you see that." He kissed her lightly, then stood away. "My turn."

She nodded and stepped over to her gear bag, stripping off her sweat-soaked leotard and tights and wiping down with a towel before pulling on a knee-length, long-sleeved fleece dress and legwarmers. Mike was aware of her watching in the mirror as he did a few more warm-up moves. His body felt strong and loose; he couldn't wait to dance. He bounced on his toes, getting into character as Paula brought the towel out to wipe up a few drops of sweat on the floor, then got set up on the chair. She raised her eyebrows; he nodded. She started the track.

Jesus, Mary, and Joseph. From the first stalking walks across the floor, he was chilling. *For someone so good-natured, he sure is convincing as a killer.* His movement had a different quality from Mary's, harder-edged. But then, he wasn't a goddess with infinite power. He'd be paying for every life he took. Paula wondered if he had any idea what this actually looked like. It was as if he knew his own savagery could rebound onto him twice as hard, but he

81

was undeterred. Her hands were trembling; she hoped the camera's image stabilization would cancel it out. *We should have had a fucking tripod*, she thought. She had to try twice to hit the stop button when he finished.

He was breathing hard, staring at her. She couldn't tell if he was still in character; decided she didn't care. She went to the door and locked it, still watching him. He moved then, getting to his feet and pulling off his clothes as he headed for his gear bag. He dropped his trunks and leotard on the floor, got out his towel and wiped his face, then grunted because she had cannoned into him. With her hands on his body and her mouth on his throat, he got an arm around her before they both went down on the crash mats stacked by the short wall.

"Turn on the music," he growled. She flailed around without looking, pressing buttons until she got 'play.' He dug in his bag for a condom. She snatched it out of his hand and ripped open the wrapper, pushed him down, climbed over him and got him ready, then sank onto him. He surged up into her, his back coming off the mat, hand going to the nape of her neck and mouth to hers, breathing in the urgent noises she made. Then she was underneath him, moaning into his mouth. In less than a minute it was over. They lay together, panting, until the song ended.

"Did we both survive?" he asked, after a while. His voice was back to its usual purr.

"I think so," she said. "Let's not tell Alison about this."

"You think she doesn't know?"

"Yeah, you're right." He disengaged and they slowly sat up, doing their best to put themselves together and erase the evidence. Paula went to her bag to get a packet of fresh wipes. "I wasn't sure what would happen here today," she said, "but I thought we might possibly need these. People expect a certain amount of funk from a crash mat, but, yeah."

He blew out a breath, imagining what that must have looked like. "It's a good thing this wasn't our first time, huh?"

"God, can you imagine? We would both be needing therapy. Like, *psycho*therapy." She pulled on some underwear and sat on the chair. Gazed at him, fidgeting a little. "This is new."

"Which part?"

"All of it."

He was dressed again, sitting on the floor with his arms draped over his knees, watching her. "Are you okay? With all of it?"

She gazed at him. "Are you?"

"I love you." *And that's the truth.*

She nodded, seeing it in his face, accepting it. "I'm pretty sure I love you, too."

"Only pretty sure?"

"Well I've never felt exactly this way before, so there's an element of guesswork." He moved his head, smiling. "What time is it?" He found his phone and held it up. "We're not working on anything else today, are we?"

"I think we're done here."

"Okay." They got up, packed up their gear, made sure the room looked more or less normal. Unlocked the door and went out.

When they got back to his place, Mike went straight to his computer to re-activate his Facebook page. Then they downloaded the camera and watched Paula's video. "Damn," she said. "I was pretty good there."

"You were great. You should post it."

"You think?"

"You don't have anything like this up. If the right people see it … well, you know." He didn't press it, simply watched his own video. After it ended he sat back, looking at Paula, proud of what he'd done but also sort of horrified. "I can't believe you didn't run out of the room. I didn't know it would look like that."

"Like what?" She knew what *she'd* seen, of course, but wondered if he saw the same thing.

"Like I was going to *literally* start killing people." She grinned at him. Mike shook his head. "And I can't believe I didn't know I had that inside me. I thought I was okay." She laughed out loud. "Are you sure I should post this?"

"Absolutely. All those fuckers in Minneapolis are going to think, goddamn, good thing he's two thousand miles away. They're going to be quaking in their hockey boots." She regarded him for another moment. "I'll post mine if you post yours. Public."

"Deal." A few minutes later, uploaded and posted, Paula put a shout-out to Alison and Mary on her Facebook page, thanking them for the choreography and linking to the video. Mike did the same. Then he added a second Facebook post: *I'M BACK, BITCHES*.

Comments poured in for the rest of the day. They ordered pizza and let the feed run, refreshing their pages from time to time to see what was being said, occasionally laughing, sometimes replying, usually letting it flow. One of Mike's former colleagues who liked the video post replied to his 'I'm back' with **From WHERE?! Holy Shit Mike**. He responded with *a couple of collisions.*

Mike's sister posted a bug-eyed emoji and his mom posted a gif of a fainting goat. Paula didn't get anything from her family, but a tidal wave of comments from Cabaret and other friends came in. Around eight o'clock, Alison posted to both of them with congratulations, tagging Mary. Another hour went by before they heard from her.

Just got back from a bloody boring job to find FB's blowing up with these lovelies. Now I have to put up my Kali version. THE ORIGINAL I might add. It's a three-way duel you tossers!

Mike and Paula both waited for the link to go live, then immediately posted replies. Paula wrote I'm not worthy, please don't kill me, all hail Kali! Mike wrote, more seriously, *Dance was my life for 24 years and this piece brought me back to it. All hail Kali.*

Nearly the last comment they both looked at was from Alison, and it tagged Mary. **Let's all get together and talk about these, soon. I have ideas.** "That sounds promising," said Mike. "But I guess I have to take you home, huh?"

"Yeah, probably. I don't have work clothes for tomorrow." She gazed at him for a minute, thinking. "Are you going home for Thanksgiving?"

"No. You?"

"No." After a moment she added, "Everything I'd give thanks for is right here."

"My God, Paula." He leaned close and put his face against hers for a moment, then kissed her. "When you say something like that it knocks me out."

"I'm trying to not be so opaque."

He kissed her again, then turned to his laptop. After shutting down the computer, he asked, "Was that usual? For you to put up something about dance and get nothing from your family?"

"Yep. That's the relationship, in a nutshell."

"Leaving aside all the stupid people in the world, no wonder you have rage."

"Had," she corrected. "I had rage. But I must have left it in the studio, because now I'm only mildly annoyed." He was half-laughing as he kissed her one more time.

A four-way text exchange led to a Wednesday night meet-up with Alison and Mary out in the Valley. Mary had moved in with her 'Green Darkness' co-star and they were all already thinking about their next project. Mike and Paula went straight from work in his car, picking up fast food on the way, talking about life in general more than dancing. *This is nice*, thought Paula. *Is this what normal feels like?*

When they got there, Mary handed around bottles of Angry Orchard and then the four of them sat down at the big dining table. "We have a couple of questions for you," she said. "First question is a pop quiz. What was different about our three interpretations?"

"Um," said Paula. "I think yours and mine were closer. We were, eh, more specific. You were in a very specific character with a very specific target. I had a specific target in mind without a specific character. I mean, it was really just me. You're a goddess, I'm a sociopath."

Mary laughed with delight, then she and Alison both nodded, looking at Mike inquiringly. He glanced away for a moment, then back at them. "I was Dresden," he said.

Alison, whose husband was a World War II buff, got the reference. "Complete, unforgivable, but possibly necessary retaliation," she said. "Did you know that's what you were doing?

He shook his head. "I think if I had *tried* to do that, I would have screwed it up. There's been this, um." Words failed.

"Magma bubble," supplied Paula. "His old company cut him loose after the crash and nobody but nobody said 'come back when you're ready.' They were all, oh too bad, time to get a real job, let's go hire a twenty-year-old."

"Bugger!" said Mary. "Any reaction from that direction?"

"The company director asked me to come back. PMed yesterday." He glanced at Paula, whose eyebrows had shot up. "It's the first time I've heard from him since I got out of the hospital. I said go fuck yourself." All three women laughed. "Probably not the wisest thing I could have said."

Paula said, "I think it was *exactly* the right thing to say." Mike shook his head, smiling.

"I'd agree," said Mary. "You can't put the genie back in the bloody bottle. Now you know what you've really got to work with, what you have available to you when the gloves come off." She blew out a breath. "When Alison told me she wanted to talk with you, and Paula this is directed to you as well, we both looked at some of your previous work. You can't go back from this sort of thing. So it's good you told that director to get stuffed. It would never have worked."

"Okay," said Alison. "Next question is multi-part. Have either of you done Latin ballroom, flamenco, or Argentine tango?"

"Not yet," said Paula. Mike shook his head 'no.'

"If I get in touch after we get somewhere with planning for the next show, would you be willing?"

"Any show with you," said Mike. "Especially if Mary's in it."

"Same," said Paula.

"Okay then. We won't keep you out here, because brainstorming at this stage would be pointless, but we'll be in touch." Alison stopped, then added, "And a word of advice?"

"What?"

"Make up proper websites with lists of your credits, your background, and some stills. You don't need more than a landing page, but you both might be hearing from people. They need to know how to find you."

"Okay," said Paula, looking at Mike. "This is so weird. This is what I wanted ten years ago."

"Maybe you're only now ready for it," Mary suggested. "Could you have done that piece ten years ago?"

"I doubt it."

"I couldn't have either. Physically, maybe, but not with the conviction it needed."

"I'm looking forward to finding my own way back," said Alison. "I left professional dancing voluntarily, but watching Mary during this process has me full of righteous envy."

All of them understood that. Paula said, "Let us know when you're ready to move. We'll look forward to hearing from you."

CHAPTER 10

On the way home, Paula looked sideways at Mike and said, "You never used to say 'fuck.' Kind of interesting."

"Yeah, well, I never used to dance like I wanted to cut somebody's throat with one of my own ribs, either."

"Jesus! That's quite an image," she said, laughing. "I mean, I like the way it sounds when you say it."

It was his turn to laugh. "I like the way it feels in my mouth. It feels like you."

Holy moly, she thought, flushing all over, squirming a little on the seat. "Damn."

"I wish we lived together," he said, taking a hand off the wheel and sliding it under her skirt, between her legs.

"Damn! So do I." She wanted to close her eyes and ride his hand, but the traffic on Ventura Boulevard was heavy and she lost her nerve. She started giggling and lifted his hand away. "That's a risky approach considering you've already almost gotten killed in a car once."

He glanced over at her. Holy crap, Paula was straight-up giggling. He did that? Why did that turn him on even more? "I could pull over."

"Or you could follow me home after we get my car."

"That could be hours in this traffic. I like the pull-over option better." He took the next turn and found a dark side street. By the time they got back on the road, the traffic jam was long gone.

Basic website setup consumed the following Saturday. The next week, they met up with Dmitri and Michelle for a first look at 'Dancing in the Dark.' Michelle greeted them at the studio, saying, "It's so great that you're willing to do this. Kenji and I are going to be traveling for a while, and I think Dmitri needed a project, you know, to kind of transition out of our thing."

"We both thought, well, we haven't done this style for a few years, but if someone like Dmitri wants us to, we are not gonna say no," said Paula.

"That's the way I felt too, when he first asked me to train in ballroom. He'll be out in a minute. What else have you been up to lately? I mean, I saw those videos of yours. Holy smokes."

"That's pretty much it. We haven't made any what you could call *plans*, yet," said Mike.

"Are the Cabaret and Mating Dance schedules set?" asked Paula.

"I think so. Julia's going to be managing Mating Dance, Stacey's taking over Cabaret. I'll make sure they send you whatever as soon as they have it."

"Thanks," said Mike. "I have some lost time to make up for."

Michelle smiled. "I kind of got that idea." Then Dmitri came out of his office and they got to work.

Paula thought, sometimes, that she had expected it to be more difficult to go from Not Dating to Dating. It seemed that everyone they knew had considered it inevitable. They had regular dinner get-togethers with friends, whose most common reaction was 'what took you so long.' Paula discovered that she literally could feed Mike anything: he was fearless about food, which made for a refreshing change from the last person she'd dated, who'd lived on smoothies and bagels. But then, pretty much everything about Mike was refreshing.

When she looked back at how simply he'd accepted her, right from the start, she couldn't quite believe it. But she also didn't doubt it. Nothing about him was artificial. Whether it was the work he'd done in rehab, the work of being a dancer, or simply the way he was built, she felt more truth from him than from anyone else she'd ever been with.

For his part, Mike felt that L.A. had started to get its hooks into him. His first few months had been lonely. The city's assets hadn't outweighed its miles of dusty pavement and endless traffic. Getting back into dancing and meeting so many dancers made him feel more at home than he'd thought he ever would. Having Paula to look forward to at the end of every week made the often-tedious office job bearable. Having her to dance with was a blessing he wasn't sure he even deserved.

He never questioned whether he should have dated more, or met more different women. After so many years as a dancer, he was well aware that finding someone you connect with at that telepathic level was not to be second-guessed. He'd had that connection only once before, with an older, already-married dancer, when he was twenty. She made the choice to end the relationship before it properly began, after a private rehearsal took a dangerous turn. He'd agreed with the decision, but he'd never forgotten how it felt to look in someone's eyes and know *exactly* what they wanted, what they needed, and how they were about to move. It was something he'd always hoped to experience again. He knew he surprised Paula sometimes, but he suspected she'd grown used to shutting down the way she wanted to be, the way she wanted to dance, because she hadn't found that person willing to take her as she was.

They worked with Dmitri three times to lock choreography, then took 'Dancing in the Dark' back to their local studios to perfect it for the January show. Tony Benedetti, studio manager Elena's filmmaker husband, dropped in to various coaching sessions and rehearsals to take footage for the Ovation series he worked on. They took video of their own and played it on the laptop in synch with the movie, to make small adjustments to lines or timing. They wanted to convey exactly the same sense of casual improvisation within the structure of the dance.

Mike's mother called on Christmas Day to check up on him. His sister lived with her, so they all got to talk. They didn't give him any flak about not coming home for the holiday. Paula got a lot of flak from her parents (as usual) and ignored it (as usual). The firm was closed that day and the day after, so they had another four-day weekend; she had no intention of feeling guilty about not going somewhere she didn't want to go. Then Mike asked, close to midnight, "You want to go somewhere? Get out of town for a minute?"

"We haven't gone to the beach yet."

"I did say something about walking on the beach, didn't I. Where's a good one?"

"Who do we even know who goes to the beach?" She said it like going to the beach was something only aliens, or tourists, would do.

"Vicky and Sharon do. In Santa Monica."

"Well, I guess if we're beach beginners, maybe we should stay local," said Paula. "Have you been to the beach at all since moving to L.A.? I have, but it's like I keep forgetting it's there."

"Nope. It does seem like something I should do."

"And take pictures and post them with a big 'suck it' to your Minneapolis people. Aren't they up to their asses in snow right now?"

She sounded so pleased about that. Mike gave her a nudge, amused. "You've got it in for them."

"Actually, I'm grateful they were so stupid, because you might not have come out here otherwise." She leaned over to kiss him, still shy about verbalizing how she felt. *But I did tell him I'm pretty sure I love him.*

"I love you, too," he said, as if he'd read her mind.

So the next day, they went to Santa Monica Beach, and it was great. There were plenty of people around, but most of the traffic seemed to center on the shopping areas. They found quiet areas to walk down on the sand, then came back to the pier area. "Some of this, you could almost dance out here," said Mike. "All the pavement."

"I guess there's dance stuff up on the pier sometimes." They went up and wandered around, then stopped in amazement at a trapeze school. "Well, I'll be damned. How did I not know this was here?" said Paula.

"Are they open?"

"I think so." They walked in and found somebody wearing a school-logo tee shirt. "Are you guys open today?"

"We don't have a class scheduled today, but one of the instructors could be here in fifteen minutes if you wanted to do a private."

Mike looked at Paula. "You want?"

"Why not?"

"Ow," he said, getting out of the car when they got back to Paula's condo. "Ow ow ow."

"Yeah, it's, ow, different," she said, a little creaky herself. "I haven't done flying trapeze before."

"But you've done all that other aerial gear. Imagine how *I* feel." He flexed his hands.

"We could get in the pool for a while. It's heated."

"Can I wear dance shorts?"

"Sure, why not?" *Wear nothing*, she thought, *I dare you.*

Again it was as if he'd read her mind. He gave her a sly smile. "Your poker face doesn't work on me anymore. So no, not unless it's dark out."

"Unfortunately, there's automated lighting everywhere out there."

"Too bad."

They went to the pool anyway, letting the support of the water help them relax out of the trapeze fatigue for a nearly-silent hour. They finally fetched up side by side on the underwater concrete steps. Mike leaned against Paula's shoulder. She intertwined her legs with his. "So you've now been to the beach."

"And mocked my snow-bound ex-friends."

"And flown on a trapeze."

"Which was a lot of fun, even if I'm sure I'm gonna regret it tomorrow." Mike leaned closer and kissed her. "Merry day after Christmas."

"I didn't get you anything."

"Yes you did." After they went upstairs, showered off the chlorine, scrounged up something to eat, got down on the floor to stretch, Mike said, "So I've been thinking about the next thing."

"What next thing?"

"The Cabaret April show. The theme was 'After Hours.' And I thought, what about 'One for my Baby.' The Dianne Reeves cover, from that movie."

Paula thought about it for roughly two seconds. "Yes. What's your concept?"

"I'm the bartender. You come in, you've been stood up or maybe dumped, you're sad. I give you a shot, it's kind of funny. That's the first verse. Then the second verse I invite you to dance. It's jazz, Gene Kelly style, with some foxtrot stuff. During the bridge we start to get close. Maybe I try to kiss you. The last verse, we separate and I know I have to let you go." He'd been watching her face. *I hope I never do.*

"I almost love it. How about at the end, I come back to you?"

"Obviously that works for me," he said, pleased.

"It's a little too sad the other way, I think. We can fake them out – make it look like I'm leaving – and then I run back and you catch me. I think the Chrome audience would really go for that."

"Okay then. Anything you want to work on?"

She looked at him almost shyly. "I did have an idea. It's kind of weird. I think it would kill if we could pull it off, though."

"Give me."

"Let me play you the music and then let's see if you can guess. You're getting awfully good at

96

reading my mind these days." She went and found her phone, plugged it into the stereo dock, called up the track and hit Play. It was Pat Benatar's cover of 'Wuthering Heights.' Mike listened, eyes closed. At the end he looked at her, went to get the printout of the Cabaret and Mating Dance schedules, and studied those.

Then he looked up. "Cabaret, October, Lunatics?" Was she really thinking that far ahead?

Paula actually bounced. "Yes!"

"Are you Cathy's ghost, on the flying rig?"

"Yes!! Jesus!" He laughed "So can I tell the Flyers? See if a couple of their rope handlers can be available?"

"Yeah, of course." He came over to her again, kneeling by her and nuzzling her neck. "You know, in case we're too sore to move tomorrow, maybe we should go fool around now."

"I like how you think." He gave her a hand up. "Ow."

"Still want to fly?"

"More than ever." Then she squealed as he scooped her up. "Jesus, you've got muscles."

"The better to fly you with." He managed to carry her down the hall, kissing her, without crashing into the walls.

Much later, with her face tucked into the curve of his neck and shoulder, Paula mumbled, "I realized that was a little overconfident."

He knew what she meant. "What, the October idea? Why would that be overconfident?"

"It's just, you know, that would be a gold-medal record, for me. To make something last that long."

"But it's different this time. Right?" She didn't answer right away. He shifted them a little so he could look at her face. "For what it's worth, I'm a faithful guy. And why wouldn't I be, when you're absolutely perfect for me? But if something changes, if *anything* changes, I'll tell you. I won't lie to you. Ever," he emphasized. His voice was low, soft and warm. As always, it made her feel as if she were wrapped in furry comfort.

She made a little gulping noise and he hugged her close again. After a minute she said, "Yes. It is different. I want this to work. And I won't lie to you, either." She kissed his collarbone. "It's been so long since I thought something might have a future, I hardly know how to behave."

"Keep doing what you're doing. I like it."

"I like everything about you. It scares me."

"I know." He kissed her again.

CHAPTER 11

January 2015

At dress rehearsal for Mating Dance: Broadway Melody, Mike and Paula got their first look at the other performances. Sam and Mateo were there with their Cinderella rumba; Vince and Kelli were dancing to 'I'd be Good for You,' from 'Evita;' and, to everyone's surprise, Julia was dancing not with her boyfriend and professional partner Ray, but with Dmitri. They were doing a jazzy foxtrot to 'Necessity,' from 'Finian's Rainbow.'

The show's lineup was usually all ballroom, but Rory was doing a strip routine set to 'Take Back Your Mink' from 'Guys & Dolls.' "I couldn't resist," she told Paula. "It's such a great song."

"Can't wait to see it. How'd you get it past Julia?"

"Made her laugh," Rory said cheerfully. "By the way, you're a ringer for Audrey Hepburn tonight. I dig it."

Mike and Paula were slotted in as the final number, which gave Paula plenty of time to get nervous. "Why are you twitchy?" Mike asked softly. "It's only a dress rehearsal. And it's not like you don't know the routine."

"It's so different from, like, *everything* I've ever done here. And I've never closed the show."

"Maybe that's because we've got a prop," he said, pretty sure that wasn't actually why. "Nobody else has anything on stage."

"Well, you can't do the routine without a bench." Paula suddenly laughed, stifling it behind her hand.

99

"What?"

"I realized this is also the first time I've been fully clothed on this stage." She was wearing a full-skirted white shirt dress much like Cyd Charisse's movie costume, though unlike Charisse, she was wearing high-heeled character shoes. Her hair was up in a twist, she'd shaped her eyebrows, and she was wearing makeup, a winged line of black eyeliner. Mike was so used to her naked face that even that slight embellishment had a big impact.

When everyone else had run through their routines, Mike and Paula took the stage, his white suit and her dress almost glowing under the stage lights. Following the movie choreography, they walked on together to music already playing. The dance was as near as possible to an exact copy of the Astaire/Charisse classic, moody and contemplative, as if they were getting to know – and trust – each other. The nature of Mike and Paula's real relationship and the absence of a significant age difference gave their action a greater intimacy, with a breath of heat in the way they looked at each other. Since there was no horse and carriage, they'd tweaked the choreography to finish sitting side by side on the bench, leaning ever so slightly together, looking up at the artificial moon.

All of the performers were still in the club and had taken seats to watch the closing number. When they finished, they received a round of applause. As they came off stage, Rory said, "Well that wasn't dreamy at all."

"Excellent partnership," said Dmitri. "I knew it."

"Thanks for that," said Mike. "It's been a real pleasure. It was a pleasure to see you dance again, too."

"I'm glad he decided to do it," Julia said, patting Dmitri on the back. "With Ray out on location, I thought I'd have to sit this one out. Besides, the students love to see him dance. I know it's not the same as dancing with Michelle."

"You are lovely dancer," he said, kissing her forehead. "It is my honor."

Kelli said "Aww," and everyone laughed, even Dmitri.

Once the January show wrapped, Mike and Paula got straight to work on 'One for my Baby.' There was so much less choreography than their previous dance that it came together faster than expected. They were at Shall We Dance one afternoon and realized they had downtime.

"Well," said Mike, "Alison did suggest working up some Latin stuff. Should we talk to Julia?"

"Does she teach Argentine tango too?"

"Guess we'll find out." A very minor amount of back and forth led to them working with Vince on Argentine tango and Julia on paso doble. They planned out a training schedule through to April.

They went to work as usual, swapped weekends based at each other's apartments, kept seeing their network of mutual friends. Mike wasn't entirely sure whether Valentine's Day was a thing for Paula, suspected it might not be, but decided to take a chance and plan something. They'd already planned to see the Underground Cabaret's February show on the fifteenth. He sent a text to Kelli to see if she had any suggestions.

Hi Kelli, I've got a kind of stupid question

LOL what?

Paula, V Day. Don't think she's the take me out to dinner kind of girl, restaurants are always so crowded here and I'll bet it's worse for Valentines

So horribly right. I'd say that's a no

But in my head we're at the six-month mark now so gotta do something. WANT to do something

Have you been to a milonga yet?

No, we're such beginners

I'd try that anyway. She doesn't get freaked out by new stuff

True. Great idea, thanks!

We like this one in the Valley. Hosts are Michael and Aida. Maybe we'll see you there ;-)

"Wondered if you'd like to go out to a milonga on the fourteenth," he said casually, on their way out of the office on the ninth. "Wanted to do a little something since, you know."

Paula said without thinking, "I usually don't do anything for Valentine's Day." Then she realized how brusque she'd sounded and looked up at him. "But it occurs to me that's because there generally hasn't been anyone I wanted to do something *with*. I'd love to go to a milonga with you."

"Good."

"Maybe I'll even get a new dress."

"You'll have to shop fast," he said, smiling. "Now that Kenji's out of town you can't just call him up and say, make me something."

"Maybe Kris can do it. You know, Mateo's sister. She works with Kenji. I'll give her a call."

Kris was delighted to get a last-minute commission. She pulled up Paula's stats from the Underground Cabaret file and got right to work, promising it would be ready on the morning of the fourteenth. She sent Paula a phone picture of the proposed fabric. Paula approved it, then called her colorist. "Shaya, I need a trim and some new color, can you fit me in?"

"You know every damn woman in L.A. is getting new hair this week, right?"

"I know. But this is my first Valentine's Day date in, like, forever. I mean literally forever. Please?"

"Oh God. Um. Can you come in at eight on Wednesday?"

"Morning or evening?"

"Morning." Shaya sounded apologetic.

Well, if that's what it took. "I'll call in sick."

"Okay, then you're on."

Paula and Mike didn't see each other again until he picked her up that Saturday night. When she came down the sidewalk he was watching, thinking, *that's for me.* She slid into the car, in her new, slinky, wine-colored dress. Eyeliner, hair up, the freshly-colored wine-and-black ends fanning out from a knot. Wearing an old pair of character shoes, carrying a new shoe bag from Worldtone. He didn't say anything at first, only leaned over and kissed her.

"You dressed up," she said, grinning. He was wearing his white suit.

"Glad I did," he said. "You look … spectacular."

"Wait till you see my new shoes."

"If they're as good as everything else, I hope this place has some kind of back room." He pulled away from the curb. "Have you eaten?"

"Yeah, I had something. Wasn't sure if this place would do food."

"Good, me too." He glanced over at her again. "Thanks for coming out with me tonight." She didn't say anything, only reached over and patted his thigh. *God, don't do that*, he thought, smiling. She must have been watching his face; he heard her laugh.

Almost the first people they saw after the hosts were Vince and Kelli, in the middle of the dance floor. "I'm surprised they're here," said Paula. "They've got a competition next weekend."

"Guess they thought, screw it, we can practice tomorrow." They claimed a table, then Mike went over to the bar to get drinks. When he got back, Paula was blatantly taking video of Vince and Kelli with her phone. "Getting some inspiration?"

"Exactly. I'm starting to recognize what the various leads feel like, but I don't think there's a 'too much' in terms of studying this stuff." She crossed her legs, calling attention to her new (black and white snake-print with crimson patent trim and three-inch spike heels) shoes. She watched Mike's gaze travel up her legs. When he got to her eyes, his had that dark look she loved. "I asked Aida," she said. "No back room. So hold that thought."

"Oh, I will." They watched the other dancers for a while, observing how a set of songs would be separated by a brief musical interlude to change partners. Then they took the plunge and got up themselves. Mike didn't try anything fancy, simply enjoyed holding Paula in the close embrace, moving with her around the floor, feeling how different their basic moves felt with different songs. At the end of the first hour, they went and got fresh drinks. As they returned to their table, Vince came over and asked Paula to dance. Mike got to Kelli five seconds before another man. "You'd be doing me a favor," he said.

She made a 'whatever' face as she took his hand. "You're looking good, considering it's only been a couple of weeks."

"Vince is a good teacher. Paula said you guys have a competition next weekend."

"Yes! We decided to try a theatre-arts routine. We worked on it this afternoon and we'll be back in the studio tomorrow, but a night off was compulsory."

"Can we come and watch?"

"Sure. I'll send you the info. So I was happy to see Paula here tonight. When she called in sick on Wednesday I thought uh-oh." She glanced up at him; he looked clueless. She laughed to herself, thinking, *you had no idea.*

At the end of the tanda, he walked her back to her table, asking, "How am I doing?"

"We didn't crash. In fact, I think you haven't crashed all night. Good floorcraft is half of good milonga, so that's very promising."

Vince was there waiting with Paula. "Lead me," he said to Mike. "I was watching that last bit."

"Uh-oh. What did I do?"

Vince shook his head. "Nothing bad. Come on." So the two men went out on the floor and Mike led Vince for a couple of songs. Paula and Kelli sat and watched, both declining invitations from other men. They could see that Vince was quietly suggesting things to Mike. Paula recognized moves from ballroom-style tango and rumba. The dancing grew gradually more confident.

"That is sexy as hell," said Paula finally. Kelli snickered. "I know, but they're both insanely good-looking and, *fuck*." Kelli giggled. "You guys ever swing?"

Kelli clamped a hand over her mouth, shaking with laughter. "That is not something we have previously contemplated," she said finally, fanning herself. "Woo!"

Paula was smiling. "I was recording you earlier. Do you want to see?"

"Sure." They stood up and went over to Paula and Mike's table so Paula could get her phone. She retrieved the video and played it for Kelli. "It's always nice to see a recording and think it looks something close to how it felt," said Kelli.

"I love watching you two. It's like every line of his body says how much he loves you."

"Awww." Kelli looked over. "Have you seen yourselves dancing before? Not on stage, I mean. Like this."

"No."

"I'll record the next one for you. You might be surprised." Then the men came back to the table and Vince invited Kelli to dance again. "I promised to

106

record them," she told him. He shrugged and sat down with her.

Mike held out his hand to Paula. "Vince gave me some suggestions. Want to try?"

"Always." They went back out on the floor.

"What did you say that made Kelli laugh so hard? I almost ran Vince into somebody." He was smiling, watching the traffic as he led her.

"I said it was totally sexy watching you and Vince, and did they ever swing."

He didn't get it at first. "You mean swing dance?" Then, "Oh!" and they were both laughing.

Vince and Kelli left at eleven-thirty; Mike and Paula stayed past midnight. They both tried other partners a few times, discovering that they'd learned more than they'd thought. They might have gone even longer if Paula hadn't felt Mike stall a little.

"This was great," said Paula, looking up at his face. "But you have a headache, don't you."

"Little bit." They sat down and he closed his eyes, took a handful of hair at the back of his head and pulled, turning his head slowly from side to side. "It's not too bad. Once Vince pointed out I could use ballroom stuff, I started to feel the music more."

"I'll give you a neck rub after we get home. And I'm driving." Before changing her shoes, Paula dug out a pill box and gave him a couple of Excedrin PM caplets, handing over her half-empty water bottle. "I'll go get another of these." She walked quickly over to the bar; Mike watched, swamped with love.

Paula made Mike sit inside till the valet brought the Jeep around. She watched him as he exited the building, noting how he flinched away from the bright

107

light over the door. Once he was strapped into the passenger seat, Paula adjusted the seat and the mirrors, fastened her seatbelt, then carefully pulled out. "This thing feels like such an elephant compared to mine."

"It's not really that much bigger."

"I know, it's just taller. But it handles like a cinder block." She drove cautiously, observing the speed limit, occasionally checking on him. He'd reclined the seat a bit and had his eyes closed. "You okay?"

"Yeah, honey, I'm fine." He opened his eyes, turning his head to look at her. "I was planning to make love with you tonight."

"It's already tomorrow. So I'll bet you will." Traffic was fairly light and they got back to Paula's complex quickly. She parked the Jeep and they went upstairs. Mike was moving slowly. Once they got into her condo, she said, "Go get ready for bed. You want anything to drink?"

"No, I'm good, thanks." He gave her a kiss and went down the hall, trailing one hand along the wall as if he couldn't quite see where he was going. *You're not good*, she thought. When she joined him he was flat on his back with his eyes closed, but not asleep. One of the bedside lamps was still on. "What time is it?" he said.

"Half past one. How are you doing?"

"Better."

She thought that was probably true; the lines of strain around his eyes had eased off. "Well, let's see if I can knock that bitch all the way back." She got in bed and sat cross-legged, laying a pillow lengthwise across her shins. Mike moved over to put his head in her lap. This wasn't the first time she'd dealt with one of his headaches. It wasn't how he'd wanted this evening to end. She started working on the neck-and-shoulder complex that tended to contribute to the headaches. He gradually loosened up and relaxed. He was nearly asleep when she took her hands away, smiling drowsily when she leaned over to kiss him. She drew her legs out from under him and stretched them out for a minute, then switched off the lamp.

It wasn't a good sleep night for Paula, so she was up before Mike. She left the bedroom quietly, went to the living area, got down on the floor to stretch. She made some coffee after a while, since they were planning to go out again that night. The aroma brought him out eventually. He was moving normally and looked rested. "Thanks for untying my knots last night," he said, leaning down to kiss her.

"You lied to me," she said, looking at him sternly. "Don't say you're fine or good or whatever when you're half blind with pain."

He laughed a little, carefully. "Yeah, okay. That one snuck up on me." He went over to fix them both mugs of coffee. They took it the same way: half and half, no sugar. "This really smells great. We have it so seldom, I always forget."

"Me too. The stuff at the office doesn't even smell like coffee compared to this." She sipped for a minute. "Do you want to go to the studio today?"

"Not unless you want to. We've got the blocking video to review for 'Baby,' and we're not performing it for two months."

"It's such a short routine. Kind of nice to throw together something like that after the other two."

"But you're itching to start something else, I can tell."

She got down on the floor again and went back to doing splits. "It seems like *forever* until October. And I can't wait to hear from Alison about whatever she and Mary are doing, but as far as I know they haven't even had a first-look about it, so who knows when that will be. I look at the schedules and honestly hate to sit anything out now that I know what it's like to dance with you."

That called for some contact. He moved in behind her, stretching his long legs out alongside hers and wrapping an arm around her waist. "I know. You want to try something for Mating Dance in March?"

She leaned her head back against his shoulder. "I have like zero inspiration for that theme. I mean, 'Hanky Panky,' okay, great song, I'm kind of assuming Julia and Ray will be doing a jive. Coming up with some other ballroom-adjacent routine, eh. That's not where my head is at with music right now."

"Then why don't we find something to work on by ourselves? We could do whatever we want and put it on video again and throw it up on YouTube. Something different."

"Well, it would pretty much have to be." She stretched down along one leg, then the other. He did the opposite, so they could see each other's faces. "You have any notions?"

"I have a notion for December. But otherwise I'm kind of at waiting and seeing. I mean, what if Alison and Mary's thing comes together and we need to block out a ton of time? Not sure if we should commit to another Chrome show."

"We could do, like, a Cabaret film festival and watch a bunch of the shows I've got on disc. See if that sparks anything. And if it doesn't, then we'll start combing through the music library."

"Okay." But while they were having breakfast, their personal *deus ex machina* weighed in; they both got a text from Kelli: **Hi guys have you watched the video I took last night? If not why not, or maybe never mind. ANYWAY I was listening to something and thought of you. Check your email. OX**

"She's supposed to be concentrating on tango, not coming up with assignments for us," said Paula. She went over to her laptop and pulled up her email. The message from Kelli said simply 'Chayanne,' with a music file attached. Paula opened it and turned up the volume. She and Mike listened to it twice. It was a gorgeous Spanish-language ballad with a strong rhythm. She raised her eyebrows.

He nodded. "I'm feeling it. What do the lyrics mean?"

"No hablo español. You would think I would after all these years in L.A. I'll find them online and throw 'em at Google Translate if necessary." She opened a new tab and typed *NO HAY IMPOSIBLES lyrics*. "Oh hey, here we go. It's kind of Spanglish." Mike came to her and read over her shoulder.

"Nothing is impossible," he said, kissing the side of her face. She turned so he could kiss her mouth. "That'll do. So what's this about a video?"

"She recorded us right after you danced with Vince." Paula looked around for her phone, spotting it on one of the side tables. They both went over to the couch and she retrieved the video. It was remarkably clear considering the low light in the club. She watched herself in Mike's embrace, moving with

111

instinctive trust in the patterns he created, their faces close together. There was the moment when they laughed. And there was the moment when he moved her with him as he pivoted, turning her out of the path of an imminent collision, holding still for a few seconds, his eyes dark and serious.

"What's the matter?" Mike asked softly. She pinched the bridge of her nose, wiped her eyes, cleared her throat.

"I said, to Kelli, that I loved watching them dance, because you could see in every line of Vince's body how much he loves her. And ... ." Her voice caught.

He put his arm around her and kissed her forehead. "Do I need to go get the magic gin?" She shook her head. "I do love you."

"I know. I love you too."

"You sure?" he said, smiling.

"Yeah, I'm sure."

"Then let's go to bed, and you can show me."

PART II: FLIGHT

The Playlist:

Way Back Into Love - Hugh Grant &
Haley Bennett (Music & Lyrics)

When the Deal Goes Down - Bob Dylan

One for My Baby - Dianne Reeves

No Hay Imposibles – Chayanne

Elevation - U2

Like a Prayer - Madonna

Hallelujah - Leonard Cohen

The Way I Am – Ingrid Michaelson

CHAPTER 12

February 2015

Paula glanced over at Mike on their way to the nightclub. She was driving; he seemed to be fine today, but the headaches always scared her, and last night's had been particularly bad. He felt her looking at him. "I have a follow-up MRI scheduled next month. But don't worry."

"It's, you know, skull fracture. That's a little beyond concussion. It's easy for me to forget how badly you were hurt, because you're so undamaged, most of the time."

He knew what she was afraid of. "They called it a linear fracture, from where the side pillar blew in and hit me. No signs of brain injury then or since, and they checked a bunch of times. There was a lot of blood at the scene. You know." He sketched a movement toward the almost-imperceptible line of the scar, where his blond hair now grew in white.

"So aside from the headaches. I never really asked. What was it like during rehab?"

"Some transient memory loss. Some balance problems. Depression."

"You had a lot of reasons to be depressed."

He smiled. "Forgetting stuff was depressing. That's gotten a lot better. The only lingering issue is the headaches and that's really only when I have to think a lot. The milonga was great, but my brain was working overtime."

"I can imagine. Anyway, this should be fun tonight. And little to no thinking required."

"I'm honestly fine now. And it's already been a pretty great day." When she glanced over at him again, he was smiling, possibly remembering how they'd spent the afternoon. A few minutes later they arrived at Chrome, turned the Jeep over to the parking valet, and walked up to collect their tickets.

The Underground Cabaret's theme for that night's show was 'That's Amoré.' It kicked off with an imaginative Latin waltz rueda de casino routine, to the song of the same title, then went forward with a variety of burlesque, dance, and circus arts performances. Paula and Mike saw several of their friends there, but they kept to themselves most of the evening. The only time Mike really paid attention to anyone offstage (other than Paula) was soon after they arrived, when he spotted an unmistakable proposal happening across the room. It gave him ideas.

The plan was for him to go back to his place after dropping Paula off. When they pulled up at her curb, she didn't get out of the car immediately, or even after a few kisses, as had become their habit. She put her head back for a moment, with her eyes closed. "Everything okay?" he asked finally.

She looked out the window briefly, then gazed at him for nearly a minute before she spoke. Her hazel eyes gleamed in the light of the streetlamp. "When is your lease up?"

His eyebrows went up and he moved his head a few degrees; he didn't know what he'd been expecting, but it wasn't that. "End of June," he said.

"Any interest in moving to Hollywood? Well, Hollywood-adjacent."

He smiled slowly, turning toward her. "I've been thinking it would be nice to find a place with a pool."

115

"I happen to know one that's walking distance from a decent studio."

"Off-street parking?"

"As a matter of fact. It's even air-conditioned."

"Sounds tempting. But there's a potential deal-breaker."

"Which is?"

"If this place doesn't have you in it, I'm not interested."

She smiled. "You don't want to know how much the rent is? Your landlord might be scamming you."

"Whatever it is, it would be worth every penny." He touched her face, turned it toward him again, looked in her eyes for a long moment. Then he closed the distance and kissed her. She wrapped an arm around his neck. After a few minutes he said, "It's going to be nice not to have to leave you after a kiss like that."

"For *real*," she said fervently. He smiled against her mouth.

The next weekend, they went out to see Vince and Kelli at an Argentine tango competition. They hadn't been in touch with Alison or Mary, so they were surprised to see both women there - and even more surprised to see that Mary was also competing, with her 'Green Darkness' partner-slash-fiancé Red, using an adaptation of the tango from that show. Red and Mary won the theatre-arts event, with Vince and Kelli taking second place.

"I've never seen anything quite like that," said Paula. "I mean I've seen some of the tango shows, but these routines were fierce. I kind of loved it."

"If we run out of other stuff to do, we could try it." He glanced around. "Let's sneak out before Alison sees us. I feel weird going over there when we haven't heard from her."

Paula nodded. "Don't want to look like stalkers." *And I don't want to go to the milonga down the hall.* She was having one of those nights when his mountain-lion walk and his perfect-for-her face were making it a challenge to keep her hands off him. She couldn't think of any good reason why she should. "Let's go home. I have a surprise for you."

He glanced over at her, wondering what she was up to. He hadn't been to her place since the week before, but a week didn't really seem long enough to have done something major. When they got there, he didn't immediately notice anything in the main living area. Then he realized she'd replaced her portrait collage of four actors with the actress version formerly in her bedroom. "Did you put the guys in back?"

"No, I don't need them anymore. You've got the best of each of them." He waved that off. "I'll probably swap this one out for something else pretty soon, too. Not sure what yet."

She didn't elaborate, only headed back to the bedroom. He followed, even more curious now, but actually took a step back when he saw what she'd done. "Wow. I mean. Wow." Where the actress collage used to hang over the bed, there was now a trio of 24x30 black-and-white images of him. He looked at Paula. She was studying the pictures, pretending she didn't know he was staring at her. "Those are from the 'Rock Star' video?"

"Yeah. Andy screen-capped them, printed and mounted. Since he was – or is, I guess – a dancer, I knew he could pick the perfect ones. They're so ferocious. I love them." Now she looked at him. He smiled a little, shaking his head, then turned back to the pictures. It wasn't a stretch to think of that performance as life-changing, even though it was in a studio in practice gear. It was the dance he'd used to announce he was back in action, to say 'you were wrong' to all those who'd discouraged him; the dance that, privately, he thought had brought him fully back to life. The pictures didn't show the big tricks or jumps. Instead, they were all caught at moments when he had just landed one of the tricks, muscles fully engaged to decelerate, face grim and focused, hair still flying, looking straight at the camera in each shot.

"He did a great job pulling those out. But I'm not sure how I feel about having me over the bed I'm in with you," he said after a minute. "Maybe we should find out."

"It's really for me," she said. "So when I'm on top, I've got four of you to look at." She slid her arms around his waist; he took her face in his hands and kissed her. Within seconds they were ripping each other's clothes off, laughing, falling over each other on the way to the bed.

Their schedule for the next two months was work at the law firm as usual, punctuated by more practice and coaching. They went out to milongas twice more, for each of their birthdays in March; Mike didn't have headaches. They had some kind of dance thing four or five nights a week, but neither of them felt like it was too much. A fun diversion was a day of being dance extras, after both of them were contacted by a casting agent looking to fill in background for a commercial.

They rented time in their local studios to start work on a jazz piece set to the Chayanne ballad and continued rehearsing their other work-in-progress set to Dianne Reeves' cover of 'One for my Baby.' Their submission of that piece had been accepted for the Underground Cabaret's April show, so they pulled from their existing wardrobes for costume. Mike would wear black dance pants and jazz shoes with a white shirt; Paula would wear a short clingy dress in sparkly blue. She'd do the routine in her Dance Paws, but needed a pair of stunt shoes to take off at the beginning. Fortunately, she hadn't yet actually chucked out all her uncomfortable high heels despite previously-lodged complaints. For dress rehearsal, she dug a silver pair out of a drawer under her bed.

When they got to the club, she was already hating those shoes again. "God I can't wait to get these fuckers off," she muttered.

"Beauty knows no pain, girls," said Mike, quoting Bernadette Peters in 'Cinderella.' They went down the stairs and headed for Cabaret principal Rory, who was looking official. "What's the show order?"

Paula looked at the printout that Rory handed her, noting the routines by their particular friends. "I see you're closing Act 1 with 'Gimme Gimme Gimme,' because of course you are. And we're ... closing the show. Again. What the actual fuck."

"Well," Mike said, determined not to laugh, "we've got props again."

"You do realize that we put that last because it's the best goddamned number we got, right?" said Rory. "I mean, don't tell anyone I said that. I mean it's the best number to close the show. If it had been Michelle

119

and Dmitri doing it, same deal. Why am I even justifying this to you."

Paula wriggled, uncomfortable but amused. "Look, I appreciate it. I'm still getting used to not being filler."

"You are a whole bag of nuts. And speaking of filler, I have to go shoehorn myself into my costume." Rory stomped off backstage.

The lighting design for the whole show was moody, giving the impression of candlelight, streetlamps, or moonlight to go with whatever music was in use (plus a mirrorball for Rory's ABBA strip routine and the disco number). For Mike and Paula's routine, Stacey had asked a lighting and projection designer they'd all met recently to do a digital backdrop with a neon effect. When the music started, the stage lights came up to show Mike already in position by a prop bar. Then Paula entered, as if through a street door. She waved half-heartedly to Mike with most of her attention on her phone, walking to a chair as if her feet hurt. Sat down, fidgeted with the straps of her shoes, finally took them off. Set her phone on the little table by her chair, looking at it again. Mike tapped her on the shoulder with a shot glass; she looked up and took the glass. He watched while she mimed tossing it back, then smacked it down on the table, flailing her hands and grimacing. The dancers hanging out in the house laughed.

Then the second verse started. Mike offered his hand, indicating the empty dance floor. Paula looked at him, set her hand in his, then stood up to dance with him. It was slow, smooth, and old-school, playing with the syncopations in the music. He moved her around with the lightest of touches, as if he knew she might not want to be touched. He started actions that she followed; when she went off on tangents he followed her. The only trick came at the end of the bridge. Paula did multiple spins across the stage, stopping in a double pirouette, then collapsing to a kneeling position on the floor; Mike did a hands-free cartwheel behind her, to land beside her with his hand on her back. She turned her head and he leaned in as if for a kiss; she turned away sharply and stood.

The last verse was Paula suddenly aware of him, Mike backing off, his action saying *hey, it's okay*, even though his face was eloquent of *stay*. As the final sung line started, Paula had collected her shoes and gone to the exit. On the word 'road,' she turned, looked at Mike, dropped her shoes and ran back to him. He caught her in a whirling spin and went to one knee, laying her across his thigh and bending close as the lights went down.

The watching dancers were up and applauding. "No wonder that's closing," Vince said to Kelli. "I'm getting trick envy. Couldn't even hear him land that."

Kelli nodded. "They are good. Has Mateo spoken to them about Alison's thing yet?"

"I don't think so."

"Let's go find him and find out."

When Mike and Paula went out to the main club floor, Vince and Kelli were waiting for them with Sam and Mateo. Mike's eyebrows went up. "Are we in trouble?"

Kelli gave him a look. "No. Mateo has some news for you."

"These guys met with Mary and Alison last month," said Mateo. "They have a concept and they've already

121

arranged with Tyrone to do another show here in August. It's called 'Gaucho' and it's based on Argentine tango. But instead of the usual semi-formal lounge scene, it's cowboys. There's a troupe and they asked me to help cast it and I wanted to ask you. Want to come talk about it?"

Mike and Paula looked at each other, then at Mateo. "Sure," they said at the same time.

"Pizza," said Vince. They all went out together, walking to the joint next door.

"So tell all, guys," said Paula. "Obviously you're in on this together."

"This show has a ménage storyline," said Vince. "Three couples. Red and Mary, Sam and Mateo, me and Kelli. Plus the chorus, which Alison said could be four but she'd prefer six; given the size of the stage, probably not more than that."

"Anyway, so Vicky's already in on a tentative basis," said Mateo. "Sharon's due next month, so they're waiting to make sure everything's okay with everybody before Vicky commits. Ray is in, since most of the prep is during his hiatus. Alison is dancing in the troupe as well as doing that choreography. Dmitri's in it too."

"Oh awesome!" said Paula.

"Red and Mary's roommate Lesley is doing costume," said Kelli. "We three couples are choreographing our duets and then everybody has to learn everybody else's because this one," she pointed at Mateo, "is going to bust up every couple and fool around with everybody before we all get back together where we started."

Mike laughed at Mateo, who was doing a little happy dance in his chair. "When does the group choreo start?"

122

"Basically ASAP," said Mateo. "But long story short, a lot of the phrases for the group are already composed. Alison's going to send out a rehearsal schedule pretty soon. She's booking space at that place on Pico, where we worked on the jumps from 'Rock Star,' and at Dmitri's."

"And when's the performance?"

"Dress rehearsal will be August second. Performances on the following three Sundays."

"So," said Vince, "are you in?"

"I'm totally in," said Paula, looking at Mike, who nodded. "We're both in."

"Cool!" said Mateo. "And then we can hog up all the slots in the Mating Dance: Milonga reboot in September."

CHAPTER 13

May 2015

A few weeks later, Mike and Paula were wrapping up another Argentine tango lesson with Vince when he looked around to make sure nobody was listening and said, "Kelli and I could use some help."

Paula said, "What's up?"

"You guys have done same-sex performances before, haven't you? Not like lead-follow practice whatever."

"Yeah," said Mike and Paula simultaneously.

"That's an acting thing, right?"

Paula nodded. Mike said, "I did a thing about ten years ago that was fully homoerotic. Serious kissing, hands everywhere, for a Pride festival. My partner for the piece was gay. He'd asked a bunch of other guys and they all said no. It's actually one of the things I'm proudest of, because it was such a challenge. It took some getting used to."

"That's the issue," said Vince. "We started working on the partner-swapping piece and dude, I was fucking *giggling*. Kelli's no better. Everybody else is acting all professional and we're, like, twelve." He looked exasperated.

Paula tried not to laugh. "You've got a limited timeline on this, huh?"

"With Red and Mary both going out of town for filming, yeah. We have the choreography to work with on our own, but for the actual face-to-face stuff we might have not much more than a few hours. We can't waste time. When we get into the ménage pieces I've got to lead *and* follow Red and Sam, and

124

lead Mateo, and it has to look real, and I can't be fucking giggling. What's the best play?"

"Probably a crash course of desensitization," said Paula. Mike nodded. "You're gonna have to, like, get all up on one of the guys and get over it." Vince sighed. "And Kelli too, obviously." She looked him over, then glanced at Mike. "You know, I was only sorta kidding back on Valentine's Day. I would happily volunteer to help with this."

"You like Kelli's face," said Mike, smiling. "And those Bambi eyes."

"I like Kelli's everything," Paula said bluntly. "She looks like one of my ex-girlfriends. And is ten times a nicer person. The obvious snag is that if you guys are too freaked out about doing this with people you know, then things get awkward between us, and I'd rather keep you as friends."

"Well, how frickin' awkward would it be to try to find people we *don't* know?" said Vince. He looked at Mike. "I really am freaked out, but I need to get over it. I want to be good in this show."

"I'm happy to help if I can. Look, if you're thinking you're uneasy because you're a homophobe and you didn't even know it, you're not. At all. What you are is one hundred percent straight and new to this," said Mike. "And for the record here, also one hundred percent straight. So anything I do will be acting, not me trying to get in your pants." Vince nodded, accepting it.

"I refuse to swear that everything will be acting," said Paula. "But I'll be professional. Where do you want to do this?"

"Uh." Vince looked undecided. 'At the studio' was clearly not the answer.

"How about my place," Mike suggested. "I'm moving out next month, so you won't ever have to see it again."

Vince shook his head, laughing. "Show business. I had to be in show business."

On their way home, Paula asked Mike, "So what happened with that routine you were talking about?"

"Nothing, really. The guy called me about a million times after we wrapped, though." He glanced over at her. "I felt sort of bad about it." She laughed. "I mean, I've had that 'wow, this must be real' thing with female partners before and I've gotten that 'whoa buddy hell no' thing, so I tried to be kind. But yeah. A million times."

Paula was still mercilessly snickering. "That poor guy. Well I mean, *look* at you. He was doomed. Is it online? I feel like I need to see this."

"It isn't. I've got it on my laptop, though."

"Guess what we're watching next time I'm over?"

On what Vince was calling D-Day (for desensitization), Mike pushed his couch all the way up against the wall, cleared the rest of the living room space at his apartment, cleaned the crappy laminate floor. He and Paula thought the best way to ease into things was to start with some dancing. When Vince and Kelli got there, they already had tango music playing. "Hi guys," said Paula. "Come on in and choose your anesthetic. We've got tequila, mandarin vodka, or magic gin."

"I keep hearing about this magic gin," said Kelli. "I'll try that."

"Tequila for me, por favor," said Vince. Paula poured tequila for him, Empress 1908 for Mike and

126

Kelli, and vodka for herself, adding a little lime juice to each. Kelli cooed over the blue-to-pink transformation. They tapped glasses and everyone drank. "Oh yeah," said Vince. "That'll help."

"The main thing to remember," said Mike, "is that *if* you get turned on, it isn't in your brain. It's not you *changing*. It's a natural physical reaction. Don't let it throw you."

"We're like bonobos down in the DNA," said Paula. "Genetically programmed to fuck anything and everything, anytime or all the time." Kelli squeaked out a laugh. "So yeah, *if*, just take it to bed with you. All it really means is that you're doing it right."

"Because the whole point of doing something like this is to turn people on," Mike added. "It's meant to be a sexy show. Each of the relationships is meant to be sexy. We've seen that in the group choreo. If you're not feeling it and you can still show it, you're doing great. If you *are* feeling it, then … well, enjoy it. And bring it home."

Vince and Kelli both nodded. He looked at her, with a hint of a smile. "I am fully prepared to get turned on by whatever you and Paula get up to."

She giggled. "Are we going first?"

"Let's all dance for a while," said Mike. Paula went into his embrace, thinking, *I haven't seen this authority before. I like it.* Kelli and Vince started dancing, and for two songs that's all they did. Then Mike released Paula, who casually cut in and took Kelli into a loose dance hold. Vince and Mike stood aside, watching. Paula wasn't an expert leader, but she and Mike had traded leads enough by now that she was able to move with some confidence. Kelli was a couple of inches shorter than Paula, shaped like a

1950s pin-up girl. Paula, enjoying this, slid her arm further around her partner. Kelli's eyes were drowsy. Her lips parted for a second, when Paula went fully into the close embrace. Mike thought, *whoa*. He'd never really watched Paula dancing with anyone else but Vince and hadn't been fully prepared for the sensuality she brought to handling another woman.

When a new song started, Paula stopped trying to actually dance. Instead she went into rhythmic walks in various directions. Weaving Kelli in and out of closed position, and then turning her to a tandem position. She bent her head and kissed the curve of Kelli's neck, wrapping an arm around her from behind. With their bodies in full contact, she did a rock step to create a reverse corté. As if by reflex, Kelli's head went back onto Paula's shoulder and her left arm went up so that her hand wrapped around into Paula's hair. Mike heard Vince inhale, feeling a little breathless himself.

Paula set Kelli on her feet again and slowly let go of her as the song faded out. She cleared her throat. "How'd that feel?"

Kelli blinked and turned around to look at Paula. "That was … totally not awkward! Woo! I pretended you were Vince." Paula grinned. "I need some water," Kelli decided, looking at Vince with hungry eyes that said 'later for you.'

"Okay," said Paula. "So obviously *personally* I don't want you to pretend I'm Vince, but for this purpose, if it works, it works. Mary's a lot taller than me, especially with her heels on. Maybe you can pretend she's Red." Paula looked at the guys. "I take it that was persuasive."

"You could say that," said Mike.

"Do you mind driving home?" Vince asked Kelli. "Because I'm gonna need a lot more tequila if that's where we're going with this."

"Or we could always go full orgy," Paula said. "After that, any dance is going to seem tame." Kelli giggled again; Vince shut his eyes and shook his head.

"That is actually not helpful right at this moment," he said. "Uno más, I'm begging you." Paula poured him the drink. He knocked it back, then looked at his student-turned-teacher.

"That's not exactly where we're going," said Mike. "Look, I don't know what, if any, notes Alison's given you guys. If it were me, I'd have everyone turning on Mateo at the end. He's caused all this trouble, right? I understand Sam ultimately comes back to him, or for him, but that last sextet, the music is kind of hard and sharp. It's like knives. Am I on track?"

"I think so," said Vince. The women retreated to the couch. Paula hadn't been expecting Mike to go this way, but she thought she could see what he was getting at. She unobtrusively got the video camera ready.

"How hard is it supposed to go? Obviously this isn't a death play like the other one. But is it supposed to stay kind of cute and light, or is Mateo going to be hurting?"

Vince said, "We haven't gotten quite that far."

"Okay. Well, like I said, if it were me, it would go pretty hard. It's almost like in 'Green Darkness' when Grendel was captured, but in this piece, the monster gets another chance because someone who really loves him is there for him. So anyway. You've got follow parts with Red and Sam. Going into that, you've had your true love tempted away. You're already hurt and confused and probably angry. So I'm going to lead, and you … be feeling that."

"Bearing in mind," Kelli interjected, "that in this setting, guys are used to dancing together. It wouldn't necessarily be about Red and Sam trying to get in your pants. It's more like everybody's thinking, what just happened, this isn't how it should be."

"Yeah," said Vince. "That's kind of where I was before. Confusion and making the best of things. I didn't get the hurt and angry bit before though. Or maybe I was thinking of that for Sam, because Mateo is his partner to start with."

"You would have gotten there," said Mike. "All we're doing is speeding up the process." He closed with Vince and they danced. They were both in jeans and tee shirts, but from the first step there was nothing casual about it. Mike used his height to control Vince in a way he never had before in the time they'd been working together. His movement was decisive and dominant. But he let a little bit of heat and softness creep in, because in the show's story, all the men had lost their lovers, and he knew that a hurt man wanted to soothe that somehow. They worked for several songs, Paula and Kelli watching with a mutual sense of revelation.

Mike finally closed a series of ochos with a sharp boleo, whipping Vince back to a spin and a corté. Vince was looking at him with an expression of total focus. There was nothing seductive about it, but it was undeniably sexy. Mike smiled a little. "That was different, huh?"

He let go of Vince, who stood back and shook himself like a wet dog. "That was definitely different." A

130

movement caught his attention. Paula was setting down the video camera. "Were you taping that?"

"I thought it might be helpful for Alison to see it. And if not, I'm gonna save it for my own enjoyment. The two of you are ridiculously hot together." Kelli was nodding. Vince's shaggy dark head with Mike's sleek blond, the completely different but equally handsome faces ... *definitely a keeper*, thought Paula.

"How are you feeling?" Mike asked.

Vince thought about it for a few seconds. "I am, okay, a little bit turned on. And I am not freaked out about it."

Paula said, "Yes!" Vince laughed. "You want another shot before you do the lead part?"

"No," he said, sounding surprised. "I think I'm good. I'll have some water, though." They all took a short break, Mike going over to look at the last few minutes of the recording. Once they were ready to begin again, Mike waited to see if Vince needed a nudge on the character. "So now," Vince said, "I'm dancing with Mateo, who has fucked me over and my heart is broken. But the little shit is really pretty and he's *trying* to tempt me, too. I'm thinking, unwilling attraction? With that anger?"

Mike nodded, moving to a position a few steps away from Vince, waiting to see what he would do. Vince let the music get in his head, then took the lead. This time Mike minimized his size with smaller, less potent movements, deliberately staying behind the music and behind the lead so that the reactions were natural. Vince was such a good leader that it was easy to stay with him. And for the first time, Vince led as if Mike were a woman. Specifically, a woman he was not happy with. There were shades of force and punishment that had Paula and Kelli looking at each other with big eyes.

Paula held the video camera still, silently cheering. She could tell after a couple of songs that Vince was building up to something. Suddenly he got there, leading a double gancho, taking it to the floor by doing a quick pivot with a long step back, lowering to his knee. Mike mirrored with a step forward so that they ended in a paired lunge. The men knelt facing each other, barely twelve inches between them. Vince's hand had gone to Mike's neck with his thumb under the corner of his jaw, forcing his head back so his throat was exposed. Then he let go and sat down on the floor.

"God *damn*," he said after a few silent seconds. Mike relaxed, sitting down and draping his arms over his knees.

"That's what I was about to say," said Paula, turning off the camera.

Kelli nodded. Her eyes were huge. After a moment, she said, "That was our choreography. But way meaner."

"How does it end when you do it?" Paula had seen the blocking video, but she knew things evolved.

"Not like that!" She looked at Vince, stretching her hand out to touch his shoulder. "How do you feel?"

"Right now I feel like I've done something I never thought I could do. A few minutes ago I felt like I wanted to fuck him to death."

Paula and Mike nodded. Mike said, "And now you know how to get there. Good work."

"Does this mean we don't get to have an orgy?" Paula said, sounding disappointed, which got the laugh she was hoping for.

132

"Have you done this kind of coaching before?" asked Vince. "Because we've been doing shows and shit for four years and no one's even suggested we needed to work on character."

"But you were always dancing together, right?" said Paula. "The two of you, dancing as yourselves. You've got your history and your lives and your dreams to draw from, whether you're playing it angry or sad or loving. It's always going to be you, unless you intentionally create a character."

"I haven't done actual coaching," said Mike when Vince looked thoughtful. "But in a company, every piece has characters. You're cast for things like an actor, and you're not usually playing yourself. You're not usually creating your own pieces, either. We always had to work out how we got to that other place. Over the twelve years I was with the company, there was a lot of talking things through. And occasionally a lot of booze." Vince made a sound of amused comprehension. "If I thought that the 'Rock Star' character was really me I'd check myself in for electroshock therapy. I got there without even realizing it."

"You had some rage," Paula pointed out.

Mike nodded. "More than I even knew." He got up off the floor and extended a hand to Vince, who let himself be pulled up.

"Thanks for this. It's going to make a huge difference."

"I'm going to copy this to Mike's laptop real quick and then you can take the SD card to Alison. I don't think we want to put this on the Dropbox," said Paula. She took care of that, and after a little more conversation Vince and Kelli left. Paula looked at

Mike. "It occurs to me that we've got almost the ideal dance situation here."

"You mean we only have to do what we want?" He smiled.

"Yeah. I've seen a lot of company pieces that I hated so much. If I'd had to dance in them in order to keep my job? What a nightmare."

"The day job pays the rent, pays for coaching, pays for studio time, and yeah. I don't have to do some derivative piece of garbage that only exists because we're obligated to do a show. I get to make dances with you." He snaked an arm around her waist, pulling her in for a kiss.

"That was really good guidance you gave Vince."

"That was really sexy dancing you did with Kelli."

"Yes, it was. Too bad they weren't up for a little orgy."

"We could have ourselves a little orgy," he suggested. She started backing toward the couch. He moved with her as if they were dancing, bending his head to kiss her. "*Really* sexy."

"You too. No one would ever know you were a hundred percent straight." He kissed her again and they stopped talking.

CHAPTER 14

Toward the end of the week, Mike and Paula both got a text from Kelli: **Sextet meeting with Alison on Sunday at Dmitri's, can you come? We gave Alison the video and the next thing I heard was a lot of SQUEEE. I think she's changed some stuff.**

Mike picked up his desk phone to call Paula. "Did you see the text?"

"Yeah. We don't have a conflict, do we?"

"I had the rehearsal room booked at Genesee, but I can cancel that."

"Okay. Talk to you later." Paula put down the phone, stared at the files stacked on her desk, and thought about how much she'd rather be dancing right now.

When they got to Shall We Dance on Sunday, the curtains were drawn across the big windows. A 'closed for rehearsal' notice was taped to the locked door. Mike pulled out his phone to call Alison, but before the call was picked up Dmitri was there to let them in. He stood back, saying "Come," and they went in. There were a dozen chairs in a big circle, eight occupied once Dmitri took his seat. Red and Mary, who were newlyweds, were holding hands in adjacent chairs. Mike avoided looking at Paula, but thought, *that's what I want.* They joined the group.

"Hi guys," said Alison. "Thanks for coming. I thought you ought to see what we're doing today. I'm hoping you can help us out with some stuff."

"And first, in case anyone was wondering, Papa Dmitri tells us Nina Simone was born Friday night,"

135

said Kelli. "Sharon is doing well and Vicky will start working in with the troupe next week."

"While in other Chrome-associated news, Andy and Victor are still breaking the Internet," said Mateo. "Did you guys see it?"

"We don't watch the show," said Paula. "What happened?"

"Big kiss! I almost fainted!" Mateo was fanning himself. Sam was laughing.

"Wow, in prime time? That's kind of major," said Mike.

Alison was smiling, but said, "That's a pretty good segue to what we are here to work on. Red and Sam have both seen the video you did last week, but Mateo hasn't."

Mateo did a diva thing. "And I'm really pissed about it, too."

"Well, here's the thing," she said to him. "I've asked Vince to dance with you, your duet. I want you to be surprised. I want you to feel what you feel, so you can use it in the show. Then we'll talk about some ideas I've had. I have some different tracks. If we have time, we'll block the opening and closing sextets so we can throw 'em on the Dropbox for Red and Mary to work with while they're out of town. Okay?" She got her own camera ready.

"Let's do it," said Vince. He and Mateo stood up and got warmed up a little. Vince wasn't looking at Mateo. Then Dmitri put on the music and they began. Mike and Paula recognized a lot of the choreography, but Vince changed the order of things to fit the new music. It started simply, with circling walks. Even here, Vince wasn't looking directly at Mateo. When he went into hold, it was predatory, fully in character. Mateo was clearly a little thrown. His own character was essentially himself, flirtatious and sweet and a bit provocative. He'd never felt heat from Vince before, and it showed in his reactions, but there was also that sense of increasing threat. Actions that were charming in Vince's blocking video with Kelli were hostile here. When Vince led the double gancho and took it down, Mateo's face was pale and his eyes were wet. They stared at each other for a second. Without warning Vince took Mateo's head in his hands and kissed him hard, then let him go suddenly and stood up, backing away. Mateo lost his balance and had to put a hand on the floor. He looked totally shocked.

"*Fuck* that was good!" said Paula, then clamped a hand over her mouth. Mike was almost as satisfied as if he'd danced it himself.

Alison had switched off the camera. Her expression was a mix of relief and excitement. "I wasn't expecting that but yeah, that was seriously good. That was a Godfather kiss." She led a round of applause.

"Jesus!" said Mateo, still on the floor. Sam went over to him and gave him a hand up. "Vince, what the hell?"

"You okay?" said Vince. He joined them, putting a hand on Mateo's shoulder. "I would have warned you, but Alison said not to."

"Jesus!" Mateo said again, cuddling close to Sam. "Where did that even come from?"

"I asked Mike for help with the character. Ever since, I've been thinking about it, how would I actually feel if you – if anyone – took Kelli from me."

"Never happen," said Kelli. Vince looked over at her with a little smile.

"I'm sorry," Sam said to Mateo. "When I saw the video I knew it was going to hit you."

Mateo was staring at Mike with disbelief. "You know, after I saw you do 'Rock Star' I knew you had a mean streak, but fuck!"

"I know," said Mike. "I'm sorry. It was the music for the closing sextet. I told Vince and Kelli last week, that music felt like knives to me. There had to be some damage."

Alison nodded. "All of you are going through some stuff in this piece, with all the breakups. Once I saw what they'd dug up, I thought it would really underscore that. At the end, everybody's back together, but nobody's getting away clean."

"You're not going to do that shit too, are you?" Mateo said, turning to Red. "This was supposed to be fun, dammit."

"No, I'm staying with how we worked it before, like I might use you and throw you away. Not like you're gonna sleep with the fishes if you ever come near me again. The contrast will play."

"Good, 'cause you could break me in half. I mean, Vince is taller than me too, but let's face it."

"That's all I have to do," said Red, smiling a little. "Just loom and shit."

Vince looked the big guy up and down. "Whereas I am resorting to venom."

"That was definitely some venom," said Kelli. "I have *never* seen you like that before."

"It will change your dancing," said Dmitri judiciously. "Going forward."

"Mary, what did you think? You've been awfully quiet," said Alison.

138

Mary looked around the circle. Her face was blissful. "I'm so bloody *grateful* to have work like this to do, and a group like this to do it with. For twenty effing years I was posing for cameras. Now this? It's a dream come true." Mike and Paula looked at each other and smiled, both of them thinking, *yep*. "Also, compared to the last thing, this one's a frolic for me. So carry on."

Alison nodded. "The thing is, it's going to change the show. I know it's a whole new angle, Mateo. How much work has gone into the ménage dances so far?"

"Hardly any," said Mateo. "We've got 'Adios Nonino,' where I do my thing, except for the finish. None of the others. And this is the first time Vince and I have even worked the duet."

"Okay, that's actually perfect. I was afraid I was going to really screw you up. Here's the new concept." She handed around copies of a new show order, with the dancers for each piece specified and some notes in the margin. "It's now three acts. 'Adios Nonino' closes Act I and I have an idea for finishing that with some impact. Fewer total numbers, but remember how you guys changed the Grendel character and it made such a difference? That's what Mike and Vince's video did for me. Sorry it's such a mess. I spent like three whole days on this. Kept having thoughts at three in the morning."

"I remember that," said Red. "That was me on the Beowulf thing."

"I've taken out the pieces where each member of the sextet had a full duet with Mateo. Except for Vince, and as you may have noticed, there's new music for that. I've added a number for the troupe in

139

Act III. That'll be tango and jazz with stepping. Like, body percussion. Nothing in hold."

"Awesome," said Paula. "We'll all still be in the jeans and shirt and vest thing, right?"

"Right, with Cuban heels. I'm sure it's well within everyone's capability, though it will take a *lot* of work to get perfectly synchronized. Um, we still have Mateo solo with the troupe, but with different music. 'La Yumba' kind of foreshadows 'Esqualo,' similar quality, like knives, like Mike said. The other new thing is this number, 'Soledad,' which is Red, Sam, and Vince each doing a solo backed by the troupe, then closing into a trio. That will end with Vince on stage alone, in full venom mode, until Mateo comes on for their duet."

"And that's gonna be like this," said Mateo. "Thanks for having us do it today. If we'd been alone I'm not sure what I would have done." He still looked a bit shaken. Sam had a hand on his back. "I mean, I would have gone home and piled all the cats on me and dived straight into a wine bottle. But aside from that." He shivered.

"I don't know all this music," said Mary. "Why these three new tracks for the ménage numbers?"

Alison said, "They're all male vocals. We're not using vocals anywhere else. And they progress. Red will dance first, his piece is more traditional milonga because his character is, can we call it negligently confident? He's sure Mary will come back to him. He's pissed and kind of lonely, but he's not worried. Then Vince dances, and his music is more sad, which will play with the audience because his duet with Kelli is such a lovely vals. It needs to be crystal clear that he's afraid he's lost her forever. Like by the end

140

of the guys' trio, it needs to be crystal clear that out of all of them, he's the one who's dangerous."

"I never would have thought he could play that," said Kelli. "He's so completely nonviolent. But I guess it was a little bit there in 'Blue Angel,' right?" She looked at Vince.

He nodded. "The difference is that I'd never be able to really hurt you. There's no character that could take me there. I guess that's why that routine didn't scare people."

"Thanks a lot!" said Mateo, looking outraged. Vince shrugged apologetically and Mateo actually laughed. "Holy moly, who knew. Fuck you all sideways."

Alison could tell from his face that Mateo was over it, so she moved on. "Anyway, so then we have Sam's ménage piece. He's dancing with four people instead of three. Red, when you dance with him he's leading, but you're practically holding him up. You could even try some lifts if you want, it doesn't take much to make Sam fly. This song 'Hoy' is, it's tragic. Dmitri, can you play it?" Dmitri nodded, went to the music system, started the track. Everyone got it as soon as the vocal came in.

"Wow," said Kelli.

"Blimey," said Mary.

"That's exactly how I would feel," said Sam. Mateo took his hand. "So when I'm dancing with the women, it's like, God, somebody, please love me. And Vince, we're friends in the show too, right? He might be all, I will fix this for you."

"Exactly," said Alison. "When you go down to the floor at the very end, he's *with* you. But he has to go, and you're left alone, destroyed. That's why I put these three numbers on their own, bracketed by short intermissions. Many drinks will be sold after that one." She sounded so pleased; the others exchanged amused looks. "Anyone who's ever been heartbroken is going to be like, I need all the vodka, right now. Anyway, it's fourteen numbers now instead of eighteen. Red and Sam both have nine, Mary and Kelli each have seven, Mateo and the troupe are in seven. Vince, shit, you're in ten. Is it too much?"

"No," he said. Alison and Kelli both smiled at his confidence.

"Great. How are we doing for time?"

Dmitri said, "Take all day. I am fascinated."

Then Mateo said, "I have a question."

"What's that?" Alison looked alert.

"How should I approach my solo? Because I'll be honest, I haven't really thought about character till today."

She glanced over at Mike. "Any thoughts on that?"

For a moment he was startled that she was even asking him. All the others were staring at him. After a second, accepting the director's invitation, he spoke to Mateo. "I think that where you're lovely and tempting and flirtatious in all your preceding dances, the solo should be arrogant. You haven't been intentionally destructive, you weren't out to hurt anybody, but you're irresistible and you know it."

"Well, okay, I like that," he said. Sam patted him, smiling. "But then Vince comes out and scares me half to death and I'm, like, chastened."

"At least," Alison said. "And that's going to be foreshadowed by what the troupe does behind you. That work for you?"

"That works."

Alison looked at Mike and Paula. "Can I ask you to work in? Like, understudy Red and Mary? Because it would really help the others if they can work with those extra bodies."

They didn't even have to consult. "Yes," they said together.

"Are you sure? Because then you are literally learning thirteen numbers, which is nuts."

Mike half-shrugged, smiling. "Remember when Mary said that thing about a dream come true?"

"The duets are on the Dropbox," said Paula. "And 'Adios Nonino.' We've got the basic shape of things already."

"And you certainly get the character. By the end of today you'll have the sextets. So. Short break, then let's get to work."

The following Saturday, Mike and Paula worked with Dmitri and Alison on the first three numbers for the troupe. Their other two members, Ray and Vicky, were also on hand. Vicky, who was a particular friend of Vince and Kelli, said as soon as she arrived, "I hear you took my pal over to the dark side."

"We showed him the way," said Mike. "He got there all by himself."

"He's pretty good, huh? I've never tried to do that in-character shit."

"You are such *a* character, you don't need to be *in* character," said Paula.

"Oh har de har."

"So how are Sharon and Simka?"

"Don't even ask or we won't get a damned thing done," Vicky said, with a goofy smile. "I could go on for hours. Right, Papa?" She looked at Dmitri. He'd been softening up to an unsettling degree ever since he and the girls decided to have a baby. Now he almost-smiled, with a sideways nod, pretending he was only mildly interested in pursuing the subject. "You're such a fraud," Vicky said, amused.

Ray said, "Julia says he's a cream puff. Crusty on the outside, mushy on the inside." Several people stifled laughter.

Dmitri looked stern. "We waste time!" Everyone saluted and they got down to business.

CHAPTER 15

On Sunday, after two hours rehearsing pieces for the show, then two more working on their Chayanne piece, Paula said, "This is a relief. It's so romantic and smooth."

"Also completely devoid of tango content. I mean I like that stuff a lot, but it can feel a little static when you're used to the whole stage."

"Yeah. I like dancing in hold with you, but being able to fling myself around like this is, whew." She folded down onto the floor to stretch. "I can't believe I'm going to say this but maybe we need to find something to do that *isn't* dancing. Or fooling around."

"Like what?"

"I don't fucking know. I never wanted to do anything outside work but dance or fool around." She didn't blame him for laughing.

"We could catch up with movies," Mike suggested. "Sit in the dark and talk. Drink magic gin."

"Oh yeah. Your agenda."

"All still valid."

"Okay. Let's do that. It occurs to me I haven't really interrogated you since … we met?"

"There was an interrogatory quality to that night at the mall."

"After the magic gin, yeah." She looked up at him. *When I completely lost my shit and you were my refuge.* His expression was so loving that her heart seemed to glitch for a second. "Maybe that's a good place to start."

Paula didn't go to the mall after work anymore, unless Mike wanted to go too. The walks she'd used to wear herself out had been replaced with dancing together, often more than ten hours a week. She still had occasional bad nights, as he still had occasional headaches. Mike thought the headaches were probably easier to deal with; at least he knew where they came from.

Now he thought that with his move to her condo imminent, there were definitely some things they needed to cover. But since one of them usually only stayed over with the other on weekends, he had to wait a few days.

That Friday after work, he packed up a Jeep-load of stuff he wouldn't be needing immediately and took it over to her place. She met him out at the gate with her key card so he could drive in and park behind her. "What are you going to do with your furniture?" she asked as they were heading up the garage stairs, each carrying a box.

"Nothing. It came with the place."

"Oh, I didn't realize that was a furnished rental. Ew."

"I got a slipcover for the couch and an antimicrobial cover for the bed, but yeah. That's why I always liked sleeping here better. Well, that's one of the reasons."

"So what have you brought this time?"

"Clothes, movies, booze."

"I approve of your priorities." They made a couple of trips to empty out the car, then scrounged up something for dinner. Paula wasn't very inclined to cook. Mike thought until he actually moved in and it was 'his' kitchen too, they weren't likely to get into a rational food routine. He tended to have his main meal of the day at lunchtime, but he'd need to solve dinner: a man could not dance on cheese and crackers alone.

It occurred to him that was a good point to start a conversation. "What's your preferred food routine?"

"High protein breakfast, high calorie lunch, whatever for dinner. Like this. An apple, cheese, maybe some bread, probably a glass of wine."

"Do you pack your lunches or eat out?" He felt like after knowing her for nearly ten months, he ought to know this; but they'd rarely even had lunch together on workdays. One or the other of them tended to have some work demand to satisfy.

"Pfft. What do you think? I guess I could save some money by packing lunches, but frankly it feels like an imposition. Stop laughing."

When he could, he said, "Eating isn't an imposition, it's a physical necessity."

"It's *boring*. Three times a day, really? For me it's easiest to get the same things pretty much every day so I don't have to think about it. I am not motivated by food."

"Yeah, I get that. Actually me neither, but since we're dancing this much I have to keep my calorie intake at a certain level. It's hard to do that without eating junk food unless I do my own prep."

She looked him over thoughtfully. A body like that did need some good fuel. "Well, once we get into a groove, if you want to take over prep I'd probably eat whatever you give me. But you really don't have to. My shitty routine seems to be working for me. It's always a breakfast sandwich and then the Cobb

147

salad. The guys down at the short order don't even ask anymore."

"Well, you haven't gotten sick since I've known you, so yeah, it must be working. Not so shitty after all."

"Just weird. But you knew that about me."

"You're not weird. Eccentric, maybe."

She made an 'I'll take that' face. "You want to go down to the pool? It's nice out tonight."

"It's always nice out."

"Yeah, yeah, Minnesota boy."

"Jersey girl." They got ready and went downstairs. Some other residents of the complex were down at the pool too, but nobody was being loud. Paula and Mike slid into the water and did a few laps, then sat on the underwater steps close together. The outdoor lighting created moody shadows from the palm and banana trees around the pool area. "This is what everybody thinks L.A. is like."

"This is what sells L.A. Nobody believes in the traffic until they get here."

"Nobody understands how *huge* it is. I got a Thomas Guide after I'd been here for about a month. Couldn't believe how long it took to get anywhere. Then I realized the metro area was bigger than Delaware and thought, oh."

"In a few years it'll probably be bigger than Connecticut."

"Ugh."

"So I thought of something to ask you." She gave him a sideways glance. "It's probably not for public consumption, though."

"Then maybe we should go back upstairs. These fuckers won't leave."

"I do love how you say that."

"I know, that's why I say it." He was smiling as he gave her a completely unnecessary hand up out of the pool. When they got upstairs, they showered off the chlorine, wrapped up in cotton robes, then sat on the couch in the dark, each with a glass of vodka and orange juice. "This is my favorite way to get Vitamin C," he said.

"Mine too." She looked at him, loving his face in the dim light from the kitchen's vent hood. She leaned over to kiss him. "So I decided to be snoopy about your family. You dropped some hints a while back that I didn't pursue for ... reasons. You don't have to tell me anything, obviously, but if you want to, I'm interested."

He looked away for a moment, then back at her. His eyes were in shadow, but she knew he was thinking, probably about how much he wanted - or didn't want - to share. She knew he loved her, but she also knew that he'd been through more shit than just the accident that had ended his professional dance career.

Finally he said, "I told you my mother lived for twenty years with an abusive alcoholic. Well, that was my dad. He went to prison for manslaughter after getting in a fight at a bar. And he died there, of a heart attack."

She nodded. "Your mom ran the business then?"

"She kind of always did. He wasn't what you would call a high-functioning alcoholic. I mean, he had five out of seven good days, I guess. It was those other two days that torpedoed everything else."

"How did she pay for your dance classes?"

"The whole family pitched in. My uncle, my grandfathers. I'm still so grateful they were willing. Because this is like from age six. And this was a community where a little boy should be wanting to be a hockey player, or at least a football player. Not a dancer."

"How did you first get interested in dance?"

"We only had basic TV, but we got PBS. Mom used to park me and my sister in front of it for hours while she was taking care of everything she had to take care of. I saw all the science and history shows, but all the classic movie musicals too, plus lots of ballet. I was a little theater geek. My sister loved it too. We'd dance around the living room together."

"Maybe your mom thought you were less likely to get hurt, or get in with a rough crowd, if you were dancing."

"Yeah, exactly. I asked her about that after the accident, because while I was half out of it I thought I heard her say she never thought I'd get hurt this bad as a dancer."

"Well, it wasn't the dancing that hurt you. All kinds of people get smashed up in car accidents."

"We straightened that out later." They'd finished their drinks. Now he put his arm around her. "So that's one of my experiences with female rage. I was only twelve when he went to prison, but I never forgot what he put her through. Or that she stayed for me and my sister."

"Is that." She stopped.

"What?"

"Is that one of the things that attracted you to me?"

"Well, there's a really long list." Starting with her face, and her body, and those eyes that saw everything. After a moment he answered seriously. "Possible. Probable, in fact. I recognized it." He looked at her; she was staring at the dark TV screen. "Did anyone ever hit you?"

"One guy. In college. Once."

"What did you do?"

"Broke his nose."

He laughed, choking it off as soon as he could. "I'm sorry, it's not appropriate to laugh at that."

"Hey, he knew I could kick him in the face. He didn't think I *would*. His mistake." She was smiling.

"Oh ow, you *kicked* him?"

"I had to, he was holding my wrists at the time. He's lucky I didn't take out any teeth." She looked up at him. "He wasn't as tall as you."

"Pretty sure you could still get my nose if you wanted to. I've seen how high that foot can go."

"I'll avoid doing that if possible. I like your nose." He had to kiss her again then. "Want to hear what else I like?"

"Well, sure."

"Let's get naked and go to bed. I like that."

"Me, too."

By the end of that weekend they'd finished blocking their troupe parts and progress videos had been uploaded to the Dropbox. The six troupe dancers would continue to meet on their own to rehearse their stepping routine, since all of them cringed at the thought of getting out of synch in performance. Alison told them, "This is the one number where absolutely no improv is allowed," and they took her seriously.

Mike and Paula put a whiteboard calendar up in Paula's kitchen, like the one Dmitri had at Shall We Dance, and wrote in all their rehearsals. "This actually is kind of nuts," said Paula when she saw what it looked like. "We have six rehearsals a week for this thing. It's a good thing the troupe choreo is set the way it is."

"If we ever want to create a show of our own, we'll have to remember that strategy," Mike commented. Paula gave him a look like *don't even*. "Don't tell me you haven't thought that."

"I admit nothing."

Alison had done a dozen phrases that were repeated multiple times throughout the show. During the featured couples' duets, the troupe couples did small, unobtrusive partner work. The same phrases, differently combined, were used for the troupe in the coda, in the featured leaders' trio, and as background for Mateo's solo. Those pieces hadn't presented much of a challenge to Paula and Mike. It was having to learn Red and Mary's full parts that had them scrambling, though not to the point of turning down another gig as extras. Paula's neighbors didn't even blink an eye anymore when they practiced on the pool deck or in the garage.

The understudy strategy worked for the rest of the cast. As the end of June approached, the sextets and ménage numbers were in good enough shape that Red and Mary would be able to step right in when they returned from their film gigs – meaning Mike and

Paula would be able to step out. Mary was due back any day; Red was expected by the third week of July.

Meanwhile, Mike and Paula had reserved one day a week to work on their Chayanne piece, which they'd taken to calling their anti-tango. It was getting to a point where they were thinking of putting it on video for their YouTube channels. After a run-through at the studio near Genesee, Mike looked at the practice tape and sighed, shaking his head.

"What's the matter?" Paula flopped down on the stack of crash mats to pummel a sore muscle.

"Nothing with the dance. I like what we're doing. I like being able to fly you."

"I like that too. I was so pissed that I couldn't swing the 540. Not enough power to get all the way around. But I guess that other trick is fine."

"Aside from the black eye."

"I did not give you a black eye."

"Well, honey, *someone* hit me in the face." He was laughing under his breath at her offended expression.

"Okay, I did hit you in the face, but it was an accident. What did your bosses say, anyway?"

"Tom said, 'trouble at home?'"

"He did not!"

Mike laughed. "He was joking. The others minded their own. They all know I'm dancing. I told them I might look a little beat up from time to time." He was smiling at her. "At least you didn't break my nose."

"They know *we're* dancing," she said. "And I told you I'd try not to."

He laughed. "Yeah, like you could avoid it. I ducked, but I went the wrong direction. I'm sure

153

everybody knows everything. There really aren't any secrets in the firm. And I wouldn't try to keep it a secret anyway."

"Nobody'd better ask, is all I can say. As long as we're not boning in the file room it's none of their fucking business." She lounged back on the crash mats. "You realize that it has now been a full fourteen months since I got called in to HR about my attitude."

"I take it that's some kind of record?"

"Yup. So what's wrong?"

"I don't want to record this here. Do you think we could get in to do it on stage at Chrome?"

"Huh. Maybe?" She liked the idea.

"Who should we talk to first?"

"How about Rory and Dana? They've known Tyrone forever, he's practically their adopted dad. And we're overdue for dinner with them."

"I'm game."

CHAPTER 16

It turned out that none of them had weekend availability for a ridiculous length of time, so they decided to do a Wednesday dinner at Rory and Dana's place in West Hollywood. Mike and Paula brought wine, French bread, and dessert; their hostesses provided everything else. When they were settled into the Tony Duquette-inspired dining den, Rory said, "I can't believe it's taken this long to achieve dinner again. I mean, I know you guys are busy, but damn."

"Things should get a little easier next month. I swear we spend half our time deciding which apartment we should be at. Mike's moving in with me in, what. Wow, three days."

"Hey, congratulations," said Dana. "How did you manage that, exactly, Mike?"

"I was invited," he said, smiling. "It surprised me, too."

"Well, you know, I was getting tired of juggling all my other boyfriends and girlfriends." Paula made a 'what can you do' gesture. "It seemed a lot less trouble to decide on one. And the obvious choice was the one who can dance."

"Plus, of course, *look* at him. I mean, even I can appreciate that," said Rory, lifting an eyebrow.

"You should see him with his clothes off." Paula sounded smug.

Dana said, "Has Andy ever hit you up to model? I mean, not that he's got a ton of time these days."

"I haven't even met Andy yet," said Mike. "He's the one who does all the Cabaret photography, right?"

"Right. Then he met Victor and they did the first edition of Mating Dance: Milonga, almost two years ago, which got some press. Andy got his first acting job in a while, then they did some other stuff together, and the next thing you know he's cast on 'Vice' and they're the gay lovers for the ages. Except right now who knows where they even are."

"They'll turn up eventually. You know, Dana got a new job." Rory nudged her, looking proud. "The guy playing the captain on Ray's show retired, Ray suggested her, and they called her in."

"No kidding!" said Paula. "That's awesome! Had you played a cop before?"

"No, but I've played lawyers, and once a military officer." She looked sideways at Rory. "They asked me to cut my hair."

Rory's mouth dropped open. "Noooooo. Did they really?! You didn't tell me that. Oh hi, Spike, it took you long enough." She picked up the fluffy orange cat who'd materialized by the table.

"That must have been some nap," said Dana. "I mean, we've got filet Oscar down here. So yeah, I told them I've been gay my whole life with long hair, why wouldn't this police captain have long hair, did they think short hair was some kind of code for lesbian, and they backpedaled so fast they fell over. They were like this." She put her hands up and made a we-never-said-that face.

Paula said, "So how's that going to work for you with the Cabaret?"

"Well." Dana shrugged. "I was never a regular, exactly, but yeah. I'm not going to have the time to work up pole routines. And we have some other evolutions to contend with."

Rory said, "Kim and Hector are moving to Seattle. Imminently. He got promoted at the cruise line and they wanted him to manage things up there."

"So," Paula said, "Michelle is AWOL, Kim is leaving, Dana is packing heat for the foreseeable future instead of climbing the pole, I'm not planning to strip again. Well, not on stage at least. That's on you, Rory. But what about Stacey, is she still going to be active?"

"To be determined. She was saying how that 'Wee Small Hours' routine in 'After Hours' might have been her swan song. The baby is taking up a lot of her time. With two full-time jobs already to contend with, there was always the chance she wouldn't be able to fit everything in." Rory glanced at Dana. "There's an awful lot of gym time required when you work on silk."

"Yeah, you can't exactly hang it up in the living room. And I'd be astonished if Michelle wanted to go back to pole." Dana waved a hand toward the front of the cottage, where her own pole was still in place. "She loved it, but she loves everything, and she never loved anything as much as she loves ballroom."

"Well, she loves Kenji that much," Rory said. "We're taking bets on who her new dance partner will be when they get back. Everybody seems to be putting their money on Vince."

"I saw that Big Bad Voodoo Daddy routine they did," Mike said. "I'd put my money there, too. So what happens to the Cabaret at the end of the year?"

"I've got to talk to Michelle and Stacey again. And Tyrone. Plus, shit, Dmitri, he's been so active with us since, golly, almost four years. We still get a lot of great submissions, but they're majority dance now, not burlesque or circus arts. As for me," Rory paused and petted Spike for a few seconds. "Quite honestly, it's getting really hard for me to stay in shape. I'm pushing forty and this body was never intended to be thin. I've been thinking for a while I might transition to stage-managing."

"I told her she could quit the day job so she has more time," said Dana. "With the new TV contract, the residuals from my first show, and the rental income from the house, we're more than fine."

"Eh." Rory wriggled. "Maybe I'm getting lazy."

Paula was a little stunned by everything she'd heard. "But, wow. Would you still want to run the Cabaret if it's only you in charge?"

"No. I liked being part of a team."

All Paula could think was that without the Cabaret, Tyrone might not book dance productions. She felt like the bottom was dropping out. Mike glanced over as if he could tell something was up, then picked up the open bottle of wine. "Anyone want some more of this? Oh, okay, everybody." He distributed the wine amongst the four glasses, emptying the bottle. "Could I offer a suggestion?"

"Sure," said Dana. "You could also go get the dessert." He took the hint and went to do that. She followed him out to make coffee. "It's decaf," she said. "I know Paula can't do caffeine at night." After a minute she added quietly, "Rory really doesn't want to quit. She's always had a complex about her body."

"Didn't she train in jazz?" Mike asked just as quietly. "Seems like it from the routines I've seen, on the DVDs Paula has."

"Yeah, she did." Dana looked at him questioningly, but he only nodded. She sliced the dessert, a chocolate and strawberry extravaganza from La Provence Patisserie. He followed behind her with plates and forks to serve it in the den.

Paula and Rory were talking striptease when they got there. Rory looked up, her hand on Spike, who had relocated to Mike's seat. "Christ, you're tall."

Mike picked up the cat, sat down on the cushioned bench beside her and kissed Rory's cheek. "You have a beautiful body. If someone said come and do a jazz routine with me, what would you say?"

"Uh. I don't know," she said. "I haven't done a straight dance number for a really long time. Like, decades."

"Well, hold that thought. So what if you were to add a couple of words to the company name, and a couple other people stepped in to help run it?"

Paula looked at him sharply, wondering what he was up to. "What words would those be?"

"I mean, I've heard how Tyrone loves that Chrome is the place to see dance in Hollywood. What if the company were to become the Underground Cabaret Dance Theater?" All the women looked at each other, then back at him. *Don't play poker with these people*, Mike thought. He could usually read Paula, but not right this minute. "I know I haven't been around very long and I don't want to be that guy who comes in telling the women what to do. So if that's an offensive idea, forget I said anything."

"It's not an offensive idea," said Rory. "Excuse me while I eat this thing for a minute." All of the women addressed their desserts, so Mike did too. Then he leaned back and watched them think. When all the plates and all the wineglasses were empty, he cleared the table. Then he brought the coffee things back to the den. The others still looked deeply thoughtful.

Paula finally said, "So who did you have in mind to help run this imaginary dance theater?"

"You and Alison." All of them sat back, clearly surprised.

"Not you?" said Paula.

"Remember, the guy telling women what to do, that's not what I'm after here. All I want is to dance." *My own stuff. With you and the rest of my people, at Chrome, in that great little theater.* He realized he needed to say that. "And frankly, I want to dance at Chrome. I missed dancing in a theater. I love these shows we do. Love having a place to create my own work. So if I can help keep this company alive, tell me how."

"I'm going to get in touch with Michelle and Stacey," said Rory. "I'll float the idea. I mean, if they don't hate it we could wrap in Julia too. She likes running Mating Dance." She was starting to look excited. Dana caught Mike's eye from across the table, shaping the words *thank you*.

"I have an ulterior motive," said Mike. "We're ready to put our new jazz piece on video and I want to do it onstage."

"I can make that happen," said Rory. "The owner's a friend of mine."

Less than two weeks later, Mike was fully moved in with Paula and Cabaret negotiations were underway. He and Paula met club owner Tyrone and Rory at Chrome on a Sunday morning. Tyrone was looking bright-eyed and interested. "Look at you, all

160

perky. You must not have been here last night," said Rory. "Was Terry running the joint?"

"Yeah, he's doing Fridays and Saturdays most of the time now. It's almost like being retired," he said, unlocking the big Art Deco door.

"How's Indira?"

Tyrone smiled. "Still perfect." He locked the door again behind them.

"Glad to hear it." The club had a slightly hungover feel to it. The only light on the ground floor was from the security fixtures by the doors. Tyrone flipped a switch to turn on the LED strip that outlined the catwalk and stairs. They started down. "Can we use the stage lights?"

"Use whatever you want. I'm going back to my office for a little while to get caught up. When y'all are ready to go, I'd like to come out and watch. I'll have my walkie turned on."

"Okay, I'll buzz you. Thanks, Daddio." Tyrone waved his hand, walking away. The others went up on stage and Rory started waking up the equipment while Mike and Paula warmed up. Mike had set their disc on the soundboard. After about ten minutes Rory said, "Ready to run it for tech?"

"Yeah, we're ready," said Paula. She took off her hoodie and threw it on a folding chair by the green room door. Her short recital dress was a tie-dyed lavender, like the tank Mike was wearing with his dance jeans. He stripped off his sweatshirt and stretched out his shoulders.

"I'll go out to the house after I start it to see what needs adjusting in the lights." Rory watched as they took their positions. When Mike gave a little nod, she started the track. About twenty seconds in, she went

161

out to the main floor to see how it looked, making notes. She'd properly watch the dance once they were doing it for the camera. At the end, she went back up onstage and made some changes to tone and angle. "I think that'll do it. Going to set up the camera now if you want to hit the green room."

"How long has Rory been doing the technical stuff?" Mike asked Paula as they headed backstage.

"They've all been taking turns for the past three years. When they had Yoshi do those extra effects for April, that was new." They each went to the bathroom, had a mouthful of water, then stretched for a few minutes until the ready light came on. "Here we go."

When they got back onstage, Rory was in position at the soundboard and Tyrone was lounging on the big banquette around the dance pole, next to the camera tripod. "Y'all ready?" he called.

Mike gave him a thumbs-up. A few seconds later the music started. Rory got out to the house as fast as she could, not wanting to miss anything. They'd put everything they had – tricks and jumps, carries, throws, assists – on a base of traveling and turning passes fitting the strong rhythm of the ballad. Mike had put his 540 in simply because he could. The piece was almost contemporary in design, though the side by side and solo phrases were unmistakably jazz. It finished with Mike holding Paula in an arched relevé arabesque that resolved to a swoony embrace and finally to the two of them holding and looking at each other.

Rory glanced sideways at Tyrone, watching him think. It was one of the best thing she'd ever seen on this stage, but it was far from burlesque. He must have felt her attention, because he looked back at her with his eyebrows up. "Damn," he said softly. "Is that what y'all meant?"

"Kind of."

"A different kind of show."

"This would be the gold standard. Not everything would be so hard core." He laughed softly. "I guess the idea is to bring the whole level up. But it's still sexy, right? Still makes you thirsty?"

Tyrone laughed for real. "It is, and it does."

Rory nodded. "We'll talk about it more soon."

Mike and Paula came down off the stage then, breathing hard, for a review of the video. Both of them were deeply satisfied. "That looks great," said Paula. "Thank you."

"If we do what we were talking about, can we use it in the company's marketing?" said Rory.

Mike said, "Of course. Thanks, Tyrone. This was fantastic. What can we do for you?"

"Just help get my girls straightened out." The men shook hands, Rory and Paula hugged Tyrone, and they all started packing up to go.

Rory said, "You guys want to come back to our place and meet Molly?"

"Who's Molly?" said Paula.

"Our temporary dog. Andy and Victor picked her up off the highway in NorCal and till they move they can't take her home. They bought a, well, it's not exactly a house. Andy says if they're lucky they'll have the power on by Christmas."

Mike was amused. "What does Spike think about the dog?"

163

"He's *crazy* about her. They're inseparable. When the boys take her home, we might have to get a dog ourselves."

"We could swing by for a while. We've got to be at Dmitri's at three."

"Plenty of time for lunch."

Later that day, after getting home from another session of troupe rehearsal, Mike decided to break out the Empress. There were things he still wanted – maybe needed – to know about Paula. They'd had some breakthroughs already, more than he'd ever really hoped for; but the more he learned, the more he wanted to learn. Watching the 'No Hay Imposibles' video before they posted it, he was amazed all over again at how much she trusted him as a dance partner. It made him want, even more strongly, the same trust in their personal relationship.

After they ate, Paula said, "You want to go down to the pool? After that thing this morning, a float would feel good."

"Sure." They got changed and went down, to find an uncommon number of neighbors out enjoying the warm July evening. Unusually, Paula didn't seem to mind. They got in the water, not swimming laps, letting the buoyancy relieve their hard-worked bodies. After a while, Paula edged closer to where Mike hung by his elbows on the pool's edge, facing the water in the deep end.

"We have some unfinished conversations," she said softly. She had her folded arms up on the ledge, head turned toward him.

He was astonished. "Yeah, we do," he said after a moment.

"You ever wonder why I never go home?"

"I haven't been home since I moved here."

"Mike, that's like a year. I haven't been home for *ten*."

His eyebrows went up; he hadn't realized it had been that long. "Then yeah, I wonder."

"The last time I went home I was twenty-five and had been here in L.A. for a year and a half. I'd turned down the Disneyland job. Decided to stop trying. I was working all those hours for the litigators. I'd broken up with somebody. More accurately, I'd been dumped because I wasn't *available* enough. I was at peak rage."

"I can imagine." He studied her face; it was turned toward him but she wasn't looking at him. Her gaze went past him to, he thought, history. "So what happened?"

"So I went home for Christmas and my parents had set up an intervention."

"A *what*?"

"An intervention. Like they do for drug addicts?" She looked at him then; he looked completely baffled, and also furious. She smiled. "Did I ever tell you how sexy you are when you're mad? Your eyebrows come down a little, your eyes narrow a little, it's like, mmm yeah. It makes your eyes look really dark. Took me the longest time to figure out."

He relaxed, sliding off the edge into the water, changing position, hanging from one arm so he could face her more comfortably. "You don't use drugs. You're not an alcoholic. There's nothing wrong with you. Did they think you were addicted to *dancing*?"

She answered indirectly. "My father works on Wall Street. My mother is a lady who lunches. They

165

were willing to put me through Smith for the MFA, they were even willing to countenance me being a professional dancer. But in *their* minds, that meant cutting-edge ballet at Jacob's Pillow. It needed to be some situation where they could tell their rich friends, and go to galas, and set me up on dates with the Ivy League progeny – the male progeny, that is – of said rich friends, trot me out once in a while looking thin and stylish."

"You *are* thin and stylish."

"But I don't wear makeup, and my hair is weird, and basically I don't do it right."

Mike was silent for a long minute. "I honestly cannot come up with anything to say that doesn't include the word 'fuck.'" Paula laughed out loud, for long enough that Mike started to laugh too. After a minute, he asked, "Does this get worse before it gets better?"

"Not really. When I walked out on their little psycho session, Dad told me I was on my own. Not to come home again until I was ready to play by their rules. And thus, I do not go home."

"But they ask you all the time."

"Well, it's not really *asking*, is it. It's complaining about how I don't go home. That's not quite the same as saying gee honey we'd really love to see you and hear about your life in L.A."

"And by the way that video was kickass, good job."

"It would be nice to hear something like that once in a while. Or, you know, ever."

They were quiet for a minute. Then Mike asked, "Do you have any brothers or sisters?"

"One of each, both older. My sister graduated from Vassar and married a lawyer. They have two

166

kids and live in Boston. My brother graduated from Harvard and *is* a lawyer. He works on Wall Street, too. He's divorced with one kid who goes to boarding school."

"You're in touch with them?"

"Off and on. Last year they both kind of asked if they were ever going to see me again."

"Would you like to?"

"I don't know. We've never been that close. Our school years barely overlapped. Jen's seven years older, Bill's four years. By the time I finished at Smith they were married. I don't feel like I even know them."

"You went to the weddings?"

"Well sure, but these weren't the kind of weddings where you sit around getting sloppy drunk and over-sharing, dishing all the family dirt with the new in-laws. These were Display Weddings."

He could hear the capital letters. "Do you connect with them on Facebook?"

"Yeah, if ever, that's where."

"We could go over there, you know. I have a little vacation time. You must have a lot, you never take any."

"I guess." She worked one of her legs in between his. "I'd rather meet your mom and your sister first."

"Want to go for Thanksgiving? They're dying to meet you." He was smiling.

"What have you told them?"

"That I'm in love with you."

She was smiling now too. "What did they say?"

"They said, 'That's all we need to know.'"

167

"God, I love them already. Let's go upstairs." They swam to the shallow end and got out, toweled off, and went up for their usual routine of a shower and a drink. Mike poured them a little of the Empress just for the hell of it.

"Want lime, or no?" he asked.

"Sure." He got the drinks ready and handed hers to Paula. "I'm going to get online for a minute," she said. "See what the feed says about that link."

"Okay."

She fired up the laptop, sipping the gin. A few minutes later, she said, "Well, I will be double dog damned."

"What?" He came over. She turned the laptop around. Her post linking to the new video had been liked by her sister and brother. And there was a comment from her brother: **That's fantastic, Paula. Great work.** Her sister had replied to that: *Beautiful!*

Paula pinched the bridge of her nose and sniffed. "That was unexpected," she said, croakily. Mike knelt by her and slid an arm around her waist. She turned to him, put her head down on his shoulder, and cried.

CHAPTER 17

"Send them something," Mike said, when Paula was calm and their glasses were empty. "Before bed. If it was me and somebody didn't answer … ."

"Yeah, you're right." She scrolled back to the comments and wrote a reply, tagging him: Thanks guys! Mike Borodin can really fly me, huh? Hope you're all well. <3

It was by then past midnight on the East Coast, but her sister Jennifer came back with a PM right away: *Bill is coming to our place for Christmas, his ex is taking Alexander to Switzerland. Could you and Mike come? Mom and Dad won't be there. They're going to the Bahamas.*

"What do you think?" Paula said, looking at Mike. "I can't call it an olive branch because the three of us never had issues, personally, but that's beyond anything. And I don't know when all this was decided, but with this much notice it's not like we can't fit it in."

"I think they want to see you. For whatever reason. I think we should go."

Paula didn't say anything, but she wrote back: We'd love to, then signed off. Later, lying in bed in the dark, she said, "You never asked me about that night last fall."

He knew what she meant. "When you broke?"

"Yeah."

"Should I have?"

"I don't know." They were quiet for a minute. "I guess I was surprised that you didn't."

169

"I kind of thought," he said slowly, "that I didn't need to. That I already understood. I mean, I wasn't sure how to deal with it while it was happening, but after ... you seemed okay. And I'd told you ... I kind of laid a lot on you. I thought it might take some time to process. I didn't know everything about you that I know now, but I got the idea that maybe no one else had ever said the things I said. And maybe those were exactly the things you needed to hear in order to let go."

She leaned over and kissed him. "I'm glad you're here," was all she said. *With me, in L.A., on Earth. Alive.* They both put in their vacation requests the next day.

Paula got another PM from her sister a week later: *Can I call you next weekend?* She wrote back Sure, Saturday is best - dress rehearsal Sunday for new show, eek! They exchanged numbers. It had been so long since they'd actually spoken that neither of them had been certain the last known digits were still good.

Over the course of that week, Paula and Mike were both doing extra rehearsals. Red was back in town, so all his routines had to be revisited with him in place instead of Mike. The troupe did their jazz + tango + stepping routine on video for Alison to fine-tune. The entire company ran 'Adios Nonino' on video with the new finish. The six featured dancers performed nearly the entire number, then the troupe danced with them into a line at the front of the stage, under a row of angled lights. Then the troupe dancers faded out to the back of the stage, where it was dark. Finally Mary, Mateo, and Kelli turned away into the darkness, leaving the three featured leaders under the lights. "That's good," said Alison, when she saw it on video.

"Excellent transition to second act," said Dmitri. "The audience will remember. Very clean."

"How's everyone doing?" Alison asked, letting her eyes travel over the group. "You feel ready?" There was a chorus of 'yes,' and she smiled. "We shared the Dropbox with Tanith and after looking things over she said, get photos at dress rehearsal. So Andy is going to leave all his unfinished business for a couple of hours and come help us out. Plus of course the whole thing's going on video."

Mateo said, "We all have costume. Is the hair situation okay?" Sam and Red both had long hair, as did Vicky, Paula, and Alison; they'd all been wearing simple ponytails during rehearsals.

"The hair situation is dope," said Alison. "No jewelry, please. For makeup we're all doing the same thing. Smudged black line under the lower eyelashes, or gray for our blond and ginger friends. And we're going to have a dozen cabaret chairs, courtesy of Andy's friend Nick."

Mary asked, "Does that mean we can actually sit down when we're not dancing?"

"That's exactly what that means. Take a load off, look jaded and dissolute. During 'Adios Nonino,' the troupe could be seated almost the entire time."

"Should Kelli and I actually be on stage during the trio? Seated?"

"I think that's a good idea. The troupe could kind of segregate you from the men." Red was smiling and shaking his head. "What? Oh crap, I'm doing the last-minute changes. Sorry. Do not suggest anything anymore, people. We are officially out of time."

171

Mike had volunteered to work late on Friday night, so they'd driven separately. Paula was home alone in the evening; she was already so used to having him there that the place felt wrong. She found herself cleaning house, as if to get ready for Jennifer's call, and finally had to laugh at herself. When Mike eventually got back, she was parked in front of 'The Tango Lesson.'

"You're not sick of tango yet?" he said, dropping his phone on the side table and leaning down to kiss her.

"The more we do it, the more obsessed with it I get."

"Me too. At the back of my brain I'm thinking when the big tricks make me feel like I need a hip replacement, maybe we go full tango." She made a sound of agreement. "I had another idea." He went over to the kitchen to hunt for a snack. This took the form of an apple with some cheese, raw veggies and hummus.

"You and your ideas! We have two numbers to work up in less than three months and I don't even know what the second one is yet."

"This one's easy. I thought, how about, since we'll be there with the tripod and everything anyway, take our camera and after dress rehearsal we could do 'Hoy' on stage."

"What, like just wing it?"

"Sure, why not?" He brought over the cutting board and sat down, setting it between them on the couch.

She smiled at him and took a piece of cheese. "Feeling tragic?"

"I wouldn't want to do that as a show number. It's too sad. But I thought at the end of the rehearsal we'll be tired, feeling a little beat up. Exactly the right frame of mind."

"If you end up with a headache, I'm going to drown you." She studied him for a second. "You want me to bring a dress?"

"The show costume's fine. After all, Alison might say no. Tyrone might say get the hell out."

"Oh yeah, that'll happen."

By the time Jennifer called the next day, Paula was thoroughly nervous. Wasn't quite sure why. As she'd told Mike, she and her siblings had never had personal issues. But she had no idea what their parents might have told them about her, or what they might otherwise know about her life in the years since they'd all lived together. She told herself to smile when she picked up the call, so she wouldn't accidentally sound grouchy. "Hi, Jennifer?"

"Hi Paula. My God it's been a long time!"

"Unbelievably long. How've you been?" They had a soothing small-talk exchange for several minutes. Paula realized that by following Jennifer on Facebook, she'd managed to keep up with the high points. It was still stunning to realize that her sister's kids were teenagers now. When they got to the end of general updates, Paula said, "So I have to confess, I'm really curious."

"About why Bill and I reached out now?"

"Yep."

"So we both saw the videos you and Mike posted late last year. Bill was on the phone to me right away,

173

going, where does that even come from? And neither of us knew. I mean, I'll get to Mike in a minute, but you seemed really, well, angry."

Paula laughed. "Yes, I was angry. I was angry for a long time."

Jennifer noticed the past tense and filed it away. "Well, I asked Dad about it. He hadn't seen the dance. I told him he should watch it because I personally couldn't imagine doing something like that, something so violent, unless I felt seriously wronged. I mean, I'd seen the 'Tubular Bells' routine a few years ago and thought, damn, but when I looked at the other stuff from that show … it didn't strike me the same way. It didn't seem personal."

"Did he watch it?"

"Yeah, he did. Then he called me back and told me about the thing they did. He didn't say he regretted it, exactly, but he seemed kind of embarrassed. I couldn't believe it."

"It seems kind of trivial now."

"I am so sorry I never knew."

"It wasn't your fault. I mean, aside from you and Bill being the perfect children. That kind of fucked me up."

Jennifer made an amused, semi-apologetic sound. "So what's Mike's deal?"

"He was nearly killed in a car accident, literally half his body was broken, and lost his place in the company he'd danced with for a dozen years. Nobody told him to come back, even when his rehab was going well. Everybody told him to give up, basically. He moved to L.A. and started dancing again. Found all these people I know who are dancing for love.

174

Then, well, that dance happened. The choreography's from a show we went to."

"He was unbelievably scary. He's not like that in real life, I'm guessing."

"He's a pussycat. Well, he's from Minnesota." Paula listened, smiling, while Jennifer laughed for a long time.

"Were you dating then?" she asked finally.

"We'd been doing dance things for almost three months, not officially dating, until basically right before we put those on video."

"Where is he today?"

"He's down at the pool right now. He'll be sorry he missed you."

"So … I have to say, if I'd met someone like that it would not have taken me three months to start officially dating."

Paula was halfway conscious of the entry door opening. "It was such a relief when he finally kissed me." She felt Mike behind her. Turned to look; he was closing the door, smiling at her. "He came in right now, do you want to say hello?"

"Sure!"

"It's my sister Jennifer," said Paula, handing the phone to Mike.

"Hi Jennifer," he said. "Thanks for getting in touch."

"It was very overdue. Bill and I are both so happy you and Paula can come for Christmas."

"I'm looking forward to meeting you all."

"We're also happy that the dances you've posted this year are not so … well, that they're different."

He laughed. "Me too."

"Anyway they're really gorgeous and we love seeing you dance with Paula. Now that I know what you sound like can you put her on again?"

"Sure thing." He handed the phone back to Paula.

"Does he always sound like that?" said Jennifer.

"Like what?"

"Like a happy snow leopard."

"Yeah, pretty much."

"Rrrrowrrr." They both snickered. "Well, I'm going to let you go now, but it was great to talk to you."

"You too."

"Can't wait to see the next thing."

"I'll keep you posted. Jennifer?"

"What?"

"I love you."

After a pause Jennifer said, sounding emotional, "I love you too."

Paula disconnected and looked at Mike. "I never told her that before."

"She'll never forget it." He kissed her, taking his time with it. "So it was a relief, huh?"

"Uh-huh. I was trying to be all tough and I-don't-need-that and we're-just-friends and it was so not working."

"Not kissing you was torture."

"This is better. Take me to bed."

A while later, lying in the dim bedroom, Paula was struck by a ridiculous mental image courtesy of Jennifer and started giggling. Mike stirred beside her. "What's funny?"

176

"My sister. She said you sounded like a ha-, happy," she giggled, "happy snow leopard."

"What does that even mean?" She wasn't looking at him, but could tell from his voice that he was smiling.

"You sound very big and possibly dangerous but also super cuddly. Seriously, with that voice you'd be a smash doing phone sex." He was doing that silent-laugh thing that she loved. "But all of a sudden I thought about this romance novel I read where the hero was a were-leopard."

"You've lost me."

"Like a werewolf, only a leopard." Her tone said, isn't that obvious. "I don't know if you've noticed, but some women like a little ferocity."

"I have noticed that, actually." He rolled over and rose up, caging her with his arms, bending his head to set his teeth on her collarbone, dragging them lightly to the hollow of her throat and then nibbling his way up to her mouth, already aroused again. He kissed her hard, then wrapped a hand around the back of her neck and pulled her up as he sat back on her thighs. She had a hand under his arm for leverage. Went for his throat with her own teeth. Avoiding a full bite, he tipped over, laughing, taking her with him so she was pinned underneath him. "No marks before dress rehearsal."

"Why not?" she said breathlessly, squirming. He reached down and hooked a hand under the top of her thigh, bringing her up to him on her hands and knees. "Fucking hell, Mike." She was still wet, or wet again; he slid right in. "God!"

He had one arm wrapped around her ribs now, holding her in place, but didn't move while she ground against him. Then he did move, fast and hard, reaching around to touch her. She screamed his name, arching up against him. The next thing he knew they were lying still, spent and gasping. He drew away slowly, lightheaded. Laid a hand on her back. "What just happened?"

"Um. I think you fucked my brains out."

He would have laughed if he could have remembered exactly what the sequence of events had been. "Are you okay?" She rolled out from under his hand and looked up at him.

"I'm fine. That was our usual, turned up to leopard." She smiled lazily. "You came really hard." She studied his face. "Are *you* okay?"

"I'm not sure," he admitted. "Feels like I lost some time."

"It went from me starting to come, to you starting to come, to over. Not really any time lost there." She sat up slowly and looked at his eyes. The pupils were normal; equal and reactive. "You look all right. Any pain?"

"No."

"Dizziness?"

"Not now."

"Vision all right?" He nodded. She scooted back, reached over, and switched on the lamp. He didn't wince. "Still okay?"

"Yeah."

"Let's see you walk." He didn't argue, only swung his legs off the bed and stood up. *So far so good*, he thought. He walked across the room and back. Paula assessed him; he looked perfectly symmetrical, as usual. "Okay. What do you think?"

He shrugged. "I guess that was the most intense orgasm I've ever had and my brain shut down for a second."

"When's your next scan?"

"Middle of September. Supposed to be the last one."

"Do you want to move it up?"

"Was it really that fast?"

She knew what he meant. "Yeah, it really was. I don't think you actually blacked out. I didn't feel you ever not *there*, if that makes sense." *You were never dead weight*, she thought, not liking her own choice of words.

"Then I guess … dress rehearsal tomorrow. And 'Hoy.' If anything funky happens, I'll move up the scan. Otherwise I'll stick to the schedule." She still looked worried. Mike abruptly remembered something. He sat down beside her and took her hand. "Listen, I'm sorry. This was my own fault. I think I'm hungry. I just realized I never had breakfast. Or dinner, really."

She closed her eyes and sighed, exasperated but deeply relieved. "And I hauled you to bed as soon as you came in from the pool. Jesus, Mike, do not fucking *scare* me like that. Do you realize if I had to call 911 I don't even have any right to go with you to the hospital?"

He studied her face now. That was something he hadn't considered. The timing could be better, but he mentally shrugged, deciding to go for it. Because it was something he'd been wanting to say for a long time, but was still kind of afraid to say, he leaned close, tipping his forehead against hers. Spoke softly, with his eyes closed. "Then let's get married." She didn't speak. He thought maybe she couldn't; she didn't seem to be breathing. "I was going to ask you in December. I already asked my mom if I could have her mother's ring. You know I love you." He pulled back enough to see her face.

"I love you too," she said, as if automatically. Then she smiled. "When?"

"Let's call out sick one day, go get the license. We could ask Rory to do the ceremony for us after 'Gaucho' wraps. As soon as we can all get together." Paula touched his face. Mike was suddenly flooded with intense happiness.

Paula's eyes were wet and he could tell she was thinking hard. "She did Vicky and Sharon's."

"Yeah, I heard." *When I asked if they knew somebody.*

"What should I wear?"

He smiled. "Anything or nothing." She laughed and shook her head. He leaned in and kissed her. "Let's go eat. And I promise I'll pay more attention."

"Yeah, do that. Please."

CHAPTER 18

The whole cast knew something was up when Mike and Paula walked into Chrome the next day. Everyone looked at them, then various people exchanged glances. Mike looked at Paula and she raised her eyebrows with a little tilt of the head, like 'you know they know,' and he said, "We're getting married." He aimed it at Rory.

She instantly did a fist-pump. "When?"

"ASAP."

"Good. Let me know when you have the license." There was a giant group hug, lots of hand-shaking, lots of kisses and congratulations. Then Alison stood back and took control. Rory and Dana went backstage to start up the technical equipment, others went back to the green room to finish getting in costume. Mike and Paula were already wearing theirs, and had done the minimal makeup at home, so they pulled over a couple of the cabaret chairs and took a load off.

A minute later, the photographer came over to them. "Hi, I'm Andy." He and Mike shook hands. "How did you like those prints?"

"They were a little alarming. But Paula likes them, so I'm good." Mike smiled as Andy laughed.

"A year ago I would have been all over you to do a session for me, but with this new gig and shit I've been up to my ass in No Time. Victor claims I danced a jig when Alison called me about doing photos for this."

"What's the plan?" said Paula.

"I'm going to shoot throughout the rehearsal and when it's done I'll do some feature shots. Someone said something about the Cabaret maybe turning into a dance theater company. I guess there'll be a new website?"

Paula glanced at Mike. "We're not sure yet."

"Well, in any case, I'll try to make sure there's good company coverage as well as highlight shots for each dancer. You've almost all got your own websites now anyway." He nodded cheerfully and went away, chatting with the others who were waiting for the call, which happened not much later.

"Okay," said Alison, when they were all assembled onstage. "Rory's already tested the projections that Yoshi did for us. She's got the final tracks and the timing for lighting changes has been marked. We're going to have 'Tanguera' as an overture, with a projected title card, like from a silent movie, on the curtain. 'Libertango' at the end for bows. Everybody feeling good?"

"Yes," said everybody.

Alison smiled. "Great. Places please for the opening sextet."

At the end of the run-through, Alison sat down with Rory and Dana to go through their notes. Andy wandered around getting some feature shots. About ten minutes later, Alison gave Mike and Paula the nod to go ahead with their improv on 'Hoy.' Rory popped back up to the soundboard to start the track for them. Dana operated the camera. Mike used bits and pieces from all the numbers they'd learned for the show, whatever came to him, not reaching for it. He let the song's sorrowful vocal wash over him and worked more from the trancey accompaniment. Paula didn't even try to think, simply followed. When he finally stopped moving, she raised her head to look at him. He smiled, and kissed her, and a moment later they realized the other cast members were applauding. They looked around as the noise abated.

Sam and Mateo were standing over by the bar with Red and Mary. Dmitri was sitting with Vicky and Alison. Ray was with his girlfriend Julia, who'd dropped in to see the rehearsal. Tyrone and his wife Indira were at the counter across the back of the room. Vince and Kelli were on one of the loveseats in the lounge area. He was leaning back in the corner of the seat; she was sitting beside him with her legs over his lap. Her head was resting on his arm, stretched along the back of the seat. They gazed at each other as though they'd forgotten they weren't alone.

"They look like they're going to go home and make a baby," said Mike softly as they started off the stage. Paula laughed under her breath. "Should we have talked about that?"

"Do you want to?" she said neutrally. He knew she didn't mean talk.

Truth, he thought. "Not in the least."

"Thank fucking God." He smiled at the relief in her voice. They arrived at the banquette where Dana was stationed with the tripod. "How'd it look?" said Paula.

"Are you sure that was improv?" Mike nodded and Dana went on. "You know, I've seen some great performers since we got wrapped into the Cabaret. I've seen some great dance numbers. I think we're damned lucky you two are in the stable."

Paula looked up at Mike again. His eyes were clear and he still had that deeply happy look he'd been wearing since the day before. *I don't know about the stable*, she thought, *but I sure feel lucky*. Then she noticed Alison had gone up on stage and was bringing the cabaret chairs into a circle. "Time for notes," she said, and they went back to work.

'Gaucho' was a complete success for Chrome and for the company. Andy printed the feature shots in poster size; Tyrone hung them all over the club during the run. There was a photo of Vince and Kelli on the loveseat, one of Red and Mary doing a trick from their duet, and one of Mateo looking implacably beautiful in his solo, with the troupe ranged behind him like a pack of wolves. Dmitri and Alison were featured in a still from the troupe's synchronized routine, Ray and Vicky in background from the men's trio, and Mike and Paula in a still from their post-show improv. The poster of Sam showed him in profile, slumped on his knees at the end of his ménage number, his head flung back and eyes closed. There were so many inquiries about buying prints that Andy offered to do a book. Alison wrote up a summary of the show, with notes on the production, then asked all the cast members to contribute observations or stories about how it had come together. They were all looking forward to seeing the finished product.

By mid-September, with the 'Hoy' video posted and voluminously commented upon, and another clear MRI in the records, Mike and Paula were well into preparation of their 'Wuthering Heights' number for the Cabaret's Halloween show. Having to rehearse in the gym with the Kung Fu Flyers was a whole new experience for Mike, but once they worked out the earthbound choreography he really got a charge out of the extra-dimensional capability the flying rig gave them.

184

After the whole routine was blocked, they had an acquaintance at the gym take video for their submission. They sent it in to Stacey, then sent a text to Rory: Ready to rock & roll.

She wrote back more or less immediately. **Got the license?**

Yep

How's Saturday? 4:00? Our place?

Excellent

Who you gonna call?

Vicky Sharon Vince Kelli Sam Mateo Alison Rob Red Mary Tyrone Indira Ray Julia Dmitri Patrick Elena Tony Andy Victor Stacey Joe + work friends Susan and Janice

in other words everybody you know

LOL yeah. Anybody else you know in & around Chrome or Cabaret is welcome, we still have people to meet

Dana says we'll get a valet company to handle the parking. Our treat.

Thanks!! But we'll buy the pizza

LMAO

"Are you nervous?" Mike asked Paula, on their way to West Hollywood.

"Not really. I was nervous at the courthouse. I've only ever been there for jury duty before."

"I haven't gotten summoned yet in L.A."

"Count your blessings. The first few times I got summoned, they sent me to fucking Van Nuys."

Van Nuys was twelve miles from her condo, a minimum of an hour in traffic. Mike would have thought she'd be sent downtown. "Are you serious?"

"Well, I only had to report there twice, but yeah. The blaspheming over Coldwater Canyon was a real high point in my history of profanity." She wasn't even kidding. "Oh awesome, the valet people are already here. That was so nice of Dana and Rory."

"I think they like you," he said, amused.

"They like you, too." They turned the car over to the valets and walked down the driveway toward Rory & Dana's cottage, then stopped in amazement as they cleared the main house. The back yard had been done up with tables and chairs, flowers, and a modest dance floor. "What in the heck." Paula turned to Mike, confused. "Is this our wedding?" He had an idea who was responsible, but he wasn't sure, so he raised his eyebrows and shook his head. They went on to the cottage.

Dana opened the door and stood back. Paula's sister stepped out. "Hi baby," she said. Paula was still confused, but now she was crying, too. Jennifer came down the steps and hugged her. "I couldn't miss it, could I?"

Several long soggy minutes later, Paula turned to Mike. "Did you tell her?"

"Yeah."

She put a hand on his face, stroked her thumb along his cheekbone, and kissed him. "You're so great. Thank you."

"You both look gorgeous," said Jennifer. "Isn't this what you wore for the 'Dancing in the Dark' thing?" Mike had his white suit on and Paula was in the full-skirted white shirt dress from the routine. She

186

was also wearing her black-and-white snake print tango shoes, because she could. Her hair was up in a knot with the red and orange ends fanned out.

"Uh-huh," said Paula. "We didn't think we could improve on Astaire and Charisse for this occasion."

Things seemed to happen fast after that. Music started while guests were still arriving. Paula and Mike mingled. Andy took pictures. People danced. At about half past four, Rory cleared the dance floor and performed the ceremony. When Mike slid a ring on her finger, Paula looked down. It was silver, set with a narrow oval of lapis lazuli. "It's temporary," he said, smiling. "Borrowed it from Andy's friend Nick's wife Lucy. It's an antique."

"And it's blue," Paula said. "Perfect."

"Alright already," Rory said to Mike. "Kiss the bride." Obediently, he did. Then he and Paula each kissed Rory. She did a fake-simper, batting her eyelashes, then said to the crowd, "There you have it, people: Mr. and Mrs. Michael Borodin. Or is it Mr. and Mrs. Paula Ross?" There was laughter, then applause. Hugs and more dancing, with Mike and Paula being passed from partner to partner. Champagne corks popped.

"Let's stick with Borodin," said Paula when she came back around to Mike. He kissed her again and she had an almost vertiginous moment of *how is this possible*. While she was still getting a grip, hardly even aware he'd gone into close embrace, Mike started dancing and she realized that the music playing was 'Palomita Blanca.' The floor cleared again around them. Paula surrendered to the music.

After the pizza and a lot more champagne, more pictures and more dancing, Paula ended up sitting beside her sister in the twilight, watching Mike talk to Ray across the dance floor. "Did you do all this?" she asked, waving a slightly drunken hand at the backyard.

"Sure did," said Jennifer, smiling. "I'm quite the party planner after all these years of organizing stuff for Adam. I called my people in Boston and got referrals. Rory helped me pull it all together at this end."

"She's so great."

"They're both great. Actually, they're *all* great. It's such a treat to meet everyone like this. Now I can go home and tell Bill that you've made yourself a family here, we don't have to worry."

"I didn't make it," Paula objected half-seriously. "I, like, fell into it."

Jennifer laughed. "And everyone is sickeningly good-looking. Our parties do not look like this." Paula snorted. "Even the DJ!"

"That's Danny," said Paula. "He produces the shows. We throw him the tracks with half-assed notes about the edits we want and he tosses back something cooler than cool. If Alison does another show next summer, I hope it's got lots of martial-arts stuff, maybe we can get Danny and Kate in it."

"Kate's his wife, right?"

"Fiancée. They're both black belts." She enunciated all those b's with special care.

Jennifer got up and went to the drinks tub, fishing out bottles of water for both of them. "When are you and Mike going home tonight?"

"I dunno." Paula took a long drink of water. "How long are you in town?"

"I'm flying back Monday morning." They looked at each other for a moment. "Are you busy tomorrow?"

"Not till evening, there's a show. We're not in it, just spectating. Do you want to come? You'd get to see a lot of these characters dance."

"I'd love to."

"Wanna hang out before that?"

"I'd love to."

"All-righty then."

"You are so buzzed."

"Yes I am," Paula agreed. She didn't care, but she drank some more water anyway.

"Everything is going to feel like an anticlimax now," said Paula on the way to Chrome the following evening. Jennifer laughed in the back seat. They picked her up for brunch and spent the day together. "After doing that show, then getting married?"

"Yeah. Kind of hard to top that," said Mike. "But we still have two performances this year, so who knows." He glanced at Jennifer in the rear-view mirror. "Mom and Beth seemed to think the wedding tango was the best we could possibly do." They'd posted the video early in the morning, before Mike called to talk to his mom.

"It was beautiful. I wish I knew how to dance like that."

"We'll teach you," he said, smiling. "When we see you at Christmas."

"You're going to need more than a holiday weekend, I'm afraid."

"They said very nice things," said Paula. "I wish we could have gotten them out here."

"They're hosting a thing when we're up there. Be prepared for a lot of parkas."

"I'm going to need to *get* a parka!"

"I've got one," said Jennifer, "but I'm going to need it myself. My husband has this lunatic idea of frying the turkey." Paula looked extremely dubious. "It's supposed to taste really good, if you don't explode it. Needless to say, this experiment will be conducted outdoors."

After they got to the club, collected their tickets, and went downstairs, they took a look at the show order to see who was dancing. Mike pointed to a set of names. "This is the couple that took third in that competition last winter."

Paula was impressed. "How do you remember all that shit?"

"The brain is working better these days. Must be all the great sex." Paula choked back a laugh, looking guiltily at Jennifer, who pretended she hadn't heard him. Mike referred to the show order again. "Andy and Victor are dancing, too. They're doing 'The Mating Game' again."

"Good, I liked that routine." She leaned over. "Oh, Ray and Julia are dancing. They're doing 'Palomita Blanca'!"

"I wonder why Vince and Kelli decided not to do it." By this time they'd been shown to a table near the bar. Drinks and snacks were on the way to keep them busy until the show started. The house music for the night was tango nuevo; they couldn't resist doing a tiny little dance around their table for a few minutes. Jennifer watched, fully envious.

190

"You guys should be in the show," said a voice Mike and Paula hadn't heard for a long time. They both looked around. Michelle was standing there grinning at them, with her husband Kenji at her side.

"Michelle! Holy shit!" Paula hugged her. "Welcome back!" Mike and Kenji shook hands, then Mike leaned over to kiss Michelle. "We were starting to wonder if we'd ever see you again. This is my sister Jennifer."

"Hi Jennifer, nice to meet you. We just got in today, but Rory pointed out that we're only a couple of months off the end of the year and plans must be made. We're going to try to set something up in a week or so. We'd like you to be there if possible."

"Absolutely, if we can. Let us know when," said Mike. "We're prepping a routine for Halloween, but the hard work is already done."

"And by the way, congratulations. We were sorry to miss the big day. But I remember how it feels, once you decide to do it. It's like, let's do it already, right?"

Paula said, "Pretty much, yeah." The house lights dimmed for a moment then. "Guess it's showtime." They waved as Michelle and Kenji went to their own table, then sat down.

Jennifer leaned over. "Really? Those two? Your gang wasn't already averaging like nine point five? She looks like Marilyn Monroe."

Paula grinned. "I know, only she can do like ten pull-ups. And he was a model back in the day."

"It's ridiculous." They both snickered as the lights went down. At the end of the show Jennifer stood and applauded with everyone else. "I really like this club. I need to find something like this in Boston.

A place to go see a show and have some drinks and not be so damn stuffy."

"Are you stuffy?" Jennifer rolled her eyes. Paula patted her hand consolingly. "There's hope. You're still young."

Jennifer blew out a breath, shaking her head. "I forget that being an adult doesn't mean all the fun has to stop. There's always so much *adulting* to do."

"Yeah." Another pat, then Paula settled back as the lights dimmed. During the show, she thought about the fact that these few days were the first time she'd really gotten to know her sister as an adult. Another thing to thank Mike for. After they dropped Jennifer back at her hotel later, with hugs and kisses and promises to stay in touch, she turned to him. "That was a good thing you did, getting her out here."

"I told her what was happening. Gave her the option. You're so used to not sharing."

"I know. I'll get better."

"I know." He kissed her. They got back in the car and went home.

CHAPTER 19

That Wednesday night, they both got a text from Rory: **Cabaret meeting at Chrome Sunday 11 a.m. plz come if poss**. They'd finished up dinner – a consistently better-organized meal these days – and both had their phones at hand. They looked at each other. Paula said, "We don't have a conflict, do we? We're rehearsing at the gym but not till four."

"Yeah, we can go. It's good that they're getting things rolling. I mean, no matter what." Mike sent a text back saying they'd both be there.

"Speaking of rehearsing. What about this December thing you wanted to do?"

Mike nodded. "I'll play it for you." He hooked his phone up to the stereo dock and located the track.

Paula listened, recognizing the song but not the singer. "Who is that? I heard the Jeff Buckley version and *hated* it, then k.d. lang and thought, oh, now I get it."

"This is Leonard Cohen. He wrote it."

"No wonder it sounds like he knows what he's talking about."

"It's my favorite version. Just the four verses. In my head, this is even closer to contemporary than the Chayanne piece."

Paula shrugged. "Contemporary makes sense when I dance it with you. I like the 6/8 time."

"Want to work on it a little bit on Saturday? It's going to come together fast, I think."

"Why don't we wait, then. I kind of want to get prepared for the Sunday meeting."

"Okay. I think I'm going to prepare to keep my mouth shut unless somebody asks me something specific."

"Nobody minds, you know. I'm not officially part of the company, but they've been letting me put my two cents in forever."

"It's that guy thing. My mom hates that so much. She's been running the business for decades, then somebody comes in and mansplains things to her."

"Offering a suggestion is not mansplaining. And, for what it's worth, you're the only person who's worked on the Cabaret shows who's also got over a decade of experience as a professional dance company member. You've got perspective that we probably need. And there I go with 'we' like I'm even in charge of anything."

He shook his head, smiling. "Alison was in a company before she got married."

"Yeah, okay. If she's there, let her talk. Now let's go to bed."

Paula checked in with Rory to see if they should bring anything to the meeting and was told that Tyrone and Indira were handling it. "Not even donuts?"

"You know Indira's a chef, right? Just you and Mike. See you there!"

When they arrived, it was to find nearly every seat in the upstairs lounge occupied by past, present, and possibly future Underground Cabaret participants. The bar was set up with finger food and coffee, courtesy of Indira and the Chrome staff. Once everyone was settled in, Michelle stood up.

"Hi everybody, thanks for coming. I'm speaking on behalf of Stacey and Rory. Also kind of for Kim today. We've been talking about the way the Cabaret shows have evolved over the past few years, and about Mating Dance, and it's time to decide what we want to do." She looked over at Tyrone. "Tyrone here gave us a place to learn and grow and he says he still wants a dance show every month. But it's time to evolve again. So." Now she looked at Mike. "Not long ago a friend of ours made a suggestion. We talked to some more people and decided to adopt a new name, which will be the Underground Cabaret Dance Theater. Julia will join the management and continue running Mating Dance. Alison will also join the management and will be framing some more traditional dance showcases and a big pro show."

Tyrone shifted forward. "Boss, you look like you have something to say." Michelle was smiling.

"We talked about trying this showcase idea and I'm cool with that. Can always change it if it doesn't work. But I was thinking. If we set aside August for a pro show, I might want to take July off y'all's calendar."

"That would actually be a relief," said Alison, "because I'll be honest, I couldn't think of a way to fill that without getting repetitive."

"It'll give us all a chance to rest and re-charge," said Michelle. "So Paula, we'd also like you on board. What do you think?"

"Would I be participating in casting all this stuff?"

"Yep. You've done the broadest range of styles of any of us and you're not scared of anything. Also, we're hoping that Dmitri and I can convince you and

Mike to take on adagio. Those numbers are really popular, but most of our ballroom couples don't do aerial. You were practically there already with your Chayanne piece."

Paula looked over at Mike. His eyebrows were up and he was smiling. "That seems to meet with the muscle's approval. And I'd love to learn adagio."

"Great. Well, it's a little early to share this news, but some of you are probably wondering. The Cabaret actually changed direction once on the advice of Vince and Kelli. Good things happened. But they are going to be stepping back for a while because she's pregnant." There was a flurry of comment and exclamation as people took this in. "Vince and I are starting to discuss whether he might want to do Smooth with me, but nothing's decided. Dmitri has some other notes about our connection with Shall We Dance."

Dmitri stood, looking patriarchal. "Mateo and Elena will compete in Rising Star Rhythm again next year. Julia and Ray compete again in Rising Star Latin. Michelle and I will teach Smooth. Vince will continue to teach Argentine tango. I will work with Alison on pro shows. Shall We Dance will be available for rehearsal." He paused, looking over at Patrick, eyes glinting. "I am told the shows are more entertaining than ballroom competition." Patrick made a 'what can I say' face. "Sam will begin to teach martial arts for dancers. Andrew and Mary will offer new movement coaching for actors. That is all." He took his seat.

"He *hates* being called Andrew," Alison noted, which produced another 'what can I say' face from Red. "One other thing you've probably all noticed is Tony hanging around constantly." Over in the corner,

Elena's husband Tony waved. "The series he directs has been extended, so he will continue to be hanging around. If you're training or rehearsing at Shall We Dance, he might ask you to sign a release. If you're asked for a private interview, or to have video taken of a private rehearsal, talk to our lawyer Randa to make sure you're okay with it."

"All right," said Michelle. "What have we not covered? Danny will still be producing us. Yoshi's on call for lighting and projection design. Andy will still create our posters. This network is getting so darned *big*." There was a general laugh. "You know what, I'm done. We're going to be brainstorming themes for the 2016 season pretty soon, send me a note if you think of something, everything will be considered."

"Martial arts," Paula said instantly. "For the pro show." She pointed at Danny and Kate, who looked startled, then at Sam and Mateo. The four looked at each other and shrugged. Paula looked over at Vicky.

"Hell yeah," said Vicky. "Michelle, you've got yourself an instigator."

"Good." She looked down at her notes. "Oh, there is one more thing." People had been starting to stir, making are-we-done noises. Everybody stopped and looked back at her. "Kenji's launching a new dancewear line and he wants to live-stream the launch here. With all of us as models."

"That's in March," Tyrone said. "Already on the schedule. Everybody stay the same size, please." He laughed richly at the dumbfounded expressions of most of those present.

"You too, Tyrone," said Michelle.

"Oh mercy," he said, and everybody cracked up.

Mike and Paula later thought of the period between that meeting and the Halloween show as their honeymoon. Their performance piece was essentially ready. They had only their December piece on the horizon, which meant they had more free time than they knew what to do with.

"Here we are again," said Paula. "Reduced to watching movies."

"We're way behind. I used to rely on movie soundtracks for new music."

"In a previous life, I would have signed up to work overtime. Now I'd rather sit and watch movies with you."

"Well, good," he said, smiling. "Where should we start? Jackie Chan?"

"You think Alison's going to go with the martial arts idea?"

"I'd put money on it."

"Jackie Chan it is, then."

But after a couple of weeks, they couldn't stand it, so they went back to the gym to brush up 'Wuthering Heights,' then into the studio to start on 'Hallelujah.' Then it was dress rehearsal for 'Lunatics,' and Andy showed up with a proof of the book for 'Gaucho.'

"Figured I'd bring this since Victor and I are dancing," he told everybody before they started running the show. "Alison had Tanith do a line edit, so it should be pretty clean. But take a minute and flip through, see what you think." He left the book on a lounge table and went backstage to warm up.

Vicky was stage-managing this time. She did a quick inventory to make sure all the performers were on hand. The show order was set and everyone was dressed and ready to go. "Okay," she said. "I've got everybody's music here and a cranky wife at home. Let's get down to business. Ann and Bonnie, you're up first."

Paula's jazz friends opened the show with 'Werewolves of London.' Then there were three moon-themed numbers followed by a mambo to 'I'm Going Bananas' before Rory closed the first act with a bendy, twisty, tricky (and scantily clad) jazz routine to 'Virtual Insanity.' She winked at Mike as she headed offstage.

"Were you a gymnast?" he asked when she got down to the main floor.

"Right up to the time I got a visit from the tit fairy. That enough jazz for ya?"

"That was all the jazz," he said. "Nice moonwalk, too. I loved it."

"Good, 'cause I've been working on it since that dinner in June and it's been torture. Thanks for nothing." She slapped his ass as she went past. Paula was laughing as they headed backstage to wait their turn. They were closing the show again.

Andy and Victor opened the second act with a jazzy foxtrot-tango routine that Dmitri had choreographed for them, set to Michael Bublé's cover of 'Moondance.' They didn't get to perform very often because of their shooting schedule, but they'd put in the work. It was sharp, showy, and sexy. The number got a round of applause from the other dancers.

Three other numbers filled out the second act and then the Flyers hooked into the rig for 'Wuthering Heights.' Stacey had requested storm-cloud and lightning effects for this one. Michelle in particular was dying to see it.

Mike was in a nineteenth-century style coat and leggings. Paula wore a flowing, slightly ragged white dress. The number started on stage; it wasn't until the first chorus began that the Flyers went to work and she lifted off. Mike heard at least a few people say "ooh" and had to suppress a smile. Then he concentrated on the woman swirling above him. Their intention was to remind the audience of the climax of 'Raiders of the Lost Ark,' when the beautiful spirits of the Ark attacked and destroyed the Nazis. Here, the ghost of Cathy would drive Heathcliff insane, repeatedly coming down to earth as if to reunite, dancing passionately, then flying away.

They weren't certain it had come across when the lights went down, because the club was silent. Then Vicky said, "Hell yeah!" and everybody else started whistling, cheering, applauding. Vicky brought up the stage lights. Paula had been lowered to the stage, Mike had gotten to his feet from his ending position; they looked at each other and smiled.

"I think it worked." Paula grinned at Mike, then winced. "Now please God, get me off this cable." The rope handlers, Alan and Brendan, came over to help her. "You guys are so awesome," she said. "That was incredible. I can't wait to see how it looks."

"It was fun," said Alan. "We always like doing these shows."

"All this work for two performances makes us feel like what we do is totally normal," said Brendan. "Practice practice practice for weeks, a day of shooting, done."

"Well, if I get my way, we're going to have a big project for you next year. Thanks so much. See you

200

on show night." The flyers shook hands with Mike, hugged Paula, and went to stow their gear.

Michelle came up to the stage. "That was seriously good," she said. "Wait till you see the video. I'm kind of glad Dmitri retired because I'm pretty sure he would have wanted to hook me into that thing."

"Calling it retirement is a bit of a stretch," said Paula. "He loves dancing too much to retire."

"You're so right. I hope we can all last that long." She turned to Vicky. "Any notes?"

"Nope. We didn't even have a wardrobe malfunction this time. Anything showing up from the house?"

"Nope. So I guess that's dress. Let's get some pizza in here!"

"I am so chafed," said Paula. They were in the greenroom after 'Lunatics' wrapped, the last to get changed so they could go join in the after-party. "Where's that olive oil?"

Mike got the bottle out of his bag and handed it to her. "Still glad you did it?" She went into the bathroom and started rubbing the oil into the red marks the flying rig had left on her skin, leaving the door ajar so they could talk.

"Are you kidding? I *love* that number. I don't know that I necessarily want to do it again." She heard him laugh. "Not for a while, anyway. Kind of like 'Rock Star,' you can't do shit like that over and over again without losing your mind."

"You've done so many different things the past few years. What did you like best?" It wasn't an idle question; they had a whole year's dancing to plan out. She took a couple of minutes to answer.

"If we're talking about what kind of things would I like to do again … Chayanne. 'Dancing in the Dark.' And 'Hoy.' Which I wouldn't have expected to put on the list, but when I think about all the tango we did, that improv of yours is the thing that sticks." She poked her head out of the bathroom. "But I'm annoyed because I really only contributed to one of those. I need to step up my game." She retreated again.

"We should look at the schedule next weekend, once we're rested up. Since you girls got the show themes set already, we've got plenty of time to think. How's the lube job coming?"

"You shouldn't say 'lube' and 'coming' unless you want to get in here with me." He went into the bathroom and closed the door. "Oh hello."

"Hi. Anything I can help with?" He nuzzled her neck. Paula giggled. About fifteen minutes later, they finally joined the party.

CHAPTER 20

The adagio number for the December show was substantially complete, but because they'd be out of town and didn't expect to be practicing over Thanksgiving, Mike and Paula wanted to really get it locked before then. They booked a session with Dmitri and Michelle the first Saturday in November.

After the first run-through, Dmitri looked thoughtful. Mike and Paula exchanged a glance; they suspected something was about to change. "I have suggestion," he said after a moment. "Come into office." They crowded in there and Dmitri got on the computer to call up a video. It was a routine he and Michelle had done several years before, to Leonard Cohen's song 'Anthem.' He pointed to the screen as he paused the video. "This."

"Oh wow," said Paula.

"Is contemporary trick, yes? I see on 'So You Think,' it was 'Wicked Game.' Michelle says she can do that, so we include it."

"Kenji cried," Michelle said. "Actually, everybody cried." The trick had Michelle running to Dmitri, leaping and spinning in the air before he caught her, on the lyric 'every heart to love will come, but like a refugee.'

"The way you hit the lyric, I'm not surprised," said Mike. He thought for a moment. "At the end of the last verse? Where he sings, nothing on my tongue but Hallelujah. Those three beats of music right after that, the spin and the catch."

Dmitri nodded, looking deeply satisfied. "I knew you would see it."

"I'm game," said Paula. "That's not too different from some of the Chayanne stuff."

"I'll show you," said Michelle. "If I can still do it." Because Mike's part for the trick was mostly 'stand here, catch flying girl' Dmitri stood back and let the two of them work it until Michelle was positive she was doing it the way she had before. Mike was taller than Dmitri, so there was an immediately necessary adjustment. By the time Michelle was satisfied, Paula had seen the launch, the spin, and the catch position enough times that she thought she understood the timing and the geometry. She got it on the second try.

Then she and Mike went through the whole routine again, making a small change to the verse to facilitate the new trick. The final chorus was going to need some extra work since the phrases they'd previously composed didn't read well following the new trick.

"I think more up and down," said Paula. "Like, you've got me but I'm running around you and then you swoop me up and over." Mike tried that. "Yeah, perfect."

Then Dmitri, shaking his head, threw them another monkey wrench. "It needs star lift."

"Shit, a star?" Paula stared at him. "We haven't done that before. Like, ever."

"We show." Dmitri had Michelle do the star lift from a standing start, getting underneath it and carrying her up as if nearly a year hadn't passed since their last adagio.

"Damn, boss," said Michelle, laughing above him. "You still work out, huh?" He huffed out a laugh and gently set her down.

204

"You as well," he said, rolling his shoulder. "I am old. Did you see?" He knelt by Michelle, who assumed the flying position as he demonstrated the hand placement. "Hands at hip and ankle. Paula, you must open the hip so that mass is all in one plane."

"I think I get the idea," said Mike, fully intending to achieve a one-handed balance at some point. "Paula?"

"Jeez you guys. Um. Let's try it."

"We'll spot you," said Michelle. It took the rest of their session time, but Mike and Paula nailed down the ideal balance points and other mechanics of the lift. Some other students, who'd been hanging around trying to watch without being obvious, gave up and applauded.

"Again next week," said Dmitri. "Whatever you bring, no more change."

Mike eased his back. "Okay. We'll practice." Dmitri nodded and went into the office. Probably heading straight for the Advil that was in Mike's immediate future.

"Really good work, guys," Michelle said. "If every base was as strong as Mike, there'd be a lot more people willing to fly." She went over to the corner and got down on the floor to stretch. "Ow."

Paula eased down next to her. "Ow is right. Jeez, I thought the flying rig was painful. I'm going to have a permanent handprint on my hip." She turned to look at Mike. He was on his phone, texting. "What are you doing?"

"Booking a massage," he said, rolling his shoulder. "That was hard work."

"Sorry. I know most flyers are smaller than me."

"You're exactly the right size." He leaned down to kiss her. "Ow."

They took the routine to the Hollywood studio during the week, to solidify the new trick and re-work the final chorus, placing the star lift on the first 'hallelujah' of the second repetition. Then they perfected the dismount and resolution to their final position, back to back on their knees, heads together, looking up. When they went back to Shall We Dance and ran it through for Michelle and Dmitri, there was satisfaction all around.

"I'm going to see if we can find a studio to practice in, in Minneapolis," Mike said to Paula as they got ready to go. "There's enough new stuff that I don't quite want to leave it for that long."

"Plus you want to get that one-handed balance. Didn't one of the guys in the company get in touch?"

"About a month ago, yeah."

"Maybe he could hook us up. It might be a little tricky finding a place over a holiday weekend."

"You're right. I'll ping him when we get home. Let's go eat." They hadn't managed to lock down a rational eating schedule during the 'Gaucho' rehearsals, but since then they'd developed a routine. They both had enough kitchen skills, and enough tolerance for repetition, to make it work. Saturday nights were usually not cooking nights, though, since they were almost always out doing something. Fortunately, Dmitri's studio was in an area packed with good restaurants. They walked down the street to a favorite Italian place, where they were surprised to see Vince, by himself, waiting for a table.

"Hey Vince, how are you? Where's Kelli?" said Paula.

"I'm hungry and she's at home. She's got this morning sickness that doesn't quit."

"Oh bummer, I'm sorry to hear that. How're you both holding up?"

"She's trying to be tough. I'm a little worried about her. My mom says 'come stay with me,' and we might do that if it doesn't ease up."

"Well, you want to eat with us? Is there anything here Kelli can eat?"

"We keep trying different things. Thanks, I'd like some company. Tell me what you've got going, I haven't been keeping up with everybody."

"You have other things on your mind," said Mike. "Want to hear about how our December routine got a star lift?"

Vince looked amused. "Dmitri and Michelle got hold of you, huh."

"Yep."

Paula had seen pictures of Mike's mother and sister, but she was still surprised when she saw them at the airport. She took a long look at Beth and then turned to study Mike. He caught her eye and nodded, clearly suppressing a smile. "I can't believe you never told me you're *twins*. What is *wrong* with you."

Beth heard her and started laughing. "He really never did? Mike, you're such a goon."

"It was probably some kind of sick test," said Paula. "Glad to finally meet you! Hi, Candace, great to see you too." Both of the Borodin women – tall, strong, and blonde – hugged her.

Candace wrapped a big knitted scarf around her neck. "Thanks for bringing him home this Thanksgiving."

"I wish we could have had you at the wedding. My sister was there, did Mike tell you?"

"He sent us pictures. She looks a lot like you."

"She's seven years older. I always thought Mike was older than Beth. I don't know why, exactly."

"Well, he *is* older … just, like, an hour older. Most people can't tell we're twins," said Beth.

"When you're in the same room, it seems obvious." Beth wasn't as tall as Mike, but she had similar facial features, a similar voice, and the same beautiful eyes. She wore her hair in a long braid. "You're the same height as our friend Vicky. I used to think I was tall," Paula remarked. "Did Mike tell you we had to find a studio? Our coach changed our December number and now we have to practice while we're here."

"Randy hooked us up," said Mike. "We're going to meet him there on Friday."

"You haven't seen him since … well, for a long time," said Candace. "Are any of the others going to be there?"

Mike glanced at Paula. "I kind of hope not. That could get awkward."

Paula shrugged. "Well, none of them were responsible for you getting booted, were they? Only the director. If *he* shows up, we might have words."

"No need," said Mike. "I'm glad he cut me. Otherwise I wouldn't have gone to L.A."

Candace said, "And on that note, pull up that scarf, California girl. Minnesota winter is not to be trifled with."

"Oh my *God*," said Paula as they stepped into the tubelike walkway leading to the parking garage. "It's *literally* freezing out here, isn't it?"

"Yep," said Mike, laughing.

They'd added a vacation day to their holiday weekend, so they got into Minneapolis midafternoon on the Wednesday. Candace and Beth took them straight back to the Borodin house, letting them unpack before offering hot drinks. They all went down to the finished basement, where there was a wood-burning stove with a group of easy chairs, and otherwise a lot of open space.

Mike was surprised. "You cleared it out."

"There was a lot of junk down here," said Beth. "I know you do that daily class thing. With two of you it was going to be an obstacle course."

Paula was looking out the basement door. It was a walkout, since the house was on a slope. The door was half glass so she could see the back yard. "You have a lot of space out here."

"We've been in this house so long," said Candace. "The newer ones going up in this neighborhood are on quarter acres, mostly. This is a full acre."

"Beth, have you always lived with your mom?"

"No, I was on my own for a while, about ten years. Came back for good about two years before Mike left town."

Paula abruptly remembered what Mike had told her about his sister. He'd never given details and she wasn't about to ask. Squarely in the category of none of her business, so she nodded and changed the subject. "Do you work at the trucking company?"

"I'm the accountant. I did that for somebody else for a while but when Mom's person retired, it seemed like a good time to make a space for myself in the company."

"What she isn't saying," Candace said comfortably, "is that I whined and complained about how hard it was to find somebody I could trust. She finally came to work with me just to shut me up."

Mike and Beth both laughed. "I had to take a pay cut," said Beth, "but since I don't have to pay rent anymore, it all kind of worked out." She watched Mike and Paula, who were both still roaming around the space, mugs in hand. "Mike, you look really good. I mean, both of you do, but … it's good to see you like this. Whole again."

He'd turned to face her, and now he smiled. "It's been kind of an incredible eighteen months."

"I wasn't sure you'd last in L.A.," said Candace. "You sounded kind of unhappy at first."

Mike looked over at Paula. "I needed someone to show me a door."

"And then kick you through it." Paula gave Candace an apologetic look. "I was a little tough on him."

"That's what it takes," his mother said. "So we're having chowder tonight because of the big thing tomorrow. Everybody's coming and they're all bringing food."

"Anything we can do?"

"Rest up. You're not going to have a moment's peace all day."

Mike took his mother seriously, so after their light dinner he and Paula went upstairs to the guest

210

room. It wasn't large, but it had a nice high ceiling. It also had its own wood-burning stove, heavy drapery over the double window, thick carpet, and a pile of quilts on the bed. A slowly-turning ceiling fan stirred the warm air back into the room.

"This is totally cozy," Paula decided, hanging up some clothes after coming back from the bathroom. "It's the way you think a B&B should be."

"And it's at the far end of the hall from Mom and Beth." Mike came up behind her and wrapped his arms around her. "Which is good because somebody can be a little loud sometimes."

She snickered, tipping her head back against his shoulder. "If you weren't so freaking sexy, that wouldn't be a problem." He ran a hand up her body to her throat, turning her face enough to kiss her. "See, it's stuff like that," she said softly. "If anybody else had me by the neck I'd be doing all my self-defense moves so fast."

He laughed into her hair. "You're scaring me." Turned her around and kissed her again.

"Yeah, you feel totally scared." She had her hands full of evidence to the contrary. "I promise not to scream out loud if, and only if, this bed doesn't squeak. If it does, then there's really no point in me being quiet, now is there?"

He laughed again, mouth on her neck, hands wandering. "It's a platform. Full of quilts and parkas."

"Excellent sound absorption," she said, a bit breathless, working her hands under his layers of clothing to bare skin.

"Let's test that." A few minutes later, naked under the covers, they stopped caring whether anyone could hear them.

The next morning, Paula came back from her shower to find Mike waiting. "I thought you'd have gone downstairs by now."

He said, "I have something for you before we go down."

"Again?" Then her eyes got big when he knelt in front of her. "Uh, Mike."

"I know it's kind of late for this. But I didn't do it right the first time. So. I wanted to say I love you. Will you marry me?" He held up the antique ring from his grandmother.

She took it from him, examining it while blinking hard and possibly sniffing a little. It was platinum filigree, with a square, flush-set diamond. "Why Mr. Borodin, this is all so sudden. It occurs to me that I love you very much, and thus I believe I will marry you. As many times as you want," she added, sliding the ring onto her minimally-manicured finger, which it suited admirably. He got to his feet and kissed her. After a while, she said, "Beth's not going to be mad she didn't get this, is she?"

"She says she likes our other grandma's ring better."

Paula was relieved. "Well, good. Now all we have to do is find her a husband. Does she want one?"

"I'm not sure. Maybe we'll get a chance to talk about stuff like that before we go home."

"Probably not today, though."

"Not a chance. Let's go downstairs."

They did have a chance to talk to Beth alone, it turned out, on Friday after their practice session. She took them over to the studio, stayed long enough to

212

think *wow* about the dance they were doing, then went down the street to a coffee shop. Mike sent her a text when they were done.

Want coffee? she texted back.

So much

LOL what's your preference, this place has it all

Big whole-milk latte for me, small decaf cappuccino for Paula, thanks!

Coming right up, meet you at the car

They waited inside until they saw her coming. Then Mike shook hands with Randy, promised to stay in touch, and they stepped outside.

"He was pretty cool," said Paula as they walked to the car. "Said nice things about the piece. I'll bet he was secretly glad when you were cut."

"Not much of a secret," Mike said, amused. "He was the next-tallest guy, so he got cast in my things right away. I appreciate that he got in touch, though. He pinged me that one time after 'Rock Star' but I didn't follow up. Wasn't in the mood then."

"Not too surprising." She glanced over at him. "And I'm sure he's competent, but I'll bet the women in the company wish he was as good-looking as you. I mean, it's not even close."

Mike was still grinning when their paths intersected with Beth's. "You look happy. How'd it go?" she said, handing the coffee tray to Mike and unlocking the car. "Crazy good from what I saw."

"It's in decent shape," said Paula. "Getting a refresher in this weekend was good, though. We're doing some new things and the body memory isn't quite set."

They all got into the car and Beth started the engine. "Anywhere you want to go?"

"Could we just drive a little? Paula's never been here before." Mike had taken the back seat so Paula could sit up front.

"Okay. Tour time." Beth headed for the river.

After a while, Paula said, "Wow. I haven't seen so much fresh water since I went to Niagara Falls."

"When was that?"

"When I was eighteen."

"Honey," Beth said seriously, "you need to get out more." Mike shook his head, laughing.

"If you ever come to L.A. you'll get an idea how far we have to go to get out! Well, at least we have the ocean. Not that we go out to look at it very often," Paula admitted.

"You guys stay busy. Mike told me about your summer schedule and it made me tired. But not too long ago I was sitting in my room reading, like I do every night, and I thought maybe I need a hobby."

"Reading is a hobby," said Mike.

"I've only ever wanted to dance," said Paula. "I like reading and watching movies, but that's basically when I'm too tired to dance."

Mike nodded. "Or to fill in the time around dancing. I'm the same way, I never had a hobby except dancing. I never read so much in my life as after the accident."

"Mom got him an e-reader then," Beth told Paula. "Loaded it up with all the Harry Potter books, lots of other things that his favorite movies were based on."

214

"She sneaked some new stuff in there too," Mike said, smiling. "That whole basement used to be full of books, Paula."

Beth nodded. "She does all her reading on her Kindle now too."

"Did you ever dance, Beth? Mike told me you used to like the dance stuff on TV when you were little."

"Eh, we were both in dance class till we were about twelve. He was obsessed with it, I just liked being with him. But he started getting so good. I got tired of being compared to him."

Mike sat forward, hand on his sister's shoulder for a moment. "I didn't know that. I'm sorry."

"*You* didn't do it," she said, surprised. "But the teacher and some of the older students, they never let up. So I quit and went out for basketball instead. It was a relief for Mom, since that was at school and didn't cost much of anything. Plus I ended up getting a scholarship for college, so it all worked out."

Mike said, "I kicked back some of the settlement. I know she doesn't need it now, but she really had to squeeze sometimes in order to keep me in class."

"Yeah, she told me you did that." Beth pulled off the road into a view stop overlooking the river, parked, and turned off the car. She looked over at Paula. "Did Mike tell you why I moved back home?"

"Not specifically. He told me in very general terms that you'd been," she paused, "assaulted. Not when, not where, not who. That's all."

"Well, that was why. It happened at my workplace, a guy I knew. So me going to work with Mom wasn't all about her guy retiring."

Paula set a hand on Beth's arm. "You don't need to tell me anything."

215

"Honey, you're my sister now. At a certain point you were going to wonder why the hell I'm still living with our mother."

"None of my business. Seriously." They shared a long look. "I told Mike about the guy who hit me in college."

"What did you do?"

"Broke his nose."

Beth produced a bark of laughter. "If I'd had to see that person ever again, I think I might have done that too. Mike was ready to beat the shit out of him. I said, stand down, caveman; if anybody's going to do that it's going to be me." After a pause she said, "I didn't file charges. I reported it, but the cops made it sound like it would never go anywhere. So I quit the job. Saw a counselor for a while. And I'm okay, but. I see what it means to Mike, to have dance in his life again. To have you to share it with. I think I'm ready for something more now. So anyway. Now I have to figure out what 'more' could be."

Mike reached over the seat again and gripped Beth's shoulder. They sat in the car, looking at the river, until they realized the daylight was going.

Beth said, "Better get back home. Mom should be well and truly napped by now."

"Your mom is great," said Paula.

"Yes she is," said Mike and Beth together. Paula rolled her eyes, muttering something about twins.

CHAPTER 21

December 2015

After the holiday, Mike and Paula got back into their work and practice routines, feeling a little pressed for time. It was only the one number, and only a two-night show, but for some reason Paula, in particular, felt a little frantic.

It wasn't until they got home from dress rehearsal that she realized why. "For fuck's sake," she said, tossing her dance bag on the floor by the couch.

"What?"

"I've been feeling all crazy, like we'd never get ready in time, and it went so well today and everything's fine, and I realized it was never about the damn dance at all. It's about going to Jen's for Christmas."

Mike glanced over at her from the kitchen, where he'd started putting together dinner. "You've been talking."

"Yeah. I've even talked to Bill."

"So what's the issue?"

"I don't fucking know." She shook her head, half-laughing. "I know it's going to be fine, they're going to love you because everybody does, our parents aren't going to be there so there won't be any of that weirdness."

"Maybe you were thinking of it as another kind of performance. Something else you had to prepare for." Paula stared at him. He was busy at the cutting board, not looking at her, but when she didn't speak for a minute he set down the knife and turned. He studied her face. "Or not."

"No, I think that's exactly right. How crazy am I?"

"You haven't seen them for a long time. It might be like when I had to move home after the accident. I'd seen plenty of Mom and Beth over the years, but even so. I really tried to put up a front. I mean, thank God Beth wasn't having it."

"That would be exactly like me, huh. Try to be all tough and oh I didn't miss you at all. I even kind of said that to you, didn't I?" He nodded. "You're so much smarter about this stuff than I am."

"Well, honey, I was in therapy for a couple of years." He was laughing silently, heading to the refrigerator. She went over and put her arms around him, squeezing, then let him go. He turned around and hugged her.

"Continue cooking," she said. "I like how you look in the kitchen."

"You like how I look anywhere." He kissed her.

"True, if egotistical."

He kissed her again, with a little more attention to detail. "You know, this will come together really fast. Maybe we should too." She laughed, but she didn't disagree.

By the time 'A Midnight Clear' wrapped, Mike and Paula had their game plan in place for 2016. Their intention was to submit for every Underground Cabaret and Mating Dance show and to try out for whatever Alison came up with for the August pro show (Paula was still hoping for kung fu). They'd gone directly to Michelle with their concept for the Mating Dance show in January. The theme was 'Movie Magic,' and they wanted to re-create the iconic Astaire and Rogers 'Cheek to Cheek' routine from 'Top Hat.' Michelle told them that Sam and

Mateo had laid claim to the climactic paso doble from 'Strictly Ballroom,' and salsa team Ricky and Anya to the finale mambo from 'Dirty Dancing,' so they had to get busy so she knew which routine would close. After talking to Kenji about the costume requirements, she texted Paula: **He's as close to having a fit as I've ever seen him**

LOL why?

With the launch in March? He's a little busy

Oh shit sorry

No worries. He's fretting but you know he loves doing costumes. Kris and the minions are on feather duty

Srsly can't wait to see it. We're starting the choreo immediately

Do that!!

Which meant, of course, that Paula had to call Jennifer and see if there was a studio where they could work over the Christmas holiday.

"We kind of screwed up," she confessed. "We decided to do this thing for a show in January, but it's a thing we cannot fuck up, because everybody in the world knows how it's supposed to look, and so we need a studio. Like, daily, or as close to that as we can get. Is there anything near you?"

"Our next-door neighbors have a ballet daughter and a home studio. I've seen it, it's roomy. I'll ask them and let you know. You're getting here Christmas Eve, right?"

"Bright and early. We're taking the red-eye, it leaves at eleven on the twenty-third."

"Ugh, okay."

"Don't worry, we'll take a taxi."

"No you will not! I'll send Oliver to get you. He just got his driver's license."

"Thanks a *lot*."

Jennifer said reassuringly, "He's been driving for a year, he knows all about snow. He might want to stop for donuts on the way home, though."

"Oh, okay then. Talk to you later." Paula disconnected, smiling. Jennifer texted back a few hours later to confirm the neighbor had granted access to the home ballet studio. She also mentioned that the ballet daughter had seen them on YouTube and wanted autographs. Paula showed the text to Mike. "She's probably going to want you to sign her boobs or something."

"A ballet girl? She probably doesn't have boobs."

"Shut up," said Paula, who rarely bothered with a bra.

"Well, you know what they say. More than a mouthful is a waste."

"You are not helping yourself here," she warned, pretending to be pissed.

There was time for one more practice hour at the Hollywood studio before the Christmas trip.

"I think this is already my all-time favorite routine," Paula said, watching their rehearsal video at the end of their session. "I love the soft-shoe. So much new stuff for us again, but the choreography is so damn good, it flows."

He smiled. "You realize that each time we do something, it's your favorite."

"You should be glad I'm not one of those people who fixates on something that happened years ago, like nothing can ever measure up."

"That's true," he said. "As long as we keep coming up with great new stuff, you'll be happy. No pressure."

She shot him an amused look. "I already can't wait for March. The waltz program?" They were planning to set a piece to k.d. lang's version of 'Bird on a Wire.'

"First we need to figure out a song for 'Hard to Get' in February. Good thing we'll have a little down time on the trip."

Paula snorted. "Yeah, on the plane. And you'll be sleeping."

"If you pick something while I'm out, that's okay."

She slapped the floor. "Oh my God I thought of the perfect thing. En Vogue, 'My Lovin,' which will be so totally ironic, because you're always gonna get it."

Mike laughed, packing up his gear. "Get your stuff together and let's go home. So I can get it."

Christmas Eve in Boston was even colder than Thanksgiving Eve in Minneapolis. "Next year we're going to Hawaii," said Paula, once they were back in the car with Oliver behind the wheel and a box of donuts on her lap. "Or at least San Diego. This is nuts."

"I apologize for my wife," Mike said from the back seat. "She's gotten soft after all those years in L.A." Oliver made an amused sound. "Have you two ever even met before?"

"No. Mom had pictures from when Paula, I mean Aunt Paula, was in high school. And I've seen some videos."

"Please do not call me Aunt anything. Paula is fine. Good lord."

"Yeah. Mike is fine too. We're not responsible adults or anything."

Oliver met his gaze in the rear-view mirror for a second. "Don't you both work in a law firm?"

"Under duress," Paula said. "It's relatively easy, and it pays the bills so we can do all our dance stuff."

"Dad seems to like it okay."

"Your dad is basically our boss, in the scheme of things. Bosses always like it better."

"Yeah, I guess." There was a complicated piece of road; Oliver stopped talking so he could concentrate. Mike and Paula looked out the windows, clueless as to where they were in the Boston area, but noticing that the houses were getting bigger and farther apart.

Mike couldn't help thinking, *this could have been her life*. He gazed at Paula. She felt the look and turned to look at him. "What?"

"Ever want a big house like that?"

She looked so appalled that Mike almost laughed. "God, no. Do you know how much work that would be?"

"Most of our neighbors have help," said Oliver. "We have a housekeeper and a gardener. Mom only gets someone else if there's a big thing, though."

"Jen likes organizing things. I'm sure the house is perfect."

"Where do you live?" Oliver glanced over at her, then returned his attention to the road.

"I bought a one-bedroom condo a few years ago. It's not far from Hollywood and it's got everything we need, aside from a dance studio."

"And one of those is in walking distance," Mike said.

"How do you figure out what you need?"

"That's a good question. I guess for the two of us, dancing has always been a top priority. Anything more than the basics costs so much in a city like L.A., or Boston for that matter. If we had a two-bedroom place, we wouldn't be able to afford all the coaching we get. Not and still save for retirement."

"I want a boat," said Oliver. "I'd like to live on a boat."

Paula asked, "Do you sail?"

"Every summer. I love it. I love the ocean."

"What do your folks think?"

"They think I'll grow out of it."

Paula and Mike exchanged another glance. Paula said, "Do they want you to go to law school, or something?"

"Yeah. Gross. I want to be a marine biologist."

Paula nodded. "I think it would be cool to have a marine biologist in the family. How about your sister?"

"Hannah hasn't decided what she wants to do yet. She's good at a lot of stuff. It makes the decision harder." Oliver signaled, even though there was hardly any traffic, turning down a side street. "That's our house."

"Holy crap," Paula said faintly. Oliver laughed. She poked him with her elbow before giving Mike a 'seriously, holy crap' look over her shoulder.

"Your mom's house seemed big to me," said Paula, "but this is ridiculous." They'd come up to their guest suite after a brief introductory conversation with Jennifer and her family. Bill would be arriving

223

later in the day. Oliver had helped with their bags and then disappeared. They stood in the big room and looked around, a little bit at a loss. "I knew Adam probably made serious bank, but damn."

"It's kind of disorienting, isn't it?"

"It's so much like my parents' house, it's giving me flashbacks."

"But your sister isn't like your mom."

"No, thank God. Which means Adam isn't like my dad. So I'm going to pretend the whole mom and dad thing doesn't exist." She caught herself in a yawn. "And apparently I'm going to have some coffee, because if I don't, I will not be making it to an East Coast bedtime. And damn if I didn't wish I could go to bed, but I'd regret it at midnight when I woke up again."

"We have our own coffeemaker up here," Mike pointed out. "And a mini fridge." He opened the refrigerator door. "With half and half."

Paula shook her head, appreciating her sister. "Of course."

They both got themselves unpacked and organized while the coffee was brewing, then got down on the floor to stretch. About halfway down their mugs, there was a knock on the door. Mike got up to answer it. "Oh hi Hannah. Is it time for us to go downstairs?"

"You don't have to if you don't want to. But if you want to go next door to practice, I could take you over there. Margaret said any time after eleven was fine."

"That would be great," said Paula. "Once it gets later in the day, I'm probably going to lose all my oomph."

"You didn't sleep on the plane?"

"Nope. I have sleep issues."

"Me too, sometimes," said Hannah. "Do you need to change clothes before we go over?"

"I don't think so. You good, honey?" said Mike. They'd both traveled in warmups.

"Yeah, I'm good." Mike collected their practice bag, with laptop, camera, and shoes. They both shrugged into their jackets.

Hannah led the way as they headed out, stopping to pick up a wax-paper bag from the hall table before going outside. "Donuts. Oliver got one for Margaret. She's super excited," she confided. "She's almost fifteen too, we're friends. Ever since she found out you were dancers and looked you up, she's been fangirling."

Paula didn't quite know what to say. Settled for, "That's nice. Did you tell her we're technically amateurs?"

"She doesn't care. She tried to get the guy in her class to do 'Dancing in the Dark' with her, but he's such a ballet snob. He's like Cyd Charisse's character at the beginning."

"She knows the part?" Mike said. "Because I could probably do it with her if she's got a couple of hours to practice."

Hannah stopped in her tracks, eyes wide. "Oh my God. She would plotz. Like, for real. I mean, she might have a little bit of a crush on you. You wouldn't mind?"

"Of course he wouldn't mind. He wouldn't have mentioned it if the idea was horrifying," said Paula, completely in sympathy with the fangirl. "The more we can both dance, the better off we are, at our age."

"You make it sound like you're old, or something."

"Dancers gotta dance, is all I'm sayin.'"

"Whatever, I'm going to text her right now. You probably aren't going to get home until dinner," Hannah warned, sounding excited.

"That's fine," said Mike, glancing at Paula, who was laughing to herself. "It will keep us awake."

The neighbors' house was less than a quarter mile away, separated from Jennifer and Adam's house by big side yards and a public greenway. They had barely begun to get used to the outdoor temperature by the time they arrived. The door was flung open before Hannah could even knock.

"Oh my God," said the slender girl standing there. "I can't even believe it. Come in, come in, oh my God."

Mike and Paula both suppressed laughter, appreciating the reaction and wanting to put the girl at ease. Paula said, "Hi Margaret. Thanks for letting us borrow your studio."

"Are you kidding? When Hannah said you were coming for Christmas I was like do they need to practice, they can use my studio, whatever, anything." She stopped talking for a moment to laugh at herself. "I'm being so uncool right now, I'm sorry."

"Did Hannah tell you what piece we're doing?"

"She said 'Cheek to Cheek.' Are you really doing that?"

"We liked doing the other Astaire piece so much that when the company posted this 'Movie Magic' theme for January, we jumped right in. Our coach said if we hadn't decided to do it, he would have done it himself."

226

"That's Dmitri Vasko, right? I've seen his pieces on the Underground Cabaret channel. He's amazing. And he's older than my dad." She made it sound like that was inconceivable; Mike and Paula again suppressed laughter. They'd gone down a hallway and up a staircase. Margaret opened a door at the end of another hall. From the amount of space, it looked as though her studio had been built over a four-car garage. The ceiling was high and there was excellent light.

"What a great space," said Mike. He crossed over to the double barre; the top rail was high enough for him. "Can we warm up for a while?"

"Sure. I'll put on some music. And would you like something to drink? A snack?"

"We had some coffee, but water would be great."

"We might have had a donut after we got back from the airport. Oliver was driving us," said Paula.

Margaret made an understanding sound. "Ollie likes those donuts. He told me he was going to stop there and he'd get my favorite for me. He's so nice."

"He is nice," Hannah said. "I lucked out in the brother lottery. Here those are, by the way, one for you and one for me. Do you mind if I hang out and watch?"

"No worries," said Paula, already at the barre. "God this feels good." They spent twenty minutes at the barre, then set up the laptop with their rehearsal video cued and started marking through the new choreography. They stopped frequently to refer to the video. Margaret and Hannah sat close together, eating their donuts, then watching and whispering. They'd been there for over an hour when Mike looked over at the girls.

227

"Bored yet?" he said, smiling a little.

Margaret said, "You're kidding, right?"

"We're ready for some music. You have a phone dock?" He pulled his phone out of his jacket pocket and met Margaret over by her sound system. She hooked in the device; Mike and Paula got into their entry position. He nodded at Margaret to start the music. After four repetitions, they were satisfied with the day's progress. Hannah was sitting back against the wall, still watching; Margaret was leaning on the counter by the sound system, looking envious.

"What is it like?" she said a few seconds after they stopped. "To have a partnership, I mean."

Mike looked at Paula. "It's the best thing in the world." Paula smiled back at him and hit the deck to stretch.

"Can you come back tomorrow?"

"We'd love to. But Hannah thought maybe you'd like to work on something."

Margaret's eyes got big. "Was she *serious?*"

"Yeah, of course. Let's take a little break and then we could work on that."

"Um, yeah. Uh, the bathroom's down the hall on the left. I'm going to go get some water." Margaret and Hannah both went down the hall. Mike and Paula heard them running down the stairs, and then there was squealing.

Paula stifled a laugh. "She's adorable. What a nice neighbor for Hannah to have."

"You're adorable." Mike pulled her up off the floor and kissed her. "I love you."

"I love you, too." She kissed him. They took turns in the bathroom, then got down on the floor again by the laptop. "Okay. Pull that over here and we'll take a look at the other thing. Do you remember it?"

"Once or twice through should do it. I'm so glad you love dancing this much."

"I love it more now than I ever did." She edged close and kissed him again, but after a few minutes heard the girls coming back and put some distance between them. "Can't corrupt the children."

"Maybe we're setting a *good* example," Mike suggested.

"Nice try," Paula said, snickering. "Turn that thing around so I can see it too." They were virtuously watching the video when Margaret and Hannah came back in, offering water. After a few minutes of chat, Mike and Paula got up to go through the routine for Margaret to see it. Then Paula sat down with Hannah and they watched while Mike started to work it with Margaret.

'Dancing in the Dark' didn't achieve perfection that day, but they promised to come back the next day and work on it some more. "This has been the greatest. The ultra," said Margaret. "Thank you so much."

"Thank *you*," said Mike. "This is going to make a big difference for us next month."

"Have you done any lift work?" said Paula as they were heading out the front door.

"No," said Margaret, looking hopeful.

"If your parents say it's okay, maybe Mike could show you a couple while we're here."

"Best. Christmas. Ever," said Margaret. Hannah hugged her friend, then they started back.

CHAPTER 22

The light was going, Paula was exhausted, and Mike was feeling the workout after so many hours on a plane. They were both hungry, too. When Jennifer saw them she said, "Easy dinner tonight. All set up in the kitchen, get whatever you want. We're all in the den. And we're heading over to a carol service at nine. Do either of you want to go?"

"Mike can actually sing," said Paula. "I can just about carry a tune, if the bucket is big enough. I will spare you."

"I wouldn't mind," said Mike, smiling. "I like carols."

"We'll do a little thing here in the morning. There's a bigger thing in the evening. I take it you had fun at the Cohens'?"

"It was great," Paula said. "Sorry we disappeared on you for the whole day. Is Bill here?"

"He's in the den. Get yourselves some food, then come join us. But seriously, whenever you need to crash go ahead."

"Thanks. We kind of promised Margaret we'd go back tomorrow."

"That's fine. I'm glad you're here."

"So are we." Paula hugged her sister before they headed for the food. They carried full plates back to the den, where they got acquainted (and re-acquainted) with Bill, chatted for a while with Adam and Jennifer, and observed that Oliver and Hannah both appeared to be studying over in a corner. Paula tipped her head toward them and asked Jennifer, "Are they in the middle of a term?"

"Yeah, there are exams in mid-January."

"I must say, you and Adam seem to have produced a fine pair of offspring. Good job there."

Jennifer looked pleased. "They are pretty rewarding. Bill's son is a sweetie too, I'm sorry he isn't here."

"Me too," said Bill. "And I have a feeling he didn't really want to go to Switzerland, but Fabienne had all these plans."

"Is the child-sharing usually trouble-free?" asked Mike.

"Usually. Most holidays he's with me, most summers he's with her. It works out all right, but we're definitely going to need some kind of plan for high school."

"Which is a couple years off," Jennifer reminded him.

"Ugh, I know." Bill looked at Paula. "Are you guys going to have kids?"

"That's a solid no," she said, with a glance at Mike. "I am just now having the dance life I always wanted. I'm too selfish to give that up, even if we had room for kids, which we don't. Plus, I mean, we both have full-time jobs. I don't know how people do it."

"Anything to add to that?" Bill asked Mike.

He shook his head. "I never aspired to be a father. I'm cool with being an uncle, though. Some of our friends have started families, and it's nice being around them."

"I guess a lot of your friends are dancers."

"Most of them," Mike agreed. "And most of them also have jobs, so everybody's busy. Our friend Vince and his wife recently got pregnant, they both have jobs, he also teaches Argentine tango. Like Paula said. I don't know how anyone does it when they have kids."

"And that reminds me, we promised Jennifer we'd teach her some tango. Not tonight," said Paula, "because I am about to go into hibernation. But that's probably a perfect after-breakfast exercise."

"Oh my goodness, really?" said Jennifer.

"Sure," said Mike. "You can do it right there in the kitchen."

"Do what now?" said Adam, tuning in.

"Tango. We'll be needing you too," said Paula, inclined to laugh at the alarmed expression on Adam's face. Then she yawned. "Oops, sorry. I think that's my cue."

"Go to bed," said Jennifer. "We'll see you in the morning."

Paula was asleep before the rest of the family left for church. Still asleep when Mike came into the guest suite after the service. She woke up when he slid into bed, though. "Hey," he said softly. "Sorry I woke you." She turned to him and pressed close. She'd put on a sleep shirt since the bed felt cold without him; he was naked. She kissed his chest and slid a hand around his back. "Or maybe I'm not sorry." She made an interested sound and did some more exploring with her hands and mouth, starting to feel quite warm. His hand went under the sleep shirt, skimming up her spine, then down to her bare bottom. "Actually I'm not sorry at all," he said after a while, mouth against her throat. He rolled her to her back, braced himself over her, and kissed her.

"Oh holy night," she said a few minutes later. Mike laughed into her hair.

232

The 'little something' on Christmas morning turned out to be cranberry waffles with scrambled eggs and ham, with mimosas for the adults and sparkling cider for the teenagers. Paula and Mike had both slept well and were at full energy. After helping clean up the kitchen, they gave Jennifer and Adam an Argentine tango lesson. Hannah and Oliver watched, apparently because they couldn't believe it was happening. Bill also watched, offering plenty of unhelpful advice to Jennifer. She finally said, "Oh my God, Bill, if you don't shut up I'm going to make Paula teach *you*." Bill, at that point, decided he had something to do in another room, but was snickering when he left.

"Okay, that's enough for now," said Paula at the end of an hour. "Except I think you should experience Mike for a few minutes. Everybody should, really." Mike waved that off.

"Uh, what?" Jennifer looked confused. Paula shook her head, smiling. Went over to her phone, which was hooked into the little speaker dock at the end of the kitchen counter. Pulled up a tango track they hadn't used yet. Mike smoothly edged Adam out of the way and took Jennifer into a loose milonga-style dance hold. Adam stood aside, looking like he didn't know whether he should feel jealous or relieved. When Paula hit play, Mike listened for a few beats and then stepped forward in the eight-count basic they'd been teaching. A minute into the song, Paula looked over at the kids; they were both clearly astounded.

"Mom's really doing it!" Hannah said. "That's so cool!"

Oliver glanced at his father and bit his lip, now clearly trying not to laugh. Adam must have noticed, because he tried to glare. Paula was watching everybody, feeling a little sorry for Adam; he was a nice-looking man, but … *yeah, my guy's gorgeous*, thought Paula smugly. When the track finished, Mike stood back and bowed a little to Jennifer; she blushed. "This is dangerous stuff," she said after a moment.

"Well," said Paula, "now you know why I like dancing with him so much."

"Uh, yeah." Jennifer looked at Adam and raised her eyebrows. "There's a thing I've been wanting to ask you. Let's go somewhere else for a minute."

Paula shot another glance at the teenagers, who now looked appalled, and it was all she could do not to laugh out loud. *Yes, kids, your parents have a sex life.* "I'm going to risk another half a cup of coffee," she said, as Jennifer and Adam left the kitchen. "You kids want anything?" *Aside from some brain bleach.*

"I don't suppose you'd let us have any of the champagne," Hannah suggested.

"How much trouble would I get in?"

"Not much," said Oliver, trying to look casual.

"You think I should believe him, Mike?"

He leaned close and murmured in her ear. "I don't think you need to worry about Jennifer and Adam for a while." She snickered.

Paula snickered. "I'm willing to risk it." She found some glasses and poured the champagne. Topped it up with orange juice for the kids, gave Mike a glass straight, and went to get her coffee. "What usually happens after breakfast on Christmas morning?"

"Not tango lessons," said Hannah. "We'll do presents whenever Mom and Dad get back to the den.

Mom usually calls her folks – your folks – around noon." She sipped her mimosa. "Hey, this is good."

"You can tell Margaret we're corrupting you over here."

"She already texted me this morning to ask when you could go over. Can I go with you again?"

"Well, sure," said Paula. "Why not? You want to come, Oliver?"

"Eh," he said. "I like Margaret and I like watching you guys dance, but I've got some exams coming up. I'd better study this afternoon."

"Well, tomorrow is another day. Hannah, I guess we could go over after your mom talks to our parents. I probably ought to be here for that." Paula leaned on Mike a little.

He took her free hand. "Are you going to talk to them?"

"I probably should."

"You don't get along, huh," said Oliver.

"I don't even know, to be honest. We haven't really spoken for years. Mostly, you know, email. Yikes, maybe I need some of that champagne."

Two surprising things happened later, the first during the call with the elder Rosses, when Paula's dad asked to speak with her privately. "Thanks for sending the wedding pictures," he said. "If we'd known that was happening, we would have liked to come. If we come out to L.A. sometime, could we see you?"

"Of course," she said, surprised. "I'd love that." After a second she said, "I'm sorry I never came home."

"We understand. Especially after talking to Jennifer." He took his own pause, then said, "We're really happy for you. And we're looking forward to meeting Mike. He seems right for you."

"He is. Thanks, Dad. We'll make it happen."

"Good. Want to put it back on speaker?"

"Sure."

The second thing was when the others were opening presents. Mike and Paula had been deterred from bringing anything, on the theory that getting themselves to Boston was enough, so they were hanging around and watching, enjoying the family's reactions to mostly silly, small gifts. Then, when Oliver and Hannah had retreated to their study corner with new books, Jennifer brought Paula an envelope.

"What's this?"

"It's from Mom and Dad."

Paula took it as if it might have been a Howler. Mike was watching. "You want me to open that for you?" She glanced over and could see that he was close to laughing. She handed it to him. He opened the envelope, unfolded the sheet of paper inside, and caught the slip of paper that fell free. His eyebrows went up with obvious surprise.

"What?" said Paula. He looked at her, apparently speechless. Passed everything to her. She read the letter and blinked at the enclosure. "Holy *shit*." The kids looked up, giggled, and looked back down at their books. She glanced over at Jennifer, then at Bill. "Did you know about this?" They shook their heads in unison. She passed everything to Jennifer, who smiled while Adam leaned close to read it, then passed it all to Bill.

"Wow," he said. "Wasn't expecting that. It's only fair, though."

"Fair?" said Mike, incredulously.

"That's what they gave each of us when we got married."

Paula said, "I can't even. No words."

"What's the first thing that comes to mind?" said Jennifer, still smiling.

"No mind right now."

Mike huffed out a laugh. "Me either. That's way outside my comfort zone." Bill handed the papers back to him; he looked at them again. "Too many zeroes." The slip was a third of a letter-sized sheet, showing a balance in a jointly-owned account. Mike read the letter once more and handed it back to Paula. "Can I get you anything, sugar mama?"

Paula and Jennifer both laughed. "Ordinarily I'd say pour me some champagne and peel me a grape," Paula said, "but we have a date with Fred and Ginger and Margaret."

On their way over, Mike glanced at Paula and said, "I've never tried to form a word having to do with money that started with 'm' except, you know, money. Can't get my head around it."

She reached for his hand and squeezed. "I'm starting to get ideas. Like, platinum wedding band for you ideas. Anniversary in Argentina ideas."

After a moment he said, "Those are good ideas." A ring for him, and an out-of-town honeymoon, hadn't been in the budget. Hannah was ignoring them, texting. As they got to the Cohen house, the door was again pulled open.

"Mom and Dad are here and they say I can do lifts as long as they can watch," Margaret said in an excited rush, then clapped a hand over her mouth and stood back. "Sorry," she said behind the hand. "Little excited."

"We have something else to show you," said Mike. "Our company Dropbox has a couple new blocking videos. I want you to see the number our friends Sam and Mateo are doing. It's up for debate whether our number or theirs should close the show."

"Have you watched it yet?"

"No. Rehearsal first. Then we'll watch this. Then we'll do some lifts. Okay?"

"So very okay," said Margaret, leading the way upstairs. She introduced them to her parents Sophie and Max, put on some music for Paula and Mike to do a quick warm-up, then sat with her parents and Hannah in chairs someone had brought up, to watch while they worked on 'Cheek to Cheek.'

After three complete run-throughs, Paula said, "That's coming together. Once more on video and then we'll move on."

Hannah worked the camera for them. "How do you use the video?" she asked, handing them the camera afterward. They watched the recording while Margaret brought them water.

"We play our rehearsal video and the movie side by side," Paula said. "That way we can really easily see where the hits and misses are."

"But then how do you fix it?"

Mike smiled. "Practice. Lots and lots of practice."

"Yeah. It's a good thing we like dancing together." Paula gave Sophie and Max a smile. They didn't look bored yet. "Okay. Time for the other thing?" She went over by the wall to stretch while Mike and Margaret started working on 'Dancing in the Dark.' She could tell that Margaret's parents were surprised by the process, but also that they were enjoying it. *Lucky girl*, she thought, *like me*, grinning at herself.

When Mike eventually said, "That's enough for today. You're doing great. We can finish it tomorrow," Paula went to the laptop and opened the Dropbox. She set the laptop on the counter and everyone crowded around.

"So what we have here," she said, "is our friends with their version of a paso doble from 'Strictly Ballroom.' Have you seen it? *No?* That's your homework. Good gracious mercy me." Hannah laughed. Paula opened the video and stood back a little so she could hold Mike's hand. "Oh, I hate them," she said when it finished. "It's so good."

"I think they should close," Mike said. "They had to create a lot of stuff."

"Maybe we could open." She looked at Mike for agreement, then closed the laptop. "Okay. Little break? Then back here for some lifts?"

Everyone seemed to agree with that program, so they reconvened in about fifteen minutes. Paula and Mike demonstrated four different lifts and got Sophie and Max's permission to work on them with Margaret. First came the fish, then a straight lift, then a supported grande jetée; all relatively basic, not requiring much from Margaret (given that she was half Mike's size) other than some self-generated lift.

"All right. Now for the big one," said Mike. "This requires different technique from the flyer.

When Paula goes into arabesque, she has to plié and then spring off the floor. My support rises with her."

"Inertia," said Hannah.

"Right, exactly. An object at rest tends to remain at rest," Mike said for Margaret's benefit. "And an object in motion tends to remain in motion. So the flyer starts the movement. The base's job is to get underneath it, carry it up, then stabilize it."

"I know that sounds gross," Paula said to Sophie. "*It* is not the flyer. *It* is the lift." Sophie looked enlightened.

"My hands are here and here." He demonstrated as Paula held the arabesque. "Now, what happens if her top leg moves?"

"She'll slip right out of your hands," said Hannah.

"Right, so the leg has to connect into that hand. It takes a lot of strength. We won't go all the way up. Margaret, come and take your arabesque."

She came over, looking nervous but very excited, and went into a nice arabesque position. Mike placed his hands and Paula said, "Connect with that leg." She could see that Margaret was concentrating on engaging the hip. "Now plié … and straight up." Margaret gave a little spring and Mike took her up to approximately shoulder height. She squealed. Sophie and Max laughed. "Hold it, Margaret." Mike took Margaret into the fish. She held her upward arch beautifully, bringing the bottom leg into piqué. Sophie, Max, and Hannah all applauded.

"That's a good day's work." Mike set the girl down. She bounced a little, completely inarticulate.

"I got that on video," said Hannah, grinning. "I'll send it to you later."

240

Mike did a quick internal survey. He'd need to stretch at home. "We'd better head out now. Paula and her family still have a lot of catching up to do. Thanks so much for letting us use the space."

"You'll come back tomorrow?" Sophie indicated her daughter. "I know Margaret wants to finish that dance."

Paula smiled. "We'll be here. Thanks."

Hannah and Oliver were talking quietly during dinner, and Hannah seemed especially thoughtful afterward. It was the seven of them, plus a colleague of Adam's who left soon after.

"He got stuck," said Adam, after closing the door. "Litigation. Short straw."

"Ugh," said Paula.

They all pitched in to clear the dining room and clean up the kitchen again. Jennifer made some coffee; Mike and Paula both opted against. They were on the floor, stretching, as soon as possible.

"Hannah says you gave Margaret a great lesson today," said Jennifer. "Sophie called to say thanks."

"Super nice family," said Paula. "And I'm totes envious of that studio."

Hannah said, "It's a lot of pressure though. Having it there staring at you all the time."

Mike and Paula looked at each other. "That's ... very acute," said Paula. "I guess it could be. Maybe it's good we have to leave home to dance."

"I decided what I want to do." Everyone looked at Hannah, with various degrees of surprise. "Oliver's going to be out on the ocean half his life, I know he is. I decided I don't want to do work that keeps me away from him." Jennifer put a hand to her mouth, eyes glimmering. "I want to be a pilot."

After a minute, Bill said, "What made you decide that?"

"Watching you guys. You lost a lot of years."

Damn, thought Paula, looking over at Jennifer, now wiping her eyes. Adam patted his wife's back. Mike moved close enough to touch Paula's hand. She edged close enough to grip his, then said, "Are you sure this kid is only, like, fifteen?" Adam laughed and Jennifer made a stifled sound.

"She's smart though." Oliver smiled at his sister.

"We'll do this again," said Mike. "In less than fifteen years."

"Less than ten," Bill suggested.

Paula shook her head. "Less than five."

"Less than three." Hannah grinned at all of them.

PART III: FACE THE MUSIC

The Playlist:

A Thousand Years - Christina Perri

Bottom of the River - Delta Rae

With or Without You - U2

A Moment - BitterSweet

Within You Without You - The Beatles

Keep it Together - Madonna

Save Me - k.d. lang

Always - Leonard Cohen

There may be trouble ahead
But while there's music, and moonlight,
and love, and romance
Let's face the music and dance.
*   -Irving Berlin*

CHAPTER 23

January 2017

The week after Mating Dance: Island Time wrapped, Paula and Mike were at Shall We Dance again to work on their waltz for the Underground Cabaret's February show. They'd done the basic choreography already, but came in to work with Michelle and Dmitri on the lifts for their adagio-style version of 'A Thousand Years.' Mating Dance show runner Julia and her partner (and new husband) Ray were there working on setting their championship paso doble to 'Obsession.' They all got done about the same time and decided to head down the street for dinner together.

Julia went out the door first. Ray was right behind her, making a joke about their song choice and how he stalked Julia back in the day. Mike followed them and Paula brought up the rear. She never forgot that snapshot: Julia looking back at Ray and laughing, Mike also looking at Ray, right before the screech of tires. After that, all she could remember seeing clearly was Ray getting an arm around Julia and throwing her back to his left, where she crashed into Mike and they both went down, knocking Paula backward into the building's wall. But Paula didn't see them land because she was looking at the SUV on the sidewalk where Ray had been a second before.

Julia was screaming, people in the studio were yelling, pedestrians were running across the street. All the commotion seemed to be happening at a distance. Paula touched the back of her head where it had struck the brick, decided she was okay, and pulled out her phone to call 911. It went to a recording. *This is incredible*, she thought dazedly, *this is horrible*. She held the phone up so she could hear if a human ever answered and looked over at Mike.

His face was ashen, pupils dilated, breath coming fast and shallow. His arm was wrapped around Julia's waist. They were both sitting on the sidewalk, Julia half in his lap, now sobbing.

"Mike. *Mike*." He looked up at Paula. *Be okay*, she thought urgently. It took a second for him to focus. He made a move, as if he were about to try to stand up. "Stay down so you don't fall down. Are you hurt?" After a moment he shook his head. "Is Julia hurt?"

He bent close to Julia's face and spoke softly to her. She shook her head, even though Paula could see that her knee and ankle were bleeding from scraping on the cement. Finally the 911 operator answered. "911, what's your emergency?"

"You probably already have calls about a crash in West Hollywood. Here's the address. Many witnesses. SUV on sidewalk. Send ambulances and a trauma team. At least one person was hit by the SUV."

She gave her name, the address again, a description of the vehicle. Then the operator asked if the driver was injured. "I don't give a fuck," said Paula. The operator calmly asked if the vehicle's engine was still running. "Shit. Yes." Paula walked on wobbly legs over to the SUV. Its right front corner was embedded in the studio window and the wall below; shattered safety glass was everywhere. The driver was sitting upright, staring out the windshield, frozen, her phone still in her hand. Paula took a picture, tamping down a flood of rage before knocking on the window. The driver hit a button and the window went down. "Turn off the car. Right now." The driver did, putting it in park and setting the brake. "Now do not fucking move, or I personally will tear you to pieces." Paula turned away from the driver and told the operator, "The engine's off now." She was asked if she could see the person who had been hit. "I think he's under the SUV," she said. Her voice didn't sound like her own; she couldn't say any more. Then she heard sirens, and a minute later the street was full of emergency vehicles, cop cars, and far too many onlookers. She disconnected and started to shake.

The next half hour passed in a nightmarish montage of half-remembered moments. Talking to people: Dmitri, Michelle, the other students and teachers. Over and over again, the police. The first time a cop came to ask her what she'd seen, she said, "Put up a screen. The SUV hit Ray Daniels. The actor. His wife is on the sidewalk behind me. Whatever is happening, please do not show the world." The cop's eyes got big and she moved fast, using her radio to get in a team to isolate the scene. The onlookers were moved further and further back. People using their phones to take pictures and videos were spoken to politely, then harshly. As people started to realize that something very bad had happened, and the level of activity around the SUV increased, the noise level subsided.

Paula was afraid to sit down by Mike and Julia, afraid she wouldn't be able to stand up again, so she stood there by the door. An EMT had crawled under the vehicle and she couldn't see or hear what they saw or said. In a few minutes, a backboard was passed under. In very little time it was extracted from the other side with a body on it, *oh God*, lifted to a gurney, then rolled quickly to the waiting ambulance. Another EMT came over. "Mr. Daniels' wife?"

"There," she said, pointing to Julia.

"Are any of you hurt?"

"I think my husband's in shock. He was nearly killed in a car accident five years ago. Are you able to take him in?"

"We can take him in the second bus." After a good look at her face, he said, "You should go too. We're heading to the ER at Cedars."

"Okay. I'll be ready in a second." Paula turned and saw that EMTs were already helping Julia and Mike up. She pulled open the door to the studio. A lot of cops were in there, taking statements. Nobody inside appeared to be hurt.

Dmitri stood by the office door, looking ten years older than he had an hour ago, arms wrapped tightly around himself. He came over to her immediately, unwinding, reaching out. "Could you see?"

She took his hands and shook her head. "They took him to the ambulance, so. I don't know what that means. I want to think he's going to be okay." Her voice broke. She took a couple of quick breaths. "I'm going in the second ambulance with Mike. I don't think he's injured, but … if he didn't have PTSD before, he's sure as shit got it now." Dmitri touched her shoulder and she kind of collapsed into his arms for a minute, biting back the urge to cling and cry. *Keep it together*, she thought, blinking hard. "I have to go. They're going to Cedars. Can you call Julia's daughter?"

"I have called." He held her face gently between his hands and kissed her forehead. "Go now. Call when you can."

"I will." She turned away and went back outside, scooping up her dance bag, half blind with fear and grief. An EMT was waiting for her, taking her quickly over to the ambulance where they already had Mike stowed. "Are you okay?" she asked him, as soon as she was inside. She was aware of the EMT wrapping a blood-pressure cuff around her arm, taking her pulse, whatever.

He shook his head. They had a cuff on him too, but he was sitting up and had regained some color. Paula sat beside him and took his hand. They were halfway to Cedars before he spoke. It was the same question that Dmitri had asked. "Could you see?"

"No." She made the mistake of meeting his eyes. He looked devastated. "Oh, God, Mike. I don't know how he could have survived." His breath hitched and he bent close, resting his head on her shoulder, shuddering. His tears wet her neck. She wrapped her free arm around his head, hid her face in his hair, and cried.

The hospital shoveled them back out around midnight. Paula couldn't help worrying about the car they'd left parked behind the studio, even though she knew Dmitri knew whose it was and that it wouldn't be towed. Maybe she worried about that because it was such a trivial, solvable problem. Neither of them was in any shape to drive anyway, so she called a taxi to get them home. Once back at the condo, she sent a text to Kelli, in response to one she'd gotten hours before that said **OMG Michelle called me R U OK.**

Hey doll. Shittiest of all shitty nights. No idea about Ray. Haven't seen Julia. No chance Mike or I will be at work tomorrow. I've got the shakes and he's a zombie.

Even though it was so late, an answer came right away. **Jesus Mary and Joseph. No news here either. Don't worry about work. Keep me posted.**

Tell me something good

Oh … Carlos and Celia are fat

Paula smiled at that. No they're not

Srsly little pigalettos

Thanks. :-) Hug Vince for us

Will do

Neither of them could sleep worth a damn. They kept dozing off, then waking up, that horrible screech and the even-worse sounds of the crash echoing for both of them. Around five in the morning they gave up entirely. Paula went to the kitchen to make coffee. Mike got in the shower. A half-hour later they sat on the couch staring at each other. "We should eat," he said.

"Yeah." Neither of them moved. After another few minutes, Paula thought, *I need to move, because he can't*. She got up, touched his shoulder, and walked into the kitchen again to put something together. It turned out to be a version of what used to be their 'normal' dinner: fruit, bread and butter, cheese. After some consideration, she also fixed them each a Cape Cod. She took one over to Mike. He looked up, surprised. "I already told Kelli we won't be in. She'll handle it."

"Thanks," he said with a sigh. "I was trying to think how we would get through the day."

"I couldn't even contemplate going to the office." Halfway down the drinks, they both felt a little more like eating. Once they got started, hunger took over. Paula took the empty plates back to the kitchen. When she got back to the couch, Mike was leaning back with his eyes closed. "Mike."

"Hmmm?"

"Did you see your crash happen?" He opened his eyes and looked at her. She could see the answer. "Oh *fuck*."

"Yeah." He smiled, sort of. "I was looking to the right, out of habit. Saw the car coming and thought, you know … well, there was no time to think anything, really, but if you can have a non-thought that's memorable, it was, I'm dead. I had this complete certainty. He was going so fast." She wrapped her hand around his upper arm and tugged him over. He let himself go, sliding onto her lap, looking up at her. She ran her hand through his hair.

"Then what?" she asked quietly.

"Next thing I knew there were EMTs everywhere and they were getting me out of the van through the driver's side. Every single move was … it was like my whole right side was on fire. I kept thinking, this is unbearable, how much more. Once I was in the ambulance they hooked up some blood and an IV, pushed some drugs. After that I kind of floated. I felt cold. I couldn't tell you how long it took to get to the hospital. Seemed like ten seconds or ten hours."

"Could you hear what they were saying?"

"Oh yeah. My vision was blurry … my right eye was full of blood, and I was dizzy … but I could hear just fine." After a minute he went on. "They thought I was dead at first. They were talking about how surprised they were to find a pulse. One of them said maybe I'd relaxed at the moment of impact, so I went with it. Like a drunk."

Paula huffed out a breath. "There's acceptance for you, I guess."

"Wasn't anything I could do. I talked about all this with a shrink during rehab. Putting words to the feelings kind of helped." They were quiet for another few minutes. "What time is it now?"

Paula picked up her phone from the side table, and woke it up. Still no messages. "Almost eight."

"I don't want to know." He closed his eyes again, turning his face toward her hand.

Paula stroked his cheekbone with her thumb, thinking if there was good news, they would have heard something by now. "Neither do I."

They spent the next few hours cuddled on the couch together, barely talking. Finally at noon both of their phones pinged with text notifications. Full of dread, Paula picked hers up. The message was from Julia's phone.

Group msg from Grace. Ray didn't make it. Mom is with his parents at their house. Will let you know about memorial. No calls please

She didn't say anything. Couldn't, at that moment. Could only think, *This is so unfair, he was only thirty-four*. Mike said, "He's dead, isn't he?" She nodded. He drew a deep breath, let it out slowly, then picked up his own phone to send a group text, to everyone except Julia.

Group msg from Mike. Paula and I are okay. We're at home today if anyone needs to talk

251

"Tough guy," Paula said shakily, after she read it.

"Not really. I cried in the shower."

"I cried while you were in the shower." She looked over at him. They both wiped their eyes. "I'm going to put some more coffee in our travel mugs, with a shitload of Kahlua. Then I think we should go down to the pool."

"Okay. I love you."

"I love you too."

They spent most of the afternoon down there, in and out of the warm water, in the sun when it hit the deck and wrapped in robes when it didn't. Friends called at intervals, to say variations of 'we're glad you're okay, isn't it awful.' Dmitri called to say they didn't need to worry about Mike's Jeep, that the studio would be closed for a couple of days and they could come for it any time. About four o'clock, when it started getting too chilly to be outside, they went back upstairs and showered off the chlorine. Then Paula ordered pizza from a local joint, with salads and tiramisu. Mike opened a bottle of wine. "Is this how alcoholism starts?" he said, half-joking.

"If you didn't get dependent after your own accident, I'm not too worried about you now. How's your hip?" Paula had seen the fearsome bruise where he'd hit the sidewalk. Hadn't brought it up only because he was moving normally.

"Sore. It's not serious." He poured the wine and set the glasses on the table. When he turned back to Paula she was staring at him. "What?"

"Inappropriate thoughts. Never mind." She looked away for a moment, then back at him. "Have I mentioned lately that I'm really glad you're alive?"

He took a step across the space between them and put his arms around her, bending his head to kiss her neck. "It's not inappropriate to want to celebrate being alive." She tipped her head back and he kissed her. It was soft and gentle at first, but when she opened her mouth he dove in. They were both breathless when he lifted his head again. "You always do it for me, Paula," he said. She could feel that it was true.

"Once that pizza gets here," she said. "Turn on the oven, we'll throw it in there to stay warm."

"Okay." He let her go, smiling a little. They both had a few swallows of wine while they waited for the pizza guy to come and go, so they could go to bed.

They both cried again after making love, and for once Paula wasn't embarrassed about it. She shied away from thoughts of Julia and what she must be going through. Just imagining how she would feel herself was enough to make her stomach clench. Eventually they got out of bed, had their dinner, then cleaned up the kitchen. They'd done next to nothing all day, but they both felt exhausted. They were back in bed by eight.

Paula woke up when she felt the bed move. At first she thought it had been an earthquake. Then she heard him, his breath harsh, and put a hand on his chest. He was shaking. "Mike?"

"I thought I was done with those," he said, voice uneven. "Nightmare. Or flashback, I don't know." He regulated his breathing and the tension slowly left his body. Paula kept the connection.

After a while, she said, "Want to tell me?"

He didn't answer immediately. Then, after a breath, "It was stuff that didn't really happen. The van rolling. Me underneath it." She slid her arm over his chest and he turned to her, pulling her tight against him. "I could see myself being crushed."

"Jesus, Mike." *Now I'm going to see that.* "What can I do?"

"I don't know. Be here," he said against her neck.

"Always." She lay still, afraid to let go of him.

CHAPTER 24

They went to work the next day, even though they both still felt like crap. Their bosses left them mostly alone to clean out their in-boxes in peace. Kelli took them out to lunch. "I'm so glad I wasn't there," she said. "It's selfish and horrible, but, ugh. How are you doing?"

"Mike's going to need therapy again," said Paula, "and I got a call this morning from the cops."

"You did?" Mike said. "What did they want?"

"The driver was complaining that I threatened her."

"*She* was complaining?" He couldn't believe it.

"The cop said what did you say, and I said it was something like, don't fucking move or I will tear you limb from limb. He asked why I said that and I said, because she had a fucking phone in her fucking hand. I texted him the picture I took at the scene and then said, tell her, please, charge me with assault. I can't wait to see what a jury would do with that. He said, that's probably all we'll need from you, thanks." Kelli was shaking her head, half-laughing despite being fully appalled. Mike was pale. Hadn't touched his food. Paula put her hand on his wrist and squeezed. "You need to eat."

"I'm not hungry."

"I know." She bullied him into eating half his lunch while forcing herself to eat most of hers. They talked about Kelli and Vince's twins, about the lessons Vince was giving a neighbor couple down in Westchester, about the ballroom training he'd started doing with Michelle. Toward the end of their break, Paula asked Kelli, "So how do you really feel about the ballroom thing?"

Kelli sighed. "I am the teeniest tiny bit jealous. But it's not really being jealous of Michelle, it's more because Vince and I haven't settled on a thing to work on yet. You might remember what that's like, when you want to dance and you're ready to dance but there's not a plan."

"Yeah, I hated that," said Paula. "Well, with Mating Dance: Milonga being an annual thing now, you should do something for that. Maybe bring back 'Palomita Blanca.'" Then she cringed inside, remembering that Ray and Julia had danced it last. But Kelli was nodding.

"That's a good idea. I could be fit by then if I have some incentive."

"When are they planning their Smooth debut?"

"California Star. They'll have had a whole year to train and then there's a good six-week break to re-work things if they need to before the 2018 season starts. Michelle was giving him crap about how Dmitri took her into her first competition after, like, two months. He gave her this sob story about how he has to commute now, and hello babies, and woe." It surprised a laugh out of Paula. Kelli gave her a half-sympathetic, half-relieved look. "You know he decided not to leave the real-estate office till later this year, so his schedule is kind of whack. Thank God for Esmeralda. He looks awfully good already, though," she added proudly.

"He's been good in everything," Mike said. "Last year I went through all your videos. His technique keeps getting better, but he's always been a great performer."

"And there is something about a sharp-dressed man," Paula said. "I'll bet he looks like a movie star in a tux."

"Yes. Yes he does." Kelli got out her phone and pulled up a promotional photo Andy had taken for the studio. Michelle looked as beautiful as ever. Vince's glossy black hair had been cut, swept back off his face to show his sideburns. The style emphasized his eyes and his admirable bone structure.

Paula made a yummy noise. "Wow, he's legit James Bond."

"Yes. Yes he is. You should hear his mother on the subject," Kelli added. "Woo! She shows this picture to *everyone*."

"My mom does that," said Mike. "With our wedding picture."

"Well, that was a movie-star moment for you two, for sure." Kelli looked at the picture again, then up at Paula. "Next time we perform I'm going to make him wear that damn tux so we can get a picture like this. Then Esmeralda will have a new one of *us* to show off. Hmph."

They went to West Hollywood after work, even though neither of them really wanted to go near it, to pick up Mike's Jeep. They approached the studio from the back, parked, and went up to the door. There was a notice taped up that said CLOSED TILL SATURDAY. "Okay," said Mike. "I guess we come back Saturday. And work on 'A Thousand Years.'"

"You're still up for that?"

"I need to dance," he said. "And you should talk to Rory and Michelle about the lineup. How we're going to handle losing Ray."

Without comment, Paula got her phone out and texted Rory. UC Love is the Drug, how are we handling?

257

A reply came almost immediately. **Michelle and Stacey thought a title card at the end. Stacey already pinged Yoshi. We'll rework the show order a little. How are you guys?**

Still shell-shocked. We're over at SWD picking up the Jeep

Want to come over for dinner? I made pot roast. You can meet Spike's new dog

Another dog?

So the cottage is getting crowded shut up

Paula showed the exchange to Mike and he nodded, his expression lightening. She texted back: We'll be right there

Rory and Dana's place was only a few blocks from the studio, so they got there in less than ten minutes. As they exited their vehicles, Dana stepped out of the cottage door holding something that might have been a very clean mop.

Mike said, "Is that the new dog?" Dana handed over the white fluffball and he cuddled it. A pink tongue swiped his face. "What a cutie."

"That's why we have her. Someone had to give her up, she was at the vet. Rory picked her up because of course she did. She kissed Rory and it was all over. Her name is Precious."

Paula smiled. "Really?"

"Hey, she's middle-aged. We don't want to change her name on her at this point. Besides, she is precious. Come on inside." Spike the cat and his other dog, the long-haired Dachshund named Oscar, were waiting politely in the front room. Paula bent down to pet them and had a shaky moment. She picked up Spike and put her face in his fur. Dana noticed. "Therapy animals available on short notice."

"Thanks," Paula said, voice muffled by cat.

They all went back to the dining den, where Rory was pouring wine. "No hugging," she said. "I start bawling every time there's hugging."

"Right," said Mike. "I'll hang onto this dog then."

"That's what they're here for. Sit, have a drink, let's talk about my new jazz piece. Thanks for nagging me, by the way."

Paula and Mike obediently sat, still holding Spike and Precious. Mike said, "Well, the thing you did for 'Lunatics' was so great. The 'Mirrorball' piece you did with Ann and Bonnie was great. And 'Tainted Love' is looking great. Then they got in touch with Paula about doing something, and since I have her all tied up - "

"In a manner of speaking," said Paula. Mike actually laughed.

He blinked, startled, as if he didn't recognize the sound. Put his free hand on Paula's thigh, as if he needed an anchor. She took a hand off the cat to wrap her fingers around his. He squeezed her hand gratefully and found some words. "Anyway. You like what you're doing?"

"Well, we started talking about it, we settled on the music right away, but there's one small problem."

"Which is ... ."

Rory looked at him sideways. "We need a man." Paula and Dana both snickered. "So very ironic. I wanna get some flight this time."

"So what is it and when are you planning to do it?" Mike had begun to relax during the conversation. He was sufficiently self-aware to think, *thank God for these people.* Precious was curled up on his lap. His free hand was under her chest and elbows; he could feel her heart beating. Her furry warmth was infinitely comforting.

"June. 'Human Nature.' Stealing pieces from Madonna but also Bollywood."

"The theme for that show is 'Cosmic,' right? We didn't have a quick concept for it ourselves."

"It's a little abstract," said Dana. "If Rory and the girls can get something on tape fairly quickly we can link people to it for inspiration."

"I don't think I've ever started to work on something so far ahead," said Rory. "But anyway. What do you think?" She looked from Mike to Paula.

"You can have him," said Paula, who thought a different style of performance, with the humor that Rory couldn't help putting in her work, might be exactly what Mike needed. "I could ping Alison about the pro show, she said last year she could have used another pair of hands."

Mike was looking at her, smiling a little, probably reading her mind. "Sure." He looked back at Rory. "Do I get to sling all three of you around?"

"If you do, Paula might not ever get you back. They couldn't shut up about you last year." Rory checked her watch. "Time to eat."

After dinner, they looked through the list of performances selected for the February show. "We still have eleven," said Paula. "And all of these songs are sick. But you had Ray and Julia opening, to hammer home the theme. What needs to go first now?"

Mike said, "'Every Breath You Take.' Everybody knows that song. And everybody knows Sam and

Mateo." After 'Gaucho,' both men had been in demand for gigs as extras and models.

"It's cool as fuck," said Rory. "They put some of that martial arts shit in there, with tango and rumba and paso and bananapants."

"Sam came on so fast," said Mike. "After 'Green Darkness.'"

"He was always good," said Dana. "Vicky said he was born to dance Latin, but yeah. He's all in now. And Mateo's choreography is getting really impressive." She drew some lines on the printout, rearranging a couple of other numbers. The others looked at it. "That's good, right? I'll clean it up and send it to Michelle and Stacey. But now I'm going to kick you out because I have an early call tomorrow." *Because rewrites, because we've lost Ray. God damn it.*

"Yes, Captain," said Paula. "Thanks for this."

"Come anytime you need critters. There's always at least one spare."

Mike picked up Precious one more time, handed her to Dana, leaned over the fluffball to kiss her cheek. "No hugs. Only love."

"Love you guys too," said Rory, clutching Oscar. "Now beat it."

The studio was full, but abnormally quiet, when Mike and Paula got there on Saturday. The big front windows were boarded up. People were in there prepping for the Cabaret, for an upcoming ballroom competition, or for imminent salsa and tango competitions. No one was talking any more than necessary. They collected a few nods of greeting, but

261

no one was hugging either. *Like Rory*, Paula thought. *None of us can stand it.*

A notice was taped to the office door. Somehow Mike and Paula knew what it would say. By mutual unspoken agreement they waited until they were done with their rehearsal before going over to read it.

> Dear friends,
>
> A memorial for Ray Daniels will be held at Chrome on Sunday morning, eleven o'clock. All studio members are welcome. No service, no flowers, just a few words to remember and celebrate his life.
>
> Thank you for your support, and for giving Ray and Julia such a happy dance home.
>
> Charlene Daniels Santiago

"Oh *fuck* it all," Paula said, pinching the bridge of her nose. Mike was wiping his eyes again. "Tomorrow." She sighed, flashing again to how she would feel. How getting past it would be so impossibly hard. Putting things off wouldn't help. Nothing would. "It's going to be rough for you."

Mike and Ray had gotten close the previous summer, when they were both working on Alison's martial-arts dance concert 'The Great Wave.' Ray had been on hiatus and hadn't taken any big summer jobs. They'd seen a lot of each other, doing the training needed for the show, learning the complex choreography. But once Ray's series was back in production, they'd mostly seen each other in passing, at the studio. "I wish I'd pushed a little harder for face time after September," Mike said.

"He was busy. They were working hard on knocking down that third championship win. And at least we had that dinner once they got back from Las Vegas." Mike didn't answer; Paula didn't pursue it. They went to collect their gear. Before they left, she poked her head into the office to see if Dmitri was there. She thought probably not, since he hadn't appeared in the main room since they'd been there, and she was right. Elena was there, so they spoke for a minute. Then Paula wrote a note for Dmitri, a quick 'see you tomorrow, let us know if we can do anything, OXO,' and went back out.

The memorial was every bit as difficult as expected. It was brief, at least. Most of the Shall We Dance and Cabaret community was present, along with many of Ray's television colleagues. Several got up to say a few words, mostly about Ray's creativity, his professionalism, his talent. Ray's sister Charlene talked about how much he had loved his life, how much he'd loved dancing, how much he'd loved Julia. "My brother was a happy man," she said, wiping away tears. "And that's what I'm going to remember." She sat down next to her husband and covered her face with her hands. Everyone was crying, including Julia, but she got up next. She looked thinner, older, and slightly glassy-eyed, as if she might have taken something to dull the pain.

"I'll never forget our first date," she said. "I'd been teaching on a weekend singles cruise and Ray came up to me as we were docking. He was so cute," she said, with a tiny, tragic smile. "He talked me into dinner even though he was sixteen years younger than me. He said, who cares? And before long I didn't care either. When he started talking about getting

263

married I thought he was crazy." Ray's parents both sort-of laughed through their tears. "I made a deal with him. I said, if we win Rising Star three times, I'll do it. You should have seen him work after that." A few more people laughed. "And then we won that third time, in Vegas, last December. My students were there, they were so in love. They decided to get married right then and there. Ray gave me that look." Julia glanced over at Charlene, who nodded, still crying, but smiling. "You know the look. And he said, we had a deal, young lady. No time like the present. So we got married too. I'm so glad we did." The last word broke in half, and she started to sag. Charlene's husband Juan got to her fast, helping her back to her seat, where she collapsed against her daughter. Her ex-husband Roger, sitting behind them, bent forward and put his arms around both women.

This is awful, thought Paula, *I never want to do this again*, weeping in Mike's arms. He was shuddering and she knew he wouldn't be able to move or speak for a while. She crammed all that grief as far down into its box as she could, trying to be steady, trying to get control. Trying to get angry again, so the box would be easier to keep closed. It was hard work and it took a while. By the time she was something approaching calm, a lot of people had left. Mike wasn't crying anymore, but he hadn't moved; his head was still pressed into the curve of her shoulder. "Guess I'm the tough guy now," she tried. He huffed out a breath.

"You always were," he said. He pulled back a little, sniffing, pressing the heels of his hands to his eyes. "God, I'm a mess."

"Everybody is." She dug in her bag for some tissues. She wasn't the only one; there was a chorus of

264

sniffling and nose-blowing that was inappropriately funny. "Jesus I wish the bar was open."

"The bar at home is." It was her turn to sort-of laugh. Mike touched her face. When she turned toward him he kissed her. "Julia's gone." Paula looked around and saw that it was true; the whole family had slipped away while everyone else lost their shit. "We can go now, if you want."

"God, yes." They took one more look at the big photo of Ray on an easel at center stage, one that Andy had taken for 'Gaucho,' and made it outside without having to talk to anyone. Then they stood in the midday sun for a while before trying to drive home. "That really was completely awful," said Paula finally. "I hope we never have to do that again."

"I wonder what she's going to do now."

"I don't know. I can't imagine." She offered to drive. Mike shook his head, unlocking the car. "Does being in the passenger seat freak you out again?" He glanced at her, didn't answer. *And there's some more damage*, she thought. She didn't say anything else, just got in the car.

Mike had another episode that night. This time his reaction didn't wake Paula up, possibly because of the Excedrin PM she'd taken a couple of hours after the two glasses of wine. He sat on the floor in the dark bedroom, stretching out of habit, trying to steady his breathing, wondering what to do. He knew he needed to talk to someone, didn't want to start from scratch with a new therapist in L.A., didn't know if it was bad enough to be worth going back to his shrink in Minneapolis. *Well*, he thought after a while, *how bad would be bad enough? Don't be an idiot.*

The next morning he told Paula, "I may need to go back to Minneapolis. Should be a quick visit. I want to talk to my shrink there."

"Did you have another nightmare?" Paula said. From the look on his face she knew he had. "Whatever you need to do. Do you want me to come with you?"

"You don't have to."

"That was not the question," she said, frowning, and he smiled.

"Okay, okay. Um … maybe not this time. I need to get in touch with her, see what she recommends. Last time, it took hypnosis to really clear it out. I didn't want to talk to, or even see, anybody after those sessions." He studied her; she looked as though she understood. *Well, she would*, he thought. *Paula's the queen of not talking*. It made him smile again. "I love you. Just so you know."

"I know. I love you too."

Paula continued to bully Mike into eating, and into taking a sedative at least every other night. He still lost weight, and the shadows under his eyes didn't go away. By dress-rehearsal day for the February show, she was truly glad he had set up a week in Minneapolis for intensive work with Dr. Nelson. "You're not supposed to actually look like a vampire, you know," she said when they finished their run-through. He was still fit, still strong enough that she hadn't worried about her own safety during the routine, but he looked unusually fatigued at the end. "I'm glad this thing is almost done so you can get out of here." He would be leaving the Sunday after the show wrapped.

"I'm glad, too. I loved making this dance, but everything feels wrong now." Then he glanced at her and shook his head. "Not everything."

"I know what you mean. It's okay." The rest of the run-through had gone well. Michelle didn't have any notes for anybody. The entire cast was subdued and there wasn't any post-rehearsal get-together this time, so everyone was getting ready to go. "We'll all be doing better by this time next month. And we're not prepping anything for Mating Dance, so forget about going to the studio."

"Bossy." He smiled a little. "Let's go. I'm hungry."

"Glad to hear it."

CHAPTER 25

Julia hadn't returned to the studio, and Dmitri hadn't volunteered any information about her plans. He was working with her private students himself. As always, he was professional; but his public face was controlled, almost grim, in a way it hadn't been for quite some time. The last time they'd been at Shall We Dance, Paula was tempted to ask Michelle if she knew what was going on, but decided to leave it a while longer. Then the Thursday after the show wrapped, she and Mike both got a text, and suddenly everything was clear.

Hi guys. FYI I am going back to Minnesota for a while. My mother's not doing so well and dad said maybe I should come. I'd like to see you both before I go. Could you come to the house on Saturday? Thx OX Julia

"That's the day before you leave," said Paula. "Not a problem, though, right?"

"Not a problem," said Mike, and sent a quick reply: *Tell us when OXO*

"Jeez, I hope her mom isn't, you know. Because that is too much. I mean, Ray is too much, but fuck."

"She might not tell us. I'm glad she reached out. I would have felt horrible if she had left without us seeing her."

"Even more horrible, you mean." *You are still so not okay.*

"Yeah." He closed his eyes briefly, taking one of those breath-managing moments that Paula was starting to associate with waking nightmares. "At least I didn't drop you during the show." There'd been one close call on the second night of performance. "I'm sorry about that."

"Yeah, you've said so a hundred times. I'm fine. I was fine. I will be fine. You, I'm not sure about." She studied him for another minute. "How've you been hanging in at the office?"

"It's easier to maintain when I'm juggling stuff all day." His phone pinged. He glanced at it. "She says three o'clock, question mark. That's okay, right?"

"Sure."

So that weekend they went over to Julia's house near Century City. They had no idea if this was a coffee or wine or food type deal in Julia's mind, so they came empty-handed and hoped she wouldn't mind. When she opened the door, she had a bottle of wine in her own hand and said, "It's good to see you. Could you give me a hand with this?" Mike took the bottle, which had a Rabbit screwed into the cork. They followed Julia inside and then to the kitchen, where he got the bottle open. "Thanks. Most of the time they don't give me any trouble, but this one was resistant."

"He's my bottle-opening fail-safe too," said Paula. She didn't ask if Julia was all right. It was blindingly obvious that she wasn't; she looked gaunt. She'd put together some fruit and cheese and crackers in her garden room. That's where they ended up with the wine. All three of them sat together on the couch, looking out at the nicely-landscaped yard. Julia asked about the February show; they talked dancing for a while. Then Paula asked, "How's Grace doing?"

"She's okay. She's got the master's program to keep her busy. And she's doing an engineering internship with Sharon's dad." Julia stopped talking, and all of them kind of stalled.

After a minute, Mike said, "So ... Minnesota. I hope your mom is okay?"

"Dad says it's oncoming dementia," Julia said with a sigh. "Her mother had it too. He wants me to see her and help him decide if he should get in-home help, or put her on the list for assisted living, or both. He's still in good shape, but he's eighty."

"Jesus," said Paula. "I'm so sorry."

"Me too," said Julia. She set her wine glass down and leaned forward over her knees, not looking at either of them. Mike set his hand lightly on her back. Julia covered her face with her hands. "This is ... I'm sorry. I need help." The words were muffled.

"Whatever you need," Mike said quietly.

"I need a body." Mike and Paula looked at each other, startled, wondering if they'd heard her correctly. Julia moved her hands so that her eyes were still covered, but she could speak clearly. The words seemed to be forcing themselves out, but came fast. "I can't sleep. I don't remember to eat. Ray ... our relationship was so physical, I feel so unbearably *empty*, I can't stand it." Tears were coming now. "Roger would. But I *can't*. I know he wants to go back to the way we were. I can't do that again. I hate this. I'm sorry."

Mike and Paula were still looking at each other. He looked shocked, grief-stricken, completely out of his depth. Paula had no idea if she looked the same. Her own initial disbelief had been swept out by that recurring loop of *how would I feel*. Before Julia had stopped speaking, she understood. "Julia … give us a minute. We'll be right back." She stood up, touching Julia's shoulder briefly, and held out her hand for Mike. He stood and followed her out, all the way back to the kitchen where she knew Julia wouldn't be able to overhear.

"Does she mean what I think she means?" Mike said, voice low.

Paula nodded. "Pretty sure. Do you think you could?"

"You *want* me to?"

"Not want, exactly. Let me try to make sense out of this." She took a moment. "If I lost you. If that happened. Once the first shock was over, I kind of think I'd be fucking everything in sight, trying to fill that giant Mike-shaped hole in my life."

His eyes filled and he looked away, blinking, taking a breath. "I don't know if I can."

"I don't know if she needs you to participate. Maybe all she needs is to hold you. But if maybe something else happens, I want you to know that's okay with me. I'll be there too." He didn't say anything. "This might be the only thing we actually can do for her." After a moment he nodded. They went back to the garden room.

Julia was leaning against the back of the couch, staring at the ceiling, but she sat forward when they came in. "Look, guys, I'm sorry, this is way beyond. Please forget I said anything."

"No," said Mike. "It's okay. If you need me … if you need us, we're here. We're here for you," he emphasized. "Do you want to go upstairs?" She looked surprised, almost fearful, but after a moment

271

she nodded. "Go on up," he said gently. "We'll be right behind you."

When they made their way upstairs and down the hall to the master suite, they found Julia lying on the big bed. The covers were pulled down, she was wearing a short robe, and her eyes were closed. Her almost-empty wine glass was on the nightstand next to a condom. Mike looked at Paula and raised his eyebrows, moving his head a little to say, are you sure? She nodded. She took off all her clothes except her briefs. Mike took everything off and they climbed onto the bed. Paula got on one side of Julia, the side away from that eloquent nightstand; Mike took the other. Then Paula wrapped her arm across Julia and kissed her cheek. Julia gripped her arm and took a shuddering breath, then turned in to Paula's embrace. They held each other for a few minutes. Then Mike moved in close to Julia's back. When she felt him there she turned around and pressed herself against him, face against his chest. Paula also turned, draping her arm over Julia to rest her hand on Mike's hip.

"You've lost weight," Julia said. "I keep forgetting you almost got hit too. Are you okay?"

"I'm okay," he said. "Well, I'm going to Minneapolis myself next week to get my head shrunk again. After that I expect I'll be okay." Amazingly, they all smiled at that. Julia raised her face. Her eyes met his, doubtfully, then she looked at his mouth. Mike felt odd, knowing that Paula was right there and watching, but she patted his hip as if to remind him it was okay, so he kissed Julia.

It was so strange to kiss another woman after so long. He didn't know if he could have initiated anything, but Julia's desperate need called a response

272

from his body. He lay there passively, keeping a hand on her somewhere, kissing her when her mouth came back to his. Her hands and mouth were everywhere. At some point it was clear that the condom needed to go on, so he did that. Without taking off the robe, Julia slung her leg over him and moved him into position. Mike thought, *she really did need a body, that's all this is, it's okay* and then he was inside her and she was riding him, head thrown back, eyes closed again.

Paula's face was close to Mike's, one hand in his hair and the other on Julia's thigh. Before long it was clear that Julia was going over. Mike's body was rigid. His eyes were shut tight and he was biting his lip. Paula breathed into his ear, "It's okay," and he shook his head slightly. One of his hands was holding Julia's upper arm and the other was gripping Paula's knee, tucked up over his thigh behind Julia, his arm and Paula's overlapping.

All at once Julia said "Oh God!" and arched back. Mike thought, very clearly, *NO*. He felt her coming and his hand left her arm and dug hard into the bed. *No. No.*

Somehow, he managed it. Julia collapsed off him to the side, rolling over his arm, then curled up, breathing hard. He lay there, still on his back, breath shallow. Paula was right up against him. She kissed the side of his face and looked down his body. *Unbelievable*, she thought. She would have touched him to finish it, but something told her he didn't want that. So she kept still, quiet, watching and waiting until he relaxed.

He sat up. Paula shifted to make room for him to get off the bed. Julia was motionless. Paula leaned closer as Mike went to the bathroom; Julia was sound asleep. When Mike came out, Paula put a finger to her lips. They got dressed in silence. Paula went down the hall to Julia's office to find some paper and a pen. Wrote a note and took it back to the bedroom. Took the glass to the bathroom and rinsed it out, filled it with water, and carried it back to the nightstand. *You poor darling*, she thought. *I'm so sorry.*

They went downstairs, put away the wine-and-cheese stuff, let themselves out. Paula unlocked the car and got in on the driver's side, forgetting for a moment about Mike's flashbacks.

He collapsed in the passenger seat and tipped his head back against the headrest, eyes closed. "That was." There were no words.

"I know. I can't believe you didn't come."

"If she'd gone any longer I don't know if I could have held it." He turned his head and looked at her. "I didn't want that. That's for you. All for you." Paula leaned over and kissed him. He wrapped his arm around her head for a moment. Then she sat back. He was still looking at her, and the look was hungry. "Can we … ?"

"Are you kidding? I'm so turned on I'm about to melt." He huffed out a laugh. Paula smiled, but said, "Do you want to get in the back?"

He looked surprised. "I forgot. I'm going to put the seat back and close my eyes, not try to watch everything."

"Okay." She started the car to take them home.

Sometime between the post-Julia sex and the bedtime sex, they both got another text from Julia: **Thank you. That helped.** Mike wrote back *Glad to hear it.* Paula wondered if Julia would try to contact Mike in Minneapolis. He read her mind. "If she gets in touch, I'll see her, but I won't do that again. Not unless you're there."

"Somehow I doubt she'll ask for that again. She'll be able to find someone there. Of course, there's no chance he'll be as awesome as you, but, you know." Paula admired him for a moment. He was a little thin, and he definitely needed some more sleep, but still. "You are a gorgeous animal. And you really are as stubborn as a mule. I still can't believe you held it. That was, like, tenth-level tantra or something." Mike snorted out a laugh, which made her smile. "You should tell your shrink about it."

"Oh shit, really?" He grimaced.

"Well, obviously I'm a dancer, not a psychiatrist, but that was the epitome of control. You're all about control, aren't you? Not in a sick way, in a managing-yourself way. Maybe that's why, or part of why, the accident knocked you for a loop. I mean, shit like that's the ultimate in being *out* of control."

After a thoughtful pause, he said, "You could be right. Okay, I'll tell her. But, ugh."

Paula patted him. "She'll understand."

"How to even say that. Our friend was killed, his wife asked me to, you know, and my wife said it was okay, so we had a sort of a threesome and it was weird, but I guess it worked?" Paula scooted close and cuddled under his waiting arm. He kissed her on the forehead, hoping it really did work.

After dropping Mike off at the airport the next day, Paula went home and called her sister. They'd been in touch since the accident, but hadn't spoken for a while. Jennifer was usually home around three on weekend afternoons; Paula caught her on the first try. "Hey Jen," she said. "I took Mike to the airport this morning and I'm second-guessing myself."

"Where did he go?"

"Minneapolis. He's doing some intensive with his shrink from before. He's been having nightmares and daymares and basically not doing well."

"Oh wow. I'm sorry to hear that. Well, it's got to be rough seeing somebody killed right in front of you like that."

"I think it's almost worse that we *didn't* actually see it. If that makes sense. It was literally like, one second Ray was there and the next second he wasn't. Just obliterated. We never saw him again. Except I did, for a second, when they pulled him out from under the truck, but that was only a shape. Jesus."

"Oh Paula. Honey, I'm so sorry. His poor wife."

"God only knows what she saw. She's not doing well, either. And she's actually also going to Minneapolis. Her parents live there and now her mother's in decline. Since she's not up to working right now, she's going home to deal with that. It's all awful."

"So you think you should have gone with Mike?"

"He said he'd rather I didn't. I think he's expecting that after his sessions, he's going to want to be left alone, and I can certainly relate to that. He's staying with his mom, but after all the therapy he went through before she knows what he needs. So I know he doesn't, like, *need* me. It's more that I need him, I guess. And having articulated that, I know it was the right thing not to go. He needs some space to deal with this shit."

"Well, I hope he can work his stuff out so you can get back to being happy together."

"Me too. So how are the kids? How's Adam?"

"Adam is training for the marathon again. Oliver is agitating to do a marine-biology thing this summer in Maine. Hannah is agitating to take Argentine tango lessons. She keeps watching your wedding dance, plus every other tango thing she can find on YouTube."

Paula thought this was great. "Does she tell you to take lessons, too?"

"She totally does. She's all, Mom, we could go together. I mean, bless her heart. Most teenagers don't want their parents anywhere near them."

"I certainly didn't. But why don't you? Take lessons."

"I might. God knows I need something more than the elliptical."

"Well, sixteen is a good time to start social dancing. Forty-four is also a good time. Hey, maybe you could bring her out here this summer. We could coach you. Throw you in the deep end. Heck, bring Adam."

Jennifer said nothing for a moment. Paula could practically hear her thinking. Finally: "I really like that idea. Hannah's doing a six-week aviation lab, but it doesn't start till July seventeenth."

"You could get a month or six weeks at one of the apartments near where they tape Dancing with the Stars, do L.A. and learn to dance. Because yeah, you were right, a holiday weekend was not long enough. What do you think?"

"I'm trying to imagine talking Adam into taking that much time off."

"When's the last time he took a long vacation? Your honeymoon, right?"

277

"How'd you guess," Jennifer said dryly. "I mean, we had a week at Disney World with the kids, but that was still ... a long time ago. We'll have a powwow. I'll let you know."

"I'd seriously love it," said Paula. "This summer will be a year and half since we've seen each other. Which seems like too long."

"You're so right. I'll let you know," she said again. "Oh whoops, here comes Captain Ahab again, and he's looking determined."

Paula stifled a laugh. "Send him to Maine." They said their goodbyes and she disconnected, wondering where the idea had come from, but really liking it. *A shrink would probably tell me I want to reinforce my connections*, she thought. *And she'd probably be right.*

Paula and Mike touched base daily while he was away, usually just a text exchange. He also called her Wednesday night to say, "Julia's in town. She got in yesterday. We're going to have coffee on Saturday before I fly back."

"I hope she's doing better," said Paula. "How are *you* doing? You sound more like yourself."

"Dr. Nelson's been working me over." There was a smile in his voice. "Apparently I have survivor's guilt."

"What, because you didn't get flattened instead of Ray?"

"Basically, yeah." The timbre of his voice dropped.

Shit. "Sorry, that was probably too blunt."

"She had me talk it through like six times, I was feeling this ... horrible *injustice*, you know? That I could survive something like that twice."

"I get it. Are you sleeping?"

"Yes, honey, I'm sleeping. I'm eating. Mom is being Mom." He knew Paula would know what that meant: meatloaf, mashed potatoes, mac and cheese, chicken and dumplings. "So I'm also walking a lot. Good thing Mom has a spare parka."

"Is there a place where you can take class?" They usually did a version of morning class on the pool deck now. Before moving in together, they'd each gone to a local studio. The older they got, the more essential it was.

"Not one I can get to and get back in time to go over to the medical center. I'm using the basement for that. Stretching a lot. What about you?"

"I'm being a lazy-ass." She smiled, hearing him laugh. "I told Jennifer she and Adam should come out with Hannah this summer. Rent an apartment and learn tango. She and Hannah are working on him. Oliver is apparently going to be happily examining fish guts on a boat in Maine."

"He's still set on marine biology, huh. That's a good idea. Do you think Bill would come too?"

"Huh." That was an interesting thought. "I don't know. I'll ping him and see. No idea what the ex was planning to do with Alex this summer." Paula was inspired. "Hey, maybe you should ask Beth."

"That's … wow, maybe I should."

"Maybe they would get along, Bill and Beth. I mean, she's almost as good-looking as you." *Pause for laugh*, she thought, smiling. *God, I love this man.* "But it's getting late for you. I love you. Go to bed. Dream of me."

"I love you too, and I always do."

Paula got to the airport early and had to drive around the loop a couple of times before her phone finally pinged to let her know Mike had made it out of baggage claim. *Finally*, she thought. *Fucking LAX.* Laughing at herself, she swung around the loop one more time and pulled up to the curb where she saw him waiting. She set the hazard lights, set the parking brake, and unlocked the car, but before he could reach for the hatch she was out of the car herself and hugging him.

He was laughing. "Did you miss me?"

"SO MUCH." She kissed him, hugged him again, then stood back so he could load his bag into the car. "That was the longest week of my life. Let's not do that again."

Bag stowed, Mike hugged her one more time, then held her face between his hands to kiss her. "I really missed you, too. I'll show you how much when we get home."

"You look so much better," she said, studying him, ignoring the impatient drivers who wanted her spot. His eyes were clear and unshadowed. "You really have been sleeping."

He glanced behind them. "We should go. You drive." They got into the car and Paula nudged her way out into the stream of traffic. "I've been better since last Saturday, actually. Maybe the thing with Julia helped me, too."

"How is she?"

"She's been sleeping. She says she eats. Her mom is going to need to go into a facility, but her dad is okay with it. It's near where they live." He paused for a moment. Paula glanced over to catch his eye. He sighed. "I kind of think Julia's not coming back to L.A. Not to stay, anyway."

"Wow, really?"

"She said she's afraid if she's here, she's going to fall back into something with Roger. And obviously they still kind of love each other, but she said it's time to think about her third act. So ... I asked if she'd consider loaning us her house for the summer. For Jen and the others."

"That's a *great* idea. I mean, if she's really not going to be here."

"She jumped right on it. I guess Grace is up for another summer program overseas. With Miguel working in San Francisco now, there wouldn't have been anybody around to keep an eye on things."

"I forgot they were still hooked in with Miguel. He's a nice kid."

"I think Julia kind of wishes he wasn't gay." He smiled, waiting for Paula to stop laughing. "She's not sure what's going on with Grace's love life."

"Grace is in career mode. She's a nice kid, too."

"Anyway, Julia will be in touch about the house. Did you hear from Bill? Beth is all for it. She hasn't had a vacation forever either. Mom told her, go, for God's sake."

"Bill's totally in, too. He'll have Alex this summer and Alex has never been to L.A., so they're both pretty excited. I'll bet when we tell Jen about the house, she'll push Adam off the fence."

Mike was still smiling, looking out the window, not even minding the traffic, except that it was taking so long to get home where he could take his wife to bed. He turned his head and gazed at her. "I realized I think of L.A. as home now."

"That's good, because you know I love you, but I am not moving to Minneapolis. I saw those weather reports. I know it's winter there, but Jesus wept." She listened to Mike laugh again and thought, *we're gonna be okay*.

CHAPTER 26

March 2017

Julia got in touch a few days later to confirm about the house. Paula sent the information to Jen, Bill, and Beth; within ten days the L.A. arrangements for the summer plan were set. With that handled, Paula turned her attention to the upcoming spring showcases at Chrome. She'd volunteered to help Alison manage the process, since she and Mike didn't currently have a dance project of their own. That went off the rails when Alison called to ask if they could revive their big piece set to 'No Hay Imposibles,' in the expectation of needing some pro-quality filler in at least one of the showcases.

"Who else have you asked?" Paula said, stalling for a minute. Out of habit, she looked at their whiteboard calendar, which was oddly (for them) barren. *We do need to do something*, she thought. *I'm getting lazy.* They hadn't done any serious dancing together for nearly a month, which now seemed like an eternity.

"Three others. I figure if we have two pro numbers in each showcase it will make up for a multitude of sins. Mary said she can work up 'Velvet Green.' Mateo said he could do 'La Yumba,' and Sam's going to brush up 'The Chairman's Waltz.' Which I'm really thrilled about, that was absolutely my favorite piece from last summer's show."

"Have you made up your mind about this year's pro show?"

"Give me a doggoned minute."

Paula made a sound that meant 'yeah, well.' "Okay, but it's March already, so, you know."

"Naggity nag. By next week, I promise. So can you do it?"

"Let me check with Mike. Probably. Hang on." Paula muted the call, then glanced over at Mike; he was looking at her, alerted by hearing his name. "Do you think we can get the Chayanne thing back in shape by April?" He raised his eyebrows and shrugged, which usually meant 'why not.' Paula rolled her eyes. "Okay, fine, keep eating. And sleeping. And going to the gym, because oh my God all those tricks." She un-muted the phone and told Alison, "It's a go."

"Awesome. I'll be in touch."

After they disconnected, Paula looked at Mike again. He was still watching her. She wanted to say 'are you sure,' but didn't. He smiled a little. "Let's go down to the gym."

The week before, Mike had met up with Rory, Ann, and Bonnie, to take his first look at 'Human Nature.' They had the basic shape of things, but wanted to add some supported elements once they got him worked in. He hadn't danced with any of them on stage before, so the first rehearsal was devoted to getting used to each other.

The next time they met, Rory wanted to experiment with some lifts. All three women were shorter than Paula, Rory by six inches, which meant his mental geometry for various moves had to be adjusted. The first time he took Rory all the way up she squeaked. The other women mercilessly laughed.

"He's so fucking tall!" she said from on high. "Shut up!"

"I'm only six one," he said, setting her down, just barely managing not to laugh out loud. "Only a foot taller than you."

284

"Yeah, only, for fuck's sake. And you had me like two feet over your head. Holy crap. What was I thinking."

"Imagine if I was Red," who was two inches taller than Mike and had a correspondingly longer reach.

"Never. Fucking never. I've lost my mind. Am I not heavier than Paula?" she demanded. "Because goddamn."

"I'm sorry to break it to you," he said, trying to look apologetic. "You're not heavier than Paula. She's taller than you. Bone weighs something." He'd actually found Rory easier to lift because she was more compact, though he'd never mention that to Paula.

"Aaaaauugh whatever. Okay, let's do it again."

At the end of the session, after Ann and Bonnie left, Mike saw Rory texting someone, then laughing. "What," he said, smiling. She handed him the phone. She'd written to Dana: **Apparently I am not heavier than Paula**

Dana had written back *HAVE I NOT BEEN TELLING YOU THIS FOR FUCKING EVER*

Mike bit his lip. Rory shrugged. "I'm, like, round, you know?"

"You're rounded," he allowed. "It's not actually a bad thing." When he got home he told Paula about it.

She made a guilty face. "I'm a little heavier than I should be. Really got lazy. And there was booze."

"There was booze," Mike agreed. "It was medicinal. You'll be fit again in no time now that we're working on that monster of a routine."

"Why did we put everything in it, again? I mean, *everything*?"

"Because we could," he said, smiling.

"Oh yeah. Hmmm."

"Hmmm, what?"

"How likely is it that I could learn to actually do the 540? I mean, realistically?"

Mike glanced over; she was serious. "Vicky got it for 'The Great Wave.' And she hasn't been dancing all her life. But she works out like a beast." He considered her for a moment. "You know *how* to do it. You need more leg power for the elevation, plus more core strength, because if you try to whip that leg over with just the thigh, you're going to tear it. If you want to do it, you'd better change your workout. Dancing alone won't get you there."

"I probably need to eat better, too, huh." He nodded and she sighed. "Why do I have to get ambitious when I'm pushing forty?"

"You're only thirty-seven. Same as Vicky. If you get it now and keep up with the work, you should be able to do it for at least ten years. Maybe fifteen. Imagine what sick routines we could do."

"Is that the goal?" she said, moving in for a hug. "Sick routines?"

"We're already doing stuff they told us we couldn't," he reminded her. "Every time we get on stage I feel like 'Rock Star' all over again."

"Speaking of monsters." She kissed him. "But such a beautiful monster."

He picked her up. "Ooof."

"Shut up!" He laughed as he carried her down the hall.

It wasn't all fun and games. The community was still very aware of the blank space where Julia and

286

Ray used to be. Elena had squeezed out some time to help manage the March edition of Mating Dance, and said she could help in the fall unless things went sideways with her competition schedule. Dmitri had recruited a new Latin specialist to take over Julia's staff position. Everyone was still avoiding the street side of the studio. Dmitri didn't even put the café table and chairs outside, as he usually did in the spring. The windows had been replaced and the wall had been repaired, but all of them *knew*.

Meanwhile, Paula couldn't seem to stop monitoring Mike, which started to get on his nerves, which made him not want to admit that he was still having occasional flashbacks and nightmares. Neither of them mentioned the fact that he was also still the primary driver.

She was aware of the nightmares, of course. She'd put herself on a strict no-alcohol regime and consequently wasn't sleeping as well. It wasn't quite the insomniac hell of her past, but she was grateful for the extra hours of gym and practice, because she was definitely back to needing to wear herself out.

The first week of April, after an exhausting rehearsal at the Hollywood studio, having missed the 540 yet again for no obvious physical reason, she flopped down on the floor next to Mike, rubbing her sore leg. "We're not quite all right yet, are we."

After a long minute, he said, "No."

"I'm sorry I keep nagging you."

"It's okay."

"No, it isn't, it's bugging you, and I'm pretty sure it's not even helping. What can I do instead? Is there anything? Or do I need to back off?" *And do God knows what*, she thought.

"I talked to Dr. Nelson again," he said, surprising her. "I asked about that. She said it would be better if there's something we can do together, something that isn't purely physical, something that's done with the intention of dealing with everything. If not actually going to a counselor ... she asked if we'd ever tried meditation."

"Huh." Paula thought about it for a minute. "I mean, no, personally, never. You?"

"No. It might be worth a try, though."

"Do we need to go somewhere, or could we do it at home?"

"She said if we want to try, she can give us some links to internet sites that can get us started. At home." He was watching her, wishing he wasn't causing her anxiety, unaware that his face told that story.

"Mike." She scooted over and wrapped around him, tucking herself under his arm, her own arms and legs bracketing his body, fitting her head into the curve of his neck. "Quit thinking you have to do something about my issues. My issues are so unimportant right now."

He kissed her forehead, wrapping his free hand around her wrist. "They're important."

"Not as important as getting you right. If you're off, I'm fucked. And not in a good way." He held her close. After a second she added, "I will do anything. So if you think maybe meditation could help, let's try it."

"Okay."

"And I'm not trying that fucking jump again until I know you're okay, because honestly I think what's keeping me from finishing it is nothing more than being afraid for you. It's like I'm afraid that extra half a turn will land me somewhere I can't get back to you."

He wasn't prepared for that. Tears in his eyes, he turned to her and buried his face in her hair. "I love you so much."

"I love you too. Let's go home. Fuck this fucking routine, we don't even know if we need to do it this month. Goddamned Alison." She held him tight for a minute more, as he started to laugh.

When they got home, Paula sent a slightly annoyed text to Alison and got a prompt reply to the effect that the April showcase schedule was set. Sam and Mary would be dancing in the pro slots. A first-look at the summer pro show could happen the following Sunday.

Thanks, Paula wrote back. All good to know. Still some issues here at home and trying to cope

I'm sorry, wrote Alison. **Keep forgetting :-(**

Our problem shouldn't be yours. Let me know if you need me, otherwise we'll be working on our shit

Good luck sweetie

See you at the show

"We're off the hook," Paula told Mike. "Till next month. So let's see if we can fix our heads. How's it going with Rory?"

"She's such a nut. You remember that Hindi Diamonds extravaganza in 'Moulin Rouge?' She's stealing from that now. Ann and Bonnie can't stop laughing. We're going to have to strip out like half of the stuff that's in at this point, or it's not going to read for the audience at all." He was smiling.

"You're having fun though. That's good."

"Yeah, it's fun."

As usual, having an issue out in the open and having a plan helped them both. Paula wasn't sure she was doing meditation right, but tried to follow Dr. Nelson's instructions. After a few nights of regular practice, she started to be surprised by what was bubbling up. At the end of the week, they went to the pro-show meeting. Alison's concept this time was a complete 180 from the previous year. It was an homage to the Miami City Ballet's 'Neighborhood Ballroom' piece by Edward Villella. There would be four set pieces based on different ballroom dance styles, with jazz, contemporary, and hip-hop. It was Alison's first time using urban dance; she was bringing in a new collaborator named Lucas Gutierrez to work with her and Dmitri. A dance friend of Ray's, Lucas had auditioned for 'The Great Wave' and ended up joining the troupe.

Once everyone was clear on the concept, they drafted a notice for an open audition at Chrome the following Sunday morning. Alison posted it in the afternoon. She sent a text to Paula and Mike later saying **fyi I'd really like to feature you in this show. Let me know soonest. We're starting group choreography now and rehearsals begin after the May showcase**

Mike and Paula discussed it, looking at their calendar. 'Human Nature' was well underway; with no project for July, they had plenty of bandwidth. Paula wrote back thanks babe we'd love to.

They didn't talk about whether they felt they were making progress until they'd been practicing meditation for about three weeks. Paula hadn't actually begun sleeping better, but her sleeplessness had been less troubling. She concentrated on her breath, noticing the little worry fish that nibbled at her brain and sending them off again. Toward the end of the third week she realized that Mike was looking more rested, more relaxed, and less wary. Maybe this shit was letting go of him. Maybe it was time to talk. She brought it up after dinner that Friday.

"So," she said. "I think the meditation is helping."

"Are you sleeping better?"

"Not really but it doesn't bother me as much. I use the time to think about shit. More meditation, I guess. Catch and release."

He smiled. "That's a good way to put it. You're getting stronger. In the gym."

"Yeah. You look better. You look ... post 'Rock Star' better." He didn't say anything; she thought he was deciding what to say. She added, "I realized I was feeling guilty."

"*You* were feeling guilty?"

She noticed the emphasis. "About being glad you were alive. Like I shouldn't hold all three feelings at the same time. Being sad about Ray, sorry for Julia, happy about you. But ... I guess it's okay to feel all of that. Isn't it?"

He blew out a long, slow breath and relaxed against the back of the couch. "Yeah, it is. I had the same thing." He stretched his arm out and she rolled into it, resting her head on his shoulder. He kissed her forehead. "I tried catch and release with the flashbacks."

"Does it help?"

"It really does. Just, oh there you are again, done with you, bye now." He shook his head, smiling a little. "It sounds so simple. The thought or the image rolls in, I breathe with it and let it go. It's a great tool."

"Who knew." They sat quietly for a few minutes. "I'm going to keep up with it too. Maybe eventually I'll be able to shut down sometime before two in the morning."

"Hope so." After another minute he said, "You want to come to the studio tomorrow and see where we are with 'Human Nature'?"

"Yeah, sure. Then maybe next time we work Chayanne, I'll try that stupid jump again."

He gave her a squeeze. "Let's watch 'The Great Wave' tonight. There's that piece we were all in, with the 540 relay. Imagine yourself doing it."

"I was *so pissed*," she said. "Me and Lucas and Red there on the sidelines with our thumbs up our asses."

"Red was pissed too. He said, quote, I'm so jealous of all you whippety fuckers, but my leg would snap right off. Mary said, never mind darling, I need both your legs." He imitated Mary's rich English-accented voice quite well.

"On the flip side, of course, he could bench-press the both of us, if we were in a small enough box."

The mental image almost made Mike laugh. "For sure. Let's get that disc."

Paula patted his leg and went to find it. The title piece for 'The Great Wave' was actually the finale. Alison had built the choreography with a team including Sam, Mateo, Danny, Kate, Mary, and Red. It incorporated synchronized kata phrases with the whole cast, punctuated by traveling passes full of martial-arts and dance tricks by individuals or smaller groups, backed by Yoshi's projections. The 540 relay ultimately included Sam, Mateo, Danny, Kate, Mary, Mike, Ray, and Vicky. The number was already one of the most-viewed videos ever posted by the Underground Cabaret community. Comments were dominated by versions of 'look at those women throwing that thing!! #BeastMode' and 'where the hell is MY Underground Cabaret.'

When the recording finished playing, Paula said, "I'm so glad we did that show. And I'm so glad Ray was in it with us." She leaned in to Mike again. For maybe the first time since the crash, thinking of Ray didn't make her feel slightly sick.

"Me too," said Mike. "I'm glad we got to know him." He pulled her onto his lap and kissed her, slow and deep and deliberate. Paula squirmed around to face him. "We have too many clothes on," he said after a while, smiling against her throat.

"As usual." She stood up, pulling him up off the couch. He came up faster than she expected and she had to step back, surprised. "Was that me?"

"I told you you were getting stronger. You're gonna be a beast for sure." She gave him a dubious look. "Okay, I helped. Give yourself a break, it's only been a few weeks. Besides," he said, scooping her up, "I'm supposed to be the monster here." She giggled all the way down the hall to the bedroom.

CHAPTER 27

By dress rehearsal for the May showcase, Paula was ready to commit to the 540. They were both feeling strong and focused. Their number hadn't been seen in a live show before, so they were also excited to perform it for an audience. Alison had slotted them in to close the show, with Mateo closing Act One.

After they got to Chrome, while they were warming up, Mike glanced over at Paula. She wore the same determined expression she'd had before her own performance of 'Rock Star,' two and a half years before. He'd been about to ask what she wanted him to do if the jump failed, but decided to keep his mouth shut. She'd landed it at the last three rehearsals; he thought it would be better to go onstage assuming it would work again.

They watched the whole first half, moderately impressed with most of the students, both half in love with Mateo by the time he finished his reworked 'La Yumba' solo. "It's totally unfair how good-looking he is," muttered Paula.

Mike nudged her. "He talked Sam into getting married."

She did a double take. "How did I not hear about this?!"

"I only heard today. Rory's going to do it for them. They'll send around an email with the details, everybody's invited."

"Like ours." Paula took a moment to appreciate that little miracle again. "When do you think Dana will finally get Rory to say yes?"

"Maybe soon. Everybody's still shaken up about Ray, it makes you think … why wait." He leaned against her for a minute. "Let's get backstage and hit the barre for a while."

"Yeah, okay."

They stayed in the greenroom for the first few numbers of the second act, then went to the wing area to wait their turn. Mike was in new dance jeans with the same tie-dyed lavender tank he'd worn for their original performance video. Paula was in her same matching lavender dress. This time she'd re-colored her hair; the ends were silver and purple. Mike admired the new muscle definition in her arms and shoulders as she bounced a little, stretching her sides. Then the dancer before them finished. She came offstage, breathing hard and shaking her head. "It was good," he told her. "Well done."

She flashed him a smile with a little shrug. "As good as it's gonna get, anyway. Looking forward to seeing you!" she added, as if she knew about them. Mike smiled, collected Paula, and went onstage.

"Nothing is impossible," Paula said under her breath, as if reminding herself. He squeezed her hand and they went to their starting positions to wait for the music.

It was a long routine, with big moments punctuating it throughout. Mike knew that Paula was getting higher this time than before. He had to gauge his own timing carefully. His body knew the shapes and the rhythm; it was a matter of initiating at the ideal fraction of a second. Halfway through, they had a pass with three parallel, synchronized tricks that came off perfectly. He smiled at the audible reaction from the watching dancers. When he caught a glimpse of Paula's face she was smiling too. A minute later came the pass with her 540. She launched, she rotated in the air, and then that leg came over and she landed it. He was right there to catch her waist and take her into a spinning carry. She was grinning down at him and he was laughing. When they were finished, the music faded out. She broke away from their closing embrace to yell "YES!!," jumping up and down, punching the air. Everyone out in the house was applauding, many of them (those who knew she'd struggled with the big trick) cheering, most of the others laughing along with her vindicated glee.

"And that's kicking your ass," said Mike, quoting from 'Charlie's Angels.' They high-fived and left the stage.

Alison sent them a copy of the video later, including everything up to their exit from the stage. Paula didn't lose a minute posting it, under the title 'Thirty-Seven.' Jennifer and Bill both sent congratulations within the hour, amid a flood of other reactions.

Monday morning at work, Paula sneaked onto Facebook and checked her feed again. A few minutes later she sent a text to Mike: You're not going to believe this. Dad posted about the video. First time ever. WTAF

What did he say?

Said 'Congratulations you were right we were wrong' with this little shrug emoji

LOL

Inorite

Did you reply?

Yeah I said 'I love you too Dad, say Hi to Mom for me' and signed off

Such a grown-up

Inorite

LOL XOX

Once the May showcase wrapped, all hands were on deck to finish 'Human Nature.' Paula also had to organize the incoming visitors. Jen and Hannah were coming out for a full six weeks, with Adam planning on four; Bill would be in town for three, but his son Alex was going to stay with Jen and Hannah for another three weeks. Mike's sister Beth was also planning on being in town for a month. All of them would be there for the Underground Cabaret's June show. Paula went over to Julia's house to meet with Grace, the day before Sam and Mateo's wedding, to make sure they were on the same page about the visitors.

"Hey Paula," said Grace when she opened the door. "How've you been?"

"Good," said Paula. Grace offered a hug, which was welcome. "Mike had to do some more therapy and we're both doing meditation. How about you?"

"Same. I talked to a counselor on campus."

"We get a note from your mom once in a while. What do you hear?"

"Looks like Grandma can move to the assisted-living facility in October, earlier than they thought. Mom still hasn't decided what she wants to do. Granddad likes having her there. She might stay." Grace looked like she wasn't sure how she felt about this. "She's been doing some teaching."

"Ballroom?"

"No, actually; acting." They'd moved through to the kitchen. Grace offered Paula a cup of tea. "Unless you have to get back to something."

"I'm free for the day. Mike's got a rehearsal this afternoon and the word was that four opinions was quite enough, thank you."

Grace made an amused sound as she put the teakettle on. "I wish I was going to be here for that."

"We'll send you the video. So what do we need to know about the house?"

"There's a full bottle of propane for the grill, eat and drink anything you find, security company number is by the alarm panel, and the panel code is right here." She opened a cabinet door to show Paula. "Here's two full sets of keys. Your family will need to coordinate those."

"Yeah, there's a potential for mayhem."

"And they really need to pay attention to the parking signs."

"That's for sure." Paula blew out a breath. "Is there anything we can do for you?"

Grace looked away for a moment. "Not really. I still miss Ray. I didn't even realize how important he was to me, you know? How much of a friend."

"We miss him too."

"Well." They looked at each other. "At least we had him for a little while."

"That's what we're telling ourselves." They hugged again, then went to sit in the garden room and talk about Japan for a while. Grace was leaving in a few days for a work/study program at Fukushima. As they were taking their tea things back to the kitchen, Paula said, "You know, your mom is really curious about your love life."

Grace looked embarrassed. "Oh shit, yeah. I've been, um. I had this thing with someone at school that

I didn't want to tell her about. Not a professor, but a TA. That went on for a little longer than it should have, but I knew from the start it wasn't going anywhere, so I didn't want to admit it."

"You're allowed to have flings, you know."

"I know. I think I was feeling … almost ashamed of myself? For wasting time on somebody I knew I didn't love."

"You're allowed to fool around with people you don't love. It's okay to be horny sometimes."

Grace half-laughed, half-shrugged. "Eh. It was a waste of time. I won't do that again."

"Well, maybe you'll meet somebody perfect in Japan." Paula studied her for a minute. Grace was twenty-three now. "Or maybe you've already met somebody perfect."

If so, Grace wasn't admitting that either. "Tell her I'm not doing anything stupid. Well, not *too* stupid, anyway."

"Okay. Stay in touch while you're gone, okay?"

"I will."

Paula had decided to give herself a free pass on alcohol for Sam and Mateo's wedding. Mike didn't particularly want to stay sober either, so they Ubered over to West Hollywood the next day. The backyard at Rory and Dana's was a near-perfect re-creation of their own wedding. Vince's mom had joined forces with Mateo's sister to set everything up.

Sam was hanging around outside as guests arrived, wearing the ocean-blue Japanese haori and loose black trousers he'd worn for the opening number of 'The Great Wave.' Mike went up and shook his hand. "Where's the other groom?"

"He's inside doing God knows what." Sam was looking completely non-nervous. "How did you feel when you did this?"

Mike smiled. "I was ready for it. I couldn't wait."

"Yeah. Ever since I said okay, we'll do it, it's been like, why didn't we do it before. We should have done this already. It's been five years."

"That's a long time."

"And I've loved him for every minute of it," Sam said. "Where did Paula go?"

"I guess she went inside. She's really happy for you. And so am I."

"You ready for that other thing?"

"Oh yeah," Mike said, laughing. "I've been practicing for weeks." He rolled his neck and shoulders. "Let's hope she doesn't put up a fight."

The backyard got crowded as more people arrived. Music was playing; people started dancing, because they could. Mateo and Sam's co-workers showed up, along with most of Mateo's family from Pomona and Sam's foster parents from Berkeley. According to the email, the ceremony was supposed to be at five. At a quarter till, there was still no sign of Mateo. Rory came out of the cottage looking like she had a big fat secret. She spoke to Sam and he laughed so hard he had to sit down. A few minutes later, Paula came out and went to find Mike.

"Is Andy set up?" she asked, looking around.

"Yeah, he's over there." Mike pointed across the yard. Andy was roaming, taking what he called 'coverage.' Somehow he always managed to get the essential shots, the ones that told the whole

300

story. Mike was sure he'd gotten a picture of Sam laughing his ass off. "What's going on, anyway?"

"Not mine to tell," said Paula, looking mysterious. "You'll see in a minute." Then Dana stepped out of the cottage and signaled to Danny, who was running music as usual. He put on his remix of 'Brush on Silk,' which had been Mateo's solo from 'The Great Wave,' and Mateo came out of the cottage. He was in full kimono, complete with wig and makeup, and looked … *gorgeous*, thought Mike. He shook his head, smiling, at the pure theatre of it. Kenji and Kris had come out behind Mateo. There were oohs and aahs from the guests as Mateo walked up to Sam and Rory, his face perfectly still and perfectly beautiful. When he got to Sam he stopped and bowed. Sam bowed back to him and they both turned to Rory, who started the ceremony.

As soon as she said, "Somebody'd better kiss somebody," Sam took Mateo's face between his hands and kissed him.

Then he said, "Hold that thought, baby," turned and picked up Rory. Mateo started to laugh.

"Hey!" Rory clutched Sam's neck, looking astonished. "What's going on, this wasn't part of the program!"

"That's what *you* think," said Sam, handing her to Mike.

"What the … heck?!"

Mike was laughing. Dana came to the dance floor and said, "They're not going to put you down until you agree to marry me."

"Dana! God damn it!"

Everyone was laughing, including Rory, but Mike didn't put her down. He turned around till he saw

301

Red, took her over there, and made the transfer. Red slung her over his shoulder. "I could do this all day," he said, patting her ass, and went to get a glass of champagne.

"Are you all insane? This is an outrage! I demand a recount! And by the way it's a long fucking way down!" Rory stopped ranting to catch her breath. Someone put a glass in her dangling hand, the one not currently smacking Red's oblivious back. "I cannot drink in this position," she said, trying to sound cold and completely failing.

"Then say you'll marry her," Red said reasonably. "Otherwise you could be in for a long thirsty night."

"Jesus! I've never seen such a heinous conspiracy! It's the fucking Ides of March out here!"

The guests had, by now, entirely given up pretending anything else was happening. Some were helping Mateo get his wig and kimono off, but most were simply drinking and giggling, watching to see how long this nonsense would go on.

Not that much longer, as it turned out. "Okay okay alright already! I give! I will marry Dana! Put me the fuck down!" Red located Dana, took Rory over there, and set her down. She managed not to spill her champagne. "Are you sure about this?" she demanded.

"Rory, you knucklehead, I've been sure for ten years. Shut up and kiss me," said Dana. Andy, of course, got the picture.

Paula was still giggling when Mike found her again. She'd landed in a group of other women, mostly talking about the magical effect of the kimono. "Need some more champagne, honey?" he asked.

302

"God, no," she said. "It's gone straight to my head. You look beautiful."

"Thanks." He leaned in to kiss her, stifling a laugh. *You're cute when you're buzzed.* "They're going to do their wedding dance in a minute."

"Oh okay." He helped her up and they went to find a good vantage point. Sam had changed into black jeans and a tuxedo-print tee shirt, which should have looked ridiculous, but didn't because Mateo was in white jeans and a white lace tee shirt and they both looked adorable. Rory and Dana were nowhere to be seen, so Danny took control of clearing the dance floor, then started their music. It was The Jive Aces' 'Bring Me Sunshine.'

"Hey, that was *our* wedding dance," said Vince, who'd fetched up beside Mike. "That's so shady." Mike huffed out a laugh. He didn't know the song, but he could see why it was getting used again; the lyrics were perfect. It went from a slow stroll to a fast lindy hop, and Sam was winging it, but he and Mateo were clearly having a ball. Mike wrapped his arms around Paula. He had a moment, thinking, *I wish Ray and Julia were here*, but he took a breath and let it go.

CHAPTER 28

A few weeks later at the dress rehearsal for 'Cosmic,' Rory marched up to Mike and said, "We have a problem."

"With the number?"

"No, it's great. Dana wants to get married."

"Yes, I noticed."

"Quit laughing. Well, since she went to all that trouble getting you he-men to toss me around, it's apparently my job to set up the thing. And I don't have a clue."

"You've put on a bunch of weddings."

"Eh," she said. "Guerrilla weddings, backyard weddings. She's been after me to do this for years, I want to give her a whole church thing."

"You should talk to Dmitri. His church does rainbow weddings."

Rory actually smacked her forehead. "Why did I not think of that?!"

"Maybe a little too much time upside down," he suggested, trying not to laugh again.

"Shut up. I have to go get into costume." She stomped off backstage. Mike went looking for Dmitri, who, to pretty much everyone's surprise, was closing the show. He'd sent Michelle a video of his concept, set to 'Within You Without You,' and she had instantly agreed to dance it with him.

Mike found Dmitri onstage behind the curtain, stretching. "Hi Dmitri. Rory wants to set up a certain long-overdue wedding. Can you get her information about your church?"

"Ah. I will send it. Your sister is here tonight."

"She's supervising the kids, since they can't come to the real show. The whole gang *wanted* to come, but that would have been excessive. They'll have to wait."

"They are enjoying the lessons?"

"Hannah and Jen are obsessed. Adam and Bill are hanging in there. Beth and Alex are ... enjoying Los Angeles."

Dmitri looked like he wanted to laugh. "They are all doing well."

"They're having fun. Looking forward to seeing your piece."

They shook hands and parted. Mike went to the greenroom to check on his group and do his makeup. Rory, Ann, and Bonnie were all wearing a belly-dance costume of full sheer harem pants with cropped tops in bright jewel colors. Rory had let her hair grow out into a three-inch Mohawk; Ann and Bonnie wore theirs in twists with the ends fanned out. All three had elaborate makeup, big witchy eyes with a painted mehndi mask across the lower face. It was like a combination of Dia de los Muertos, Kabuki theater, and Hindu temple art.

Mike was wearing black leggings and a sleeveless black tee, having gently but firmly rejected a request, which may or may not have been serious, to do the dance in the nude. Rory had asked him to do the same sort of facial makeup the women were wearing. It took him about twenty minutes, even with the mehndi stencil. "I used to be faster," he said, glancing at the clock as he started on his eyes. "Out of practice."

"No worries," said Rory. "They haven't even started yet."

"Dmitri's going to send you some stuff about the church."

"Thanks." She was fidgeting.

He glanced at her. "Are you nervous?"

"Sorta. Little bit. Don't really know why," she confessed. "We've been working on this damn thing forever and I know it's together."

"It's more complex than your other things."

"Yeah."

"It's a good piece, Rory," he said. "You'll see."

"Yeah." She fidgeted some more. "I want to say thanks."

"For what?" Mike set down the makeup brush and met her eyes in the mirror.

"For making me see that I could do this again. That I could still do it. That I didn't have to settle for, you know, being the best stripper in L.A."

"Did you think you were settling?"

"Not at first. It was fun. But once the Cabaret evolved and people started bringing the art, well. You know."

"Yeah, I know." He was about to say something else, but she must have read his mind.

"Don't you dare say something mushy. This makeup is not waterproof."

He stifled a laugh and picked up the brush again. "Right." Before he touched the brush to his skin she reached out and tugged his hair, then patted his shoulder, then turned away to scoop up Ann and Bonnie and take them out to the stage. After finishing his makeup, Mike joined them for a mark-through of the routine. Then they all went out to the house to

306

watch the first act and wait their turn to open the second.

His sister leaned over when he sat down beside her. "That makeup is *sick*. Was that Rory's idea?"

"The whole thing was Rory's idea. The rest of us have been contributing, but she's got some pent-up creativity so we're just going with it, for the most part. I've been editing. And lifting."

"You are really buff. This is so different from the stuff you're doing with Paula, huh."

"Yeah." He glanced over at Beth and she flinched back a little. "What's the matter?"

"You really don't even look like you. A little scary. God, don't smile, that's even worse." Mike turned away so he could laugh without freaking her out. Hannah and Alex were a few feet away at another table, looking at him. He made a Maori haka face and they both laughed. A few minutes later, Vicky started running the rehearsal.

Alison's new collaborator Lucas was opening the show with a hip-hop number set to 'God,' by Tori Amos. It was his first time with the Cabaret since they'd all gotten acquainted the previous summer. The first half finished up with a few technical notes from Vicky and short comments from Michelle, who'd been watching from the house. Mike went behind the curtain with Rory and the others for a final warmup before the Act Two run-through started.

Their 'Human Nature' number used a set piece, a forty-by-forty-inch plywood box with open front and back. All four dancers entered through the box, Mike coming in last and staying down on the floor. His character for the dance was, according to Rory, a Leviathan lizard of doom. At first Mike hadn't been entirely sure what that meant, but as they'd developed the piece it had become clear. His role was to give the women various kinds of support for their moves, but he never danced with them in unison. He was in and out of the box throughout the first half, providing a shoulder, an arm, a leg, or his back, lurking animalistically in between his interactions with the women. In the second half of the song, he came off the floor to give them carries, assists, or lifts.

Rory, Ann and Bonnie were all cheerful goddesses of destruction. They were funny, but in a way that said 'wow, people, you are really fucking things up; we're going to annihilate you and start over.' The iconic Madonna track hadn't been edited at all. They all thought it was perfect as it stood. As it started to fade out, the women exited backward through the box. Then Mike vaulted onto the top of the box, staying low like a lizard with one leg dangling like a tail, glaring at the audience before the stage went black. During the blackout, he and Vicky quickly got the box offstage so the next number could enter. He smiled at her, listening to applause from the other dancers. She murmured, "Eww, don't do that, that's so creepy."

"So how did it look?" he asked quietly once they were in the wing area.

"Pretty bitchin' from this side. I can't wait to see the video. But yeah, seriously creepy. That mask thing. Eww."

He turned away again and stifled a laugh. "I'll go get this off. Nobody wants to look at me, I'm developing a complex." She shrugged, like *what did you expect*. Mike rolled his eyes and went back to the greenroom to get cleaned up and changed. He gave half his attention to the monitor, wanting to get back

308

out to the house to see Dmitri and Michelle's number. Once the worst of the makeup was off, he went on out and took a seat near Beth again. Paula was there now too, with the teenagers. She held up a hand for a fist bump, then gave him a thumbs-up, as did Hannah and Alex. He held her hand while they watched the closing number.

"God, it's good to see them dance again," Paula said, applauding, when it was over.

"It really is. What were you and Alison talking about before Rory caught me?"

"Oh, stuff for the pro show. Now that we're in rehearsals it's time to start editing. What did you think of Lucas' thing?"

"I liked it. Not your father's hip-hop."

"Yeah, that's what I thought. He and Ray were kind of close, huh."

"Lucas had a lot going on last year, too. It was a good piece to work all that out. What did you think of our makeup?"

"Creepy as fuck!" Hannah and Alex pretended to be shocked. "Sorry, kids. Well, wait till you see it for yourself. But seriously, it completely changed the number. Your animal-style stuff, with those freaky lifts Rory and the girls came up with, kind of came across more circus without it."

"Not circus any more?"

"Not at all. It was still cool before, but it's like hello Hiroshima now. It's great you decided to do the routine. Would've been very different without you."

"Maybe it's Rory's 'Rock Star.' And as I recall, I was drafted." He was smiling. Paula reached over to wipe away a line of makeup he'd missed, thinking, *you weren't about to say No*, then turned his face toward her so she could kiss him.

"I did kind of volunteer you for it. Are they ever going to do notes? Oh, okay, here comes Vicky." There was a short recap of Act Two before, according to Cabaret dress-rehearsal tradition, pizzas were delivered. With a number of new performers, the post-notes gathering lasted longer than usual. Eventually Mike and Paula got themselves and Beth and the kids together and returned to Julia's house. The others all wanted to know about the dress rehearsal, but since they were going to see the show for real very soon, Mike and Paula bailed as soon as they could.

"These guys will tell you all about it. More lessons in a couple of days," Paula reminded them. "Practice! Use that great studio space! I'd be in it every day if we lived here. We'll see you soon. Call if you need anything."

"We're good," Jen assured her. "Take Mike home, he looks tired." She winked.

"Yes ma'am." Paula gave a round of hugs and they eventually made it out to the car.

"What was that wink about?" said Mike, sliding into the driver's seat.

"He looks tired is code for you look like you want to jump his bones."

"When did she come up with that?"

"I don't remember. Probably the day after the wedding." She glanced over at him, smiling, as he made the turn onto Santa Monica Boulevard. *I do want to jump your bones.*

"And is it accurate?"

"Always." She considered him. "You don't actually look tired. You still look kind of jazzed."

"It was a jazzy day."

"How many times did you have to practice that vault?"

"You don't want to know. It took me way too long to figure out I needed to add the roll, so the trailing leg wouldn't keep banging into the side."

"That was a hell of a bruise."

"Still is." She put her hand on his thigh, sliding it down to his knee. He glanced over at her. "Want to put some arnica on it for me later?"

"I'd be delighted. Can I rub anything else for you?" She slid her hand back up. "Hmm, I guess so. Drive faster."

He caught her hand and lifted it away, laughing.

All the visitors except the teenagers went to the second night of 'Cosmic,' and stayed for the after party. The couples were sitting together. Instead of spacing themselves between the others, Bill and Beth ended up sitting next to each other. Mike glanced at Paula, who had also noticed. "What are Hannah and Alex doing tonight?" Mike asked when they all had drinks in hand.

Jen said, "They walked over to Century City for dinner and a movie. Hannah told us not to hurry back." Bill raised his eyebrows inquiringly. "She and Alex are bonding."

Paula said, "That's good. Do the boys get along?"

"Oh sure," said Adam. "They all spent some time together last summer before Fabienne took Alex to France."

"What's Alex think about all the globetrotting?"

"He's over it," said Bill. "He's so polite all the time, but yeah. He thinks she's about to get married again. I hope she does, maybe she'll leave him with me more."

"What's the plan for high school?" asked Mike. "Will he still be at the boarding school?"

"Eh. He could go there if he wants to. I keep trying to get him to say what he actually wants, because there are other options. I almost wish he was one of those angry teenagers who's yelling all the time, at least I would know what's on his mind."

"Huh," said Jen. "Is he admitting to anything he wants to focus on? Oliver's been all about the ocean forever, Hannah came down for aviation eighteen months ago. It's about time, if there's any pre-college prep work he wants to do."

"I'm hoping this getaway will help him sort things out," said Bill. "And being able to talk with Hannah can only help. I really appreciate being able to leave him with you the next few weeks."

Paula said, "When we were over in Boston for Christmas, Oliver said Hannah took longer to decide because she was good at so many things."

"That was nice of him," said Adam.

"He's a nice kid," Mike agreed. "Is Alex good at a lot of things?"

"Yeah, he is," said Bill. "Maybe that's the problem."

"Maybe he needs a change of scene," said Beth, who'd been quiet up to now. "Someplace where nobody's watching. If I'd gone to boarding school, I'd have made a clam look talkative."

Mike was looking at his sister with considerable interest. He glanced over at Paula and she made a quick 'what the fuck' face that almost made him laugh. He said, casually, "There's a really good school near you and Mom."

Beth shrugged. "Just sayin.' Minneapolis would probably be a culture shock after New York, or wherever he goes now."

"Connecticut," said Bill, also looking at Beth with interest. Mike realized it wasn't the first time over the past three weeks that he'd caught that particular expression. The implications were delightful.

"A kid who's willing to do tango lessons with his cousin and aunts and a complete stranger has to be pretty adaptable," Beth said, now looking at Mike with a half-exasperated smile.

Bill frowned, slightly suspicious. "Is there some kind of alien telepathy going on here?"

"They're twins, Bill," said Paula. "They did this to me a bunch of times that first Thanksgiving."

Beth came out with it. "This is an invitation, Bill. If Alex wanted to go to the Great White North for a year, or two, or whatever, we have a big house. Pretty sure my mom would be all for it. I mean, you're a lawyer, you could figure out how to work it to get him registered, right?"

Bill seemed to be considering it. "There's a guy in my firm with a lot of experience in that stuff. We handle some complex divorces; kids' educations tend to be the subject of major negotiations." He gazed at Beth for a minute, watched closely by Jen, Adam, Mike, and Paula. "Of course, you'd have to deal with regular visits from me."

Beth looked around at all of the others, then back at Bill. "That's kind of the whole point." She rolled her eyes at Mike, who was laughing. "I mean, I had to say something, because you're about to go back to New York, right?"

Bill was blushing a little. Mike said, "She played center, Bill. You've got to move fast to get past her."

"Jesus, Mike!" Beth was now also blushing.

"Tell you what," said Jen. "Why don't we go back to the house. Then if this conversation needs to proceed between Bill and Beth, it can do so without so many people chiming in. Okay?"

"Oh my God Mike, I was *stifling* myself," said Paula when they were finally on their way home. "I didn't know whether to laugh till I puked, or scream KISS HER ALREADY."

"I have a feeling that's going to happen." Mike was smiling in the driver's seat.

"Yeah, no doubt." She giggled. "It would be so cool if that worked out. I wonder if Bill would move to Minnesota? Because I'm pretty sure your sister would not dig New York." She dug out her phone and sent a text to her brother: Was great having you out here. We'll keep an eye on Alex. KEEP US POSTED wink wink

An answer came back before they got home. **What the hell just happened**

LOL I dunno did you kiss her??

NOYB

That means yes

LOL can't a person get a little privacy

Srsly? No

LMAO thanks for setting all this up. Uh you didn't actually set that up did you?

314

Facilitated not orchestrated

Fine distinction

We'll be interrogating Beth later

OMG help

Love you big brother

Love you little troublemaker

Paula dropped the phone in her bag, grinning.

CHAPTER 29

Mike and Paula were back over at Julia's house before the end of the week, catching up with Beth and Adam one more time in a non-lesson setting before they left. It seemed like a good opportunity to see if there were any updates about Alex, or Bill, or both. Mike pinned Beth down in the garden room while everyone else was in the kitchen. "So," he said.

"So, okay. I've been texting with Bill. I've been talking to Mom. Bill's been talking to Alex and to Fabienne. Nothing's decided yet, but wheels are turning."

"And in the meantime? Paula couldn't get Bill to confirm, but was there ... something?" He knew there was; Beth's face was an open book for him.

She rolled her eyes, shook her head, but finally looked back at him, grinning. "Okay so he kissed me."

"And you didn't hate it, obviously."

"Obviously."

"Well, that's a start." He gazed at her affectionately. "Has Alex coughed up any actual preferences?"

"Something to the effect that he'd kill to play hockey."

Mike made an understanding sound. "Figure skating wasn't getting the job done, huh."

"Well, he's going on fifteen. If he was serious about competition, he'd already be ranked. We looked at some of his videos and he said yeah, my technique doesn't suck, but my heart's not in it. I told him to think about what he liked about it and how that could apply elsewhere. That's when he came back with hockey. He likes skating, but he wants to be on a team, is what it comes down to, I think."

"What did Bill say about that?"

"He's all for it. I hear Fabienne about had a seizure, but he's working on her." She paused for a moment. "He thanked me for getting Alex to talk. I told him, the kid didn't want to disappoint you or his mom. I guess that school is pretty cutthroat. Everybody's got to be the best at something. It doesn't leave a lot of room for teamwork."

"Guess not. Well, this is all very interesting. But back to you. How did you like the lessons?"

"I mostly liked them because we all got to spend so much time together. You can really get to know somebody."

"Yeah, apparently." She laughed. He hugged her for long enough that she started to squirm and giggle. They went to join the others.

Two weeks later, just as rehearsals for the summer pro show were reaching full intensity, it was time to say goodbye to Jennifer, Hannah, and Alex. "So what's your opinion of L.A., now that you've had the whole tourist experience?" Paula asked. "Still think I was crazy to move here?"

"Not a chance," said Jennifer. "I mean, when we saw that whiteboard of yours I definitely thought you were crazy - " she paused for a laugh " – but I don't know that you could have done what you're doing here, anywhere else. Tyrone and the Cabaret, I don't know if that could exist where we grew up."

"I'll bet it could," said Mike. "A lot of us hear from people who are trying to set up something

317

similar. It is tough, though. A stage venue has to make money. Tyrone was an entertainment booker before he bought that club, so he knew how to get in acts that would sell drinks, which make money."

"And the Cabaret was sexy from the start, so the drinking crowd kind of dug it. By the time the Cabaret had evolved, so had the audience," said Paula.

"I remember what you told me and Margaret," said Hannah. "About being willing to accept that sometimes you couldn't make a living doing what you really loved. But that didn't mean you couldn't do it *at all*."

"What's she up to this summer?"

"Dance intensive at Cornell. She knows she's probably not going to hit company level, but she wants to be the best she can be."

"But back to L.A.," said Jennifer. "It's too big. It's too dusty. The traffic is unspeakable. The ocean is hard to get to. But Disney Hall is the most beautiful concert venue I've ever been in. The Hollywood Bowl was magic. The Getty Villa. The fabulous architecture everywhere. The gorgeous people everywhere. The *food*, oh my God. And I really love your community. Everybody is so great."

"When your friend died," said Hannah, then hesitated.

"Go ahead," said Mike.

"A guy at school died in a skiing accident and his friends totally fell apart. Did your people pull together?"

"Yeah, pretty much. We've all been making that extra effort to get face time. To tell, and show, people how we feel about them. Sometimes it's tough, because we've got people living everywhere from Van Nuys to Westchester."

"Which is basically from Mars to Uranus," said Paula, getting a laugh from the teenagers. "But when you work together as closely as dancers do, you have to trust each other. That's hard to maintain at a distance."

Jennifer nodded. "Like any family." After a minute she said, "This has really been great. I'm so glad we could all come out."

"Me too," said Paula. "And I'm glad we got to do it now. So. Saturday, airport, right?"

"Right. Back to Boston. Back to reality."

"Back to my lab," Hannah, with a little regret. "I wonder if learning tango will help me be a good pilot. I'm sure it'll help Alex play hockey." He looked doubtful. She said, "Guess we'll find out."

The following weekend Paula checked in with her brother by phone. They'd had a grueling rehearsal earlier and she was lying on the couch. "You sound weird," said Bill.

"We got flogged through this whole damn show for three hours. Maybe four. It's kind of a blur. Dress rehearsal's next week. We just ate and now I cannot remain upright."

"Where's Mike?"

"We're both wrecked, and we're going to a wedding tomorrow, so he's already in bed. I think he's asleep."

"Tell me about the show."

"It's called 'Face the Music.' The biggest show so far, sixteen numbers, eighteen dancers. Four acts, each one's based on a different ballroom style, but it's like, here's every way you can use that style. Mike and I are doing three group numbers and three duets."

"No wonder you're tired."

"Dmitri's new Latin guy is doing *seven* numbers. He's a sex bomb, you'd better be glad Beth didn't get a look at him." She paused, smiling, for a laugh from her brother. "Anyway, we cheated a little for one of ours, we're using 'A Thousand Years,' which we did earlier this year as an adagio."

"I remember, I saw it."

"It's more ballroom-y now. Which turns out to be *harder* because, duh, big dance, small stage. If these group numbers come off with no collisions, it will be a small miracle." She yawned. "Sorry. So how's the whole negotiation coming?"

"Fabienne came around. The paperwork's getting done. I have to tell you." He stopped, laughing.

"What?"

"We were all on the phone and Fabi was going on about how dangerous hockey was and Alex actually lost his temper. I swear, I wanted to high-five him."

Paula giggled. "Have you been out to Minneapolis yet?"

"Um," he said.

"Bill," she warned.

"Going next weekend."

"Staying at Candace's house?"

"No, in a hotel."

"Uh-huh," she said. "That means you're thinking of asking Beth to spend the night with you where her mother isn't right down the hall."

320

"It does not!" But he was laughing.

"It totally does. Carry on, my wayward son."

"You're such a nut."

"And now that we've established that, I'm going to crawl over to the kitchen for some medicinal gin. I think I've earned it."

"And then do your meditation."

"Always. Love you bro."

"Love you too."

Paula disconnected and laboriously sat up, setting down the phone. "Ow." Then she heard a soft laugh and looked up. Mike was leaning against the wall where the kitchen turned into hallway, wearing sweatpants and no shirt. "Oh hi honey. I thought you were asleep. You look delicious."

He smiled. "I thought I heard something about medicinal gin."

"And the thought revived you?"

"Sufficiently," Mike said, coming over to give her a hand up, gently tugging her close and wrapping an arm around her. "I'll bet with a little magic gin and a little meditation, you'll be able to sleep."

She rested her head against his shoulder, breathing him in. Her hand went around his ribs and her thumb absently rubbed the scar there. "I'll bet you're right." He did that thing where he put his hand on her throat, tipping her head up to kiss her. A few minutes later she said, "Who needs magic gin anyway. Let's just … meditate." He said something against her hair that made her smile. They went back down the hall together.

"You know something weird," Paula said to Mike the next day, on their way to West Hollywood.

"Hmm?"

"This is the first wedding I've been to that's actually in a church. Jennifer and Bill both did country-club things. We were in the backyard, then Sam and Mateo were in the backyard."

"That's the total?" he said. "Four?"

"Can you believe it?"

"It seems like aside from dancing, all I did from age eighteen to twenty-eight was go to weddings. Or be in weddings."

"I was not exactly wedding-guest, let alone wedding-party, material during that timeframe. How often did drunk girls propose to you?"

He couldn't help smiling. "Once or twice."

"And how often did drunk girls proposition you?"

Smiling more broadly, eyes on the road ahead. "A little more than that."

"I'll bet." Paula admired the antique ring on her finger for a minute. "I'm really glad you ended up with me."

"So am I." Mike couldn't do what he wanted at that exact moment, but as soon as they handed the Jeep over to the valet he turned to Paula and hugged her. "I'm really glad," he said quietly, then kissed her. "I love you."

"I love you, too." She stood back a little to admire him. "And *wow*, I mean really." He was wearing his white suit, which never failed to make her swoon a little.

"Wow yourself." Paula had a new Sixties-style pencil dress courtesy of Kris, in an orchid pink that flashed iridescent in the sun, with a cropped jacket in purple lace that matched her shoes. Her hair was up in a sleek twist. The whole look was classy, chic, and very sexy. "That's not your usual style, but I really like it."

"I was reading these romance novels set during the space race and had some fashion envy," she said. "Had to go through the closet and get rid of a couple of things. Ever since we squeezed you in, I've been on a strict one-in, two-out regimen."

"Sorry about that." He set a hand lightly on her back and they headed for the door.

"I had a ridiculous amount of clothing, it's been good for me." She tipped her chin up and gave him that look through her eyelashes that had bewitched him from the start. "Everything about you has been good for me."

"Don't look at me like that, we're walking into a church." He was smiling. She edged closer, hip to hip. Then they were inside, looking around the lovely space full of their friends, taking a program from Randa and being photographed by Andy, then being escorted to their seats by Ann, watching Bonnie make a few adjustments to the flowers at the pulpit. A few minutes later, music started playing. Paula looked at the program; it was from Ian Anderson's 'The Secret Language of Birds.' The celebrant entered from a side door, and then a procession started.

First came Kim and Hector, back from Seattle for the event. Then Stacey and Joe, followed by Charlene and Juan, then Michelle and Kenji. All of the women wore shades of purple. They took places at the front, with the men going to seats. Then the music changed and Tyrone brought Rory down the aisle. She was wearing traditional Indian costume, with the blouse and skirt in peacock blue and the sari in silver-gray. Some kind of signal was passed. Everyone stood up to watch Dana come down the aisle, escorted by Dmitri, who was in full tuxedo. Dana was wearing a sparkly white two-piece, with an off-the-shoulder cropped top and a trailing mermaid skirt that made the most of her body. Her hair was in a complicated up-do ornamented with peacock feathers, she wore pearl chandelier earrings, and she carried a small bouquet of white roses with more peacock feathers. "Wow," breathed Paula. Mike squeezed her hand. He noticed four older people he didn't know, following Dana down the aisle and taking seats in the second row. *Must be their parents,* he thought. He looked at the front again, almost dazzled by the six women standing there in front of the celebrant.

He leaned close to Paula and spoke almost soundlessly. "This picture would look great in our bedroom." She made big eyes at him, nodding. Another signal passed from front to back and all the guests sat down.

"Dearly beloved," began the celebrant. Paula leaned against Mike, half-listening to the service, knowing if she paid too-close attention she'd start crying. Rory and Dana said their vows and exchanged rings. Each of them was invited to kiss the bride, which made everyone laugh. Finally music started again. All six women turned around for a picture, then Dana and Rory came down the aisle together, holding hands and grinning. They went out the front door while the other women re-joined their husbands.

Paula wiped away a few stray tears and checked the program. The reception was, of course, going to be held at Chrome, officially starting in about an hour.

They found Tyrone and confirmed they could head over any time; he was on his way himself, with Indira at his side. "Did you loan Rory that beautiful sari?" asked Paula.

"I did," Indira said, smiling. "I offered some jewelry but she said she was the groom, it wouldn't be appropriate. Didn't Dana look wonderful?"

"Sensational. It's funny how you can know, objectively, that someone is really good-looking but you see them in a different context and think, whoa." Everyone agreed. "I'm so happy they did that."

"It's about time," Tyrone said. "We'd better head over to this party. Y'all coming?"

"We wouldn't miss it," said Mike. They all went outside to wait for their cars. Mike was holding Paula's hand again. "It's just shy of three years since I met you," he said, gazing at her. "I never could have imagined everything that's happened."

"Mostly good," she said. "We haven't wasted much of that time."

"I don't think we've wasted any." He let go of her hand and pulled her tight against his side. "Is there going to be dancing at this reception?"

"I'll bet there is."

"Do you think I can convince my wife to dance with me?"

She looked up at him, smiling at the love in those beautiful eyes, and said, "Always."

THE END

325

If you enjoyed FACE THE MUSIC, please consider leaving a positive rating or review. It really helps! Thanks for reading.

Want more? Vince and Kelli's story is SMOOTH, available at Amazon. Discover this world of romance at www.thelastories.com

Author's note: Empress 1908 gin was not released until 2017. Therefore, my characters could not have been drinking it in 2014/2015. You will forgive this flight of fancy once you try it.

*****

About the Author

Alexandra Caluen lives in a small purple house with her husband, a bottle of Laphroaig, a lot of books, and nine pairs of ballroom shoes. She works in patent law and has enough hair for three people.

www.ingramcontent.com/pod-product-compliance
Lightning Source LLC
Chambersburg PA
CBHW030601180626
46816CB00005B/1631